THE VALLES CALDERA

GARY L. STUART

BOOK TWO IN THE ANGUS SERIES

For information about this title or to order other books and/or electronic media, contact the publisher:
Gleason & Wall Publishing
7000 N. 16th Street, Suite 120, PMB 470, Phoenix AZ 85020
www.garylstuart.com
gary.stuart@garylstuart.com

ISBN: 978-0-9863441-2-1 (print)
ISBN: 978-0-9863441-3-8 (eBook)

Printed in the United States of America

Cover and Interior design: 1106 Design

Other Books by Gary L. Stuart

The Ethical Trial Lawyer

The Gallup 14

Miranda—The Story Of America's Right To Remain Silent

*Innocent Until Interrogated—The True Story of the
Buddhist Temple Massacre and The Tucson Four*

AIM For The Mayor—Echoes From Wounded Knee

Ten Shoes Up

Anatomy of A Confession—The Debra Milke Case

CHAPTER 1
Angus–April 1883–Riding the *Rio de los Pinos*

IN EARLY APRIL 1883, the snowmelt down into the *Rio de los Pinos* was a mighty pretty sight. Tucson, the steadiest horse I ever rode, was stepping easy along a little shale embankment when it gave way and dumped us into water so cold it burned my skin. I was not paying any particular notion to our path, giving my attention instead to a cloud formation high up over a snow-covered peak a mile or so away. I'd decided it resembled a white horse chasing down a spotted calf. So, you can imagine my surprise when, of a sudden, I found myself grabbing for the saddle horn as we cartwheeled down the slope smack into the river. The current carried us a quarter-mile from Colorado on the north bank to New Mexico on the south. The wreck lamed Tucson and put

1

me afoot. Took us two days to reach the nearest town, what with him walking on three legs, and me barely stumbling on two. Finally, we presented ourselves to the suspicious-looking family running a small sheep ranch six miles north of Tierra Amarilla. I talked them into a buckboard ride into town, with Tucson in tow on a lead rope, and my saddle and tack dumped in back. There was no conversation among us. It was an embarrassing situation—riding a buckboard is low-living, if you ask me. There was more bad news waiting for me at the sheriff's office. A fuzz-faced deputy handed me a telegram from the US Marshal up in Denver. It was dated a week before. Course, Marshal Ramsey didn't know just where I was, so he sent the telegram to six different towns north and south of the Toltec Gorge. It didn't matter where I was; he found me. And, I felt obliged to do as Marshal Ramsey said.

Seems I was wanted in Denver, MY SOONEST—or so it said in the telegram. Big day for me—a telegram I never thought I'd get—and a new horse, one I never thought I'd need. JB, who owned the livery stable, confirmed my suspicion. Tucson had a torn fetlock. He could stand and maybe trot with nobody riding him. But, the man said in a somber tone of voice, "this fine animal should be pastured for the rest of his days." That near tore my heart out. Didn't know then it would be No Más that would heal me. I needed a stout, mountain-raised horse to make the seventy-mile ride north to Alamosa, Colorado. Once there, I figured on taking the train the rest of the way to Denver. I'd rather ride the whole way, but Marshal Ramsey had said SOONEST in his damn telegram.

How I'd get No Más? Horseback, that's how. With a little snake oil lathered on my aching shoulder, I borrowed one of

JB's horses and rode out to the Cross S Ranch, eight miles east of town. I'd cowboyed on that spread nine years back, and figured they'd sell me a horse that might be half the horse Tucson had been before the Rio de los Pinos lamed him. John Avery, owner of the Cross S, had gone to Santa Fe to buy some new stock, but Catalina, his range boss, said he had a three-year old gelding named No Más available for almost no money. He wasn't the sort of man that ever gave a horse away, especially when the boss was off the property. Catalina, a plain speaker, allowed as how he'd let me have this fine piece of horseflesh for the miserly sum of five dollars if I promised never to bring him back. He'd bucked off three good cowboys, and showed no promise for nosing cows out of boggy ground or sagebrush thickets.

I was looking for a horse that had a personality like an Indian canoe—you know, one that did pretty much what you told it to do. How pretty a horse is means nothing to me. The most important thing was a horse that won't come undone when I'm riding a far-off ridgeline alone and we come on a twenty-five pound bear cub, or a seven-hundred pound bull elk. Second thing was a horse that didn't pay no never mind to what I hung on him—saddles, ropes, bags, scabbards, slickers, gunny sacks with feed, game, or ammo. Last, a horse I'm going to trust will always let me sit crossways on the saddle, knee cropped over the saddle horn, and he'll ground tie anywhere I stop. But it wouldn't be in this stock pen that I'd find out if No Más had any of these features. They'd show up later, or not. I wanted him broke, but not broke to death. We couldn't learn anything from one another that way. I was looking for a horse with no discrepancy between what I wanted and what he was willing to do.

All that said, No Más had a beauty in him. Black as wet granite, with three white socks of unequal length, and dark eyes that changed color every time I looked at him. Long-bodied, so I figured him as a horse with a stride to cover fifty miles a day, depending on the availability of food and water. He'd prove to be a good-moving horse, but at the moment only showed a bad frame of mind. They had him backed up in a split-pine holding corral facing down two cowhands. Neither one looked comfortable. No Más stomped and snorted so much you'd think he was intending on killing these boys before suppertime. His upper lip snarled back to reveal yellowed teeth clinched so tight he could break his own jawbone. He was barrel chested, black footed, and stood about fifteen hands high with every nerve and muscle in him lit up and twitching. Standing stiff-legged with his butt wedged into the corner of a ten foot cuttin' chute, the two cowboys were trying to get close enough to slip a head-stall on him. He was having none of it, and his wide, flickering eyes were telling them to back up. For a long minute, none of us moved. I was two lengths away with a rope in one hand and a gunny sack in the other. The cowhands got his message, but because a stranger was present, they stood their ground. No Más flicked his head my direction, puffed up, and flared blood red nostrils at me. I dropped the rope with a flick of my wrist, and muttered softly to the men to let me try him. Standing stock still, I waited till they climbed the rail. It was an awkward climb over a five-foot fence since they insisted on looking back at No Más over their shoulders till they flopped over onto safe ground on the other side.

Tucking the gunny sack into the back of my belt, I showed him empty hands. Acting like it was me that was lame; I eased down into a squat over my spurs, settled myself, and waited him out. Rocking a little on haunches, my breathing returned to normal. I tried an old trick, pursing my lips and blowing softly in his direction. After three or four minutes, I started nodding my head slowly up and down. He still stood leg-locked, but I could see the tenseness slipping away starting at his throat muscles. He still glared at me, but dropped his head down just a little. His ears flicked back and forth, and he snorted on every other breath. He quit staring at me, and pawed the ground with one foot. I stood up and did the same. I backed up five feet, he came forward one. I inched the gunnysack out of my back belt, fished out a handful of mixed cane sugar and grain, and stood still. Horses can smell anything sweet from ten feet off. He shuffled his feet as if he wanted to come, but his eyes kept flicking at the cowboys sitting on the top rail. I asked them, quiet-like, to get out of his line of sight. They did. And No Más gave me his full attention. It was my first test.

He circled me with slow steps as I moved, always turning to face him, but hiding the gunnysack from view. The closer he got, the further away I moved. While still tense and angry with them, I hoped he'd mellow some with me. Just let me stay in the corral with you, I thought. I aimed that thought in his direction. He quit quivering, but still gave me the black-eye stare. Five minutes later, I got overconfident and a little too close. Hearing the swoosh of a looped rope outside the corral, he bolted sidewise. I lost my footing trying to get out of his way, and his big butt knocked me aside. I took another trip to solid ground. Turtle-like, I rolled toward him and sat up on my boot heels. The cowboy haunch seemed to settle him some, almost as if he recognized it. That got me to thinking about the cowboy that'd started him as a colt. He began plowing the ground around me in tight, little circles. I got it—he was not angry with me—it was those two boys who'd piled off the rail, but were now standing, ropes in hand, five feet behind the fence.

"Go on, git," I said to them, showing No Más my back for the first time.

He watched them walk away, and then lowered his head slightly, in my general direction. Inhaling deep as I could, I gave him a low whistle. I emptied the gunny sack's offering—four handfuls of cane sugar mixed with last month's grain—onto the ground and climbed back up on the rail to watch. There's two things all horses have in common. They want to feel safe. They like sweet grain. With me up on the top rail, he could focus on the smell of grain. It calmed him down like a light spring rain early in the morning. But, No Más wasn't through with me yet. I spent the next hour alternating between sitting on the rail, and stepping down into the corral to walk around without paying much attention to him. I got a little closer with each pass. Finally, he had me inside his head. I wasn't a threat. He let me come up close, rub his chest, knead the soft muscles behind his ears, and breathe on his neck. I stood with one arm up under his chest rubbing the other side of his shoulder. Within minutes, the fear evaporated like dew drying out in the sun. I could tell he'd carry me from one sundown to another. All I had to do was to remember to tie on a gunny sack and ride with a loose set of reins.

The next morning, shy of five dollars, with my saddle cinched down, I rode No Más out of the corral at a slow trot. Moving him into an easy lope, we headed for the Rio Grande. And, for whatever Denver had in store for me.

CHAPTER 2
Angus Gets a New Assignment

WE SPENT PURTIN' NEAR four days riding up the Rio Grande to Alamosa. I stabled No Más at the livery stable there, and caught the train north to Denver. The US Court House in that city was not my favorite place. Big, heavy, and closed in. I'd rather be riding a riverbank. That's what I told him.

"Yeah, Angus, I know," Marshal George Ramsey said, "but this is 1883; times have changed. Colorado has been a state since 1876. New Mexico, your stompin' grounds, is still just a territory. You know the ground down there. I've got work for you to do there. Again."

My boss, the right honorable George Ramsey, is *the* US Marshal for Colorado. That makes him the top federal law dog for two hundred miles in any direction. He's got four deputies, counting me, except I only work part time.

No more'n I have to. And, mostly, he assigns trouble down in the New Mexico Territory to me. He was giving me that sideways look of his again. I'd been ridge-riding down in the northern New Mexico canyons for the last six months, minding my own business, avoiding all manner of people, and their troubles. I sure as hell hadn't been minding his business for six months, not since I turned that old coot Tom Emmett loose in the mountains. Since then I'd had no thoughts of work of any kind and especially not for the US government.

Marshal Ramsey laid it out simple-like. There was some trouble brewing to the south, and he wanted me to ride down and take a look. Hell, I always liked that part. Just me, a pony with a good head, and a stout mule to pack my kit. And, when the riding weather ranged from crisp to cold, well, that's all it took to get me back on the job. So, I gave him a nod.

"You still got your badge, don't you?"

"Yes, I do. Right here in my vest pocket. It's been in my saddle bag since we last talked about turning Tom Emmett loose. As I recall our conversation six months ago, you said we both needed to think on that some before you'd give me a new assignment."

"Angus," he said, putting a match to the bowl of his pipe and wheezing in a puff of gray smoke, "you made the right decision letting Emmett go. The federal government still wants his hide for robbing a federal mail car down near Las Cruces, New Mexico territory. But, it has no claim to him for robbing a train up in Union County, New Mexico. You made the right call on that one, and the guys in the suits at the US

Department of Justice back east agree with me. But, this time, Angus, I need you out in the open. Not hiding your badge this time. Out in the open—be a nice change for you."

I'd ridden those last two assignments with the badge in my saddle bag, not on my vest. This was to be my first, by God, *official* job as a deputy US Marshal.

"Out in the open? You know, you and I think differently about what being out in the open means to a man."

"Yes, sir, Angus, we surely do. But, this time, I'm deputizing you for all of New Mexico to see. Official. I'm going to announce your assignment by telegraph to a man you will soon meet, Perfecto Armijo. He's the sheriff of Albuquerque. I want him to know you're a senior, federal law enforcement officer out of this office. He may pay you no never mind, but you've faced that problem before. And, of course, I will also send a courtesy telegram to Dave Knop, the US Marshal for the Territory of New Mexico. Only met him once, but Washington says he's trustworthy, and gets the job done on time. Time is important in Washington, even if it ain't to you."

"Yep," I said, and started to ask him a question, but he raised his palm up toward me. That's his way of saying hold up, I ain't finished talking.

"Angus, I am sending you back down to New Mexico to handle some politics and some law. You're good at law, but I don't have a feel for your politics."

"That's because politics and law ain't the same. Don't mix. Not in my mind."

"Well, without the law everything would be political, just remember that down in New Mexico. And, get down there promptly, hear?"

"Okay, but what's the law part?"

"Well, the Territory of New Mexico has a prisoner who came from here, or at least this was his last stop before he moved down there a year or so ago. His name is Milton J. Yarberry, and he was the town marshal in Albuquerque until he shot a citizen down there, summer before last. They tried him, convicted him, and the judge gave him the death penalty. He's gonna hang soon, damn soon, so you need to get down there before they stretch his neck, talk to him, and try to sort out Colorado's piece of this."

"Well, hell, George, something don't make sense here. He murdered somebody almost two years ago and he still ain't hung? I thought justice was swift down there."

"Seems like he has friends and one of 'em is the sheriff of Albuquerque who made Mr. Milton J. Yarberry a deputy sheriff of Bernalillo County, and talked the city of Albuquerque into making him the town's first marshal. Then, some good lawyers took up his defense, and finally, just a week ago, the Supreme Court of New Mexico issued an opinion that upheld the jury verdict and the court's death sentence. The politics of it come in because the governor, man named Lionel Sheldon, a Republican, issued a death warrant—the same day, January 25, 1883. The hanging's scheduled for February 9, so you need to make haste if we're gonna close up the Colorado piece of this."

"What would that be, Marshal?"

"It would be you interrogating this fellow in his prison cell before they drop his ass down the hanging chute; that's the Colorado piece."

We jawboned it for almost an hour. Best as I could make it out, this Yarberry was more gunman than lawman; leastways that's what he was up here. He showed up in Canon City, Colorado in 1878, and partnered up with a man named Tony Preston in the salon and brothel business, although there was a respectable side to it. Seems they had a variety theater that was real popular with the miners and locals over there.

His partner, Preston, got himself shot in March of 1879 by a bartender at the Gem Saloon. Yarberry inserted himself in the fracas and fired back, but apparently was a bad shot—three bullets fired, no hits. Yarberry joined the posse and they tracked the bartender down. That's how Yarberry started his law career: one of many in a posse, most of 'em drunk. He got into scrapes of one kind or another, mostly involving brothels they owned. He shoehorned himself into law jobs in boom camps that followed building the Santa Fe Railroad. There was talk of Yarberry's financial misdeeds involving the railroad.

Yarberry's last foray into Colorado law was down near Trinidad or somewhere south of there. By then, Yarberry had a female partner named 'Steamboat.' Rumor had it they were in the brothel business together. Yarberry departed a day after a freighter named Nuget was found robbed and murdered twenty miles from town. They said Nuget was hauling trade goods, mining equipment, and a federal payroll. The local law suspected Yarberry, but he absconded before the investigation was finished. It's still open. The federal government pays close attention to missing federal payrolls. That made it my boss's problem. Seems like after Preston got himself shot, Yarberry turned his attention to Preston's wife, a younger woman named Sadie. All three of them, Yarberry, Steamboat, and Sadie ended up in Albuquerque in 1880, which led, more or less, to Yarberry's shooting that citizen in 1881. Somehow, Sadie and her part-time husband, Tony, figured into the shooting of another man, name of Campbell. It all made my head hurt some, but Marshal Ramsey was of a mind to get it sorted out, and he told me to head south, soonest.

"So, I'm to interrogate a man who may have come from Colorado, but was a convicted murderer in New Mexico, with a hanging coming up? It ain't plain to me why I'm doing this."

Giving me a look with his head tilted sideways, he said, "Why? Well, in the first damn place, because it's an assignment, that's why. Here's a packet of papers you should read. They came to me from the by-God Department of Justice in Washington, District of Columbia. And, my orders are to get someone down there in that rough territory we can trust to get at the core of a rotten apple. Peel it back for me, Angus. I'm counting on you."

Shaking his head at me, he passed over a leather satchel and a deputized warrant to investigate the case, officially titled "New Mexico versus Milton J. Yarberry," and situated in Bernalillo County, New Mexico. He also handed over a government draft for funds to advance my 125 dollar monthly salary "not to exceed six months from and after this 28th Day of January, 1883."

Not answering my why question told me the answer. The law in Washington does not see this Yarberry fellow as one of their own, but New Mexico does. Washington wanted to close that file on the stolen federal payroll, but New Mexico did not care about that, or any other federal payroll. Never mind. My badge and a six-month grub stake put me horseback, and soon enough I'd be riding the Rio Grande.

Back at the hotel, I shuffled the batch of papers in the satchel. The fat one, tied on top with a brown string, was a court opinion that made my head hurt just reading the first twenty pages, so I put it aside until after breakfast.

Over morning coffee under the domed-glass breakfast room at the St. Elmo, I pushed the last of the toast to one side and gave the damn thing my best effort. The front part of it was in legal language. The words were English, but the meaning was for judges, lawyers, and such. Not deputy marshals. The January 9, 1883, opinion had its own title: *The Territory of New Mexico, Appellee vs. Milton J. Yarberry, Appellant*, 2 N.M. 391 (1883). Chief Justice Axtell wrote it, I guess. Or maybe not. He sure wasn't Mark Twain, now there's a man can write. Anyhow, he was wordy and took some pleasure in announcing legal principles in long sentences and longer paragraphs about criminal offenses, evidence, hearsay, defendant's rights, and big things like jurisdiction and New Mexico's organic act, whatever 'n hell that means.

I ordered more coffee and kept at it. Lots of yammering on paper, though short on what really happened. But, in my mind, the story played out more or less simple. Yarberry, the lawman, met up with two fellers he knew on June 18, 1882, in Albuquerque. They were sitting on a bench when they heard a shot down an alley. Yarberry, wearing his marshal's badge and toting a .44, led the other two to the head of the alley. They saw a man running away from them. Yarberry ordered him to stop. He paid them no mind. That's the simple part.

Somehow, Yarberry and a man name of Boyd drew down on the fleeing man, cocked their hammers, and fired at the same time. The running man, name of Charles D. Campbell, collected six balls, all from behind, all piercing his back, and making big blowout holes in his chest and belly. He fell forward and expired at the scene, or so Judge Axtell said in his rambling way. Yarberry did not know the man they shot, and did not bother to examine the body. He just casually walked down the block to the nearest saloon and ordered drinks.

One witness said Yarberry ordered the deceased man with the six lead balls in him to "hold up your hands." He didn't. They commenced to firing. They were armed. Campbell was not. Another witness recounted as many as ten or twelve shots fired "instantly," with six hitting their mark—Campbell's spinal column.

According to Judge Axtell, a citizen asked Marshal Yarberry, "Why did you do this?"

His answer: "I did it, and there he lies," pointing back to the alley.

His defense: "He shot at me, but I was too quick for him, and I downed the son of a bitch." I put the court opinion back in the brown envelope, paid the breakfast bill, $1.90, left a quarter tip, and headed for the train station.

CHAPTER 3

Angus Takes No Más to New Mexico

WHEN I GOT OFF THE TRAIN in Antonito, I sent JB, the livery man in Tierra Amarilla, a telegram, saying it might be a month before I would come back and pick up Tucson. I didn't get a response, but didn't count on one, anyhow. Livery stables make a living taking care of horses that need time to heal. Then I checked on No Más. The slow-talking old man at the barn said he'd been off his feed a little, but was otherwise no trouble. I bought a pack mule and put him in the same stall with No Más for the night. The next afternoon, just before sundown, I saddled up No Más, strapped my tack and the food stores I'd bought in town, and headed south. Four hours later, we were close to the New Mexico border. The night sky glistened with stars, just starting to flicker at No Más, the pack mule named Black Jack, and me. I love the night sky, but I ain't sure a horse has ever even looked up to see stars at night. When you're in the saddle, they mostly pay attention to where they're steppin'. When picketed, or standing in a corral, they have other things to think about. Stars ain't on their minds. Mules ignore the night sky, too, but don't seem to mind me gawking up when I'm horseback, unless it puts tension on the lead rope. They'd told me in Antonito that the mule was called Black Jack because he'd once been used in the famous Black Jack mine near Gallup, New Mexico. How he'd got himself from there to Colorado was a mystery. But, Black Jack brayed with the best of them. That happened every time I pulled too tightly on the lead rope. We bedded down around midnight, and slept until the sun came up next morning.

That day we covered thirty-five miles up from the flat prairies of Southern Colorado onto the lee side of Cumbres Pass. We topped out at just under ten thousand feet. The long, dark valley below was in New Mexico. The railroad line was out of sight, but not out of mind. I remembered another starry night here two years ago. I'd been running from Standard H. Plumb, and his gang—he called it a posse—not two miles from here. They shot Tucson, my best horse. But, that's another story. Seems like I was always getting Tucson into one scrape or another.

No Más was a fast-breaking, run-till-you-drop kind of horse. He wasn't a mountain horse that stepped around boulders; he preferred jumping over them. His ears picked up at what he likely thought were close sounds. But, up this high, sound carries a far piece. This late in winter, the lakes were all frozen above seven thousand feet. They rumbled, then groaned, and bits of ice always seemed to be popping like cannon shot.

Black Jack was hauling a light load, about 150 pounds. Under the diamond hitch tarp, I'd snugged stores, an extra rifle, tent covers, and tools. They rattled and cranked into the night, alerting critters for miles around. The critters scattered away in silence, but Black Jack and No Más knew they were about, and both were flicking their ears this way and that.

I clicked my tongue against my cheek to let No Más know I was not worried about those strange night sounds, and gave him a little pressure with my knees to push him up onto a piece of flat ground. It looked to offer some rocky cover from the prevailing south-to-northwest wind, which always came up early in the morning at this height. Dismounting, I maneuvered No Más and the mule into a six foot crevice and spring-knotted the both of them to the last of the jack pine at this altitude. Then, I scraped out a small hole in the frozen ground and filled it with pine needles and scrub oak twigs. Covering it with a loose tarp, I used the other tarp to cover my bed roll and me.

I wasn't worried about covering No Más or Black Jack. Horses handle cold weather better than people do. I figured the temperature at maybe twenty-five degrees. Horses with good winter coats are snug at fifteen degrees. In summer, they feel just as comfortable at sixty degrees. That's what horse doctors say is a horse's comfort zone—fifteen to sixty. Same for me, but I do like a good ground cloth under me if I'm down on the ground in winter. Its wet weather or strong winds that present a danger for horses. With the tarp over me, and snugged up against my saddle I easily drifted off to sleep. No need, I thought, to build a cook fire now—it'll be light in five hours—time enough for cowboy coffee, a half-dozen bacon strips, and a hunk of sourdough bread warmed up in the coals of an early-morning fire. I figured on staying here until the early afternoon; I had this little space all to myself. Or, so I thought.

The American wolf, sometimes called a timber wolf, or a lobo in New Mexico, is a 100-pound, big-jawed, nervous animal who keeps to himself under normal circumstances. But, when hungry enough, and when his blood is up by the howling of three or four others in a pack, he will get your attention. He did mine. My first thought at hearing him, just above us on a rock ledge, was that I should've built that damn fire.

From a distance, they look almost majestic, loping along a ridge line, or circling up through a stand of ponderosa pine. But, up close, like now, I could see his big head settled on a long, slim body. The moonlight made his eyes look wide, and his viselike jaws, long hooked fangs, and the stillness in the night were paralyzing. I'd fired at a few lobos over the years, just to scare 'em off, but until now had never felt the need to kill one, before he killed me.

Holding my breath, I realized he hadn't even seen me. It was Black Jack that had his attention. The dang mule was lying on his side, asleep between the boulders six feet from me, but less than two jumps for a big wolf. No Más, downwind about fifteen feet, had not yet picked up the wolf's scent. I figured he'd go crazy when he did. The wolf would either run or attack. *Don't chance it, Angus. You got less than ten seconds before all hell breaks loose.*

I reached for the new Winchester .44-40 I'd bought in Denver. It was alongside my bed roll. But, I knew if I jacked a shell into the chamber, I'd wake up the mule, startle No Más, and turn the wolf's attention on me. So, not having a better plan, I decided to aim, but not ready myself to fire. I eased up into a sitting position, stocked the rifle butt against my left shoulder, and lined up the tip of the barrel. And there I sat. The wolf, No Más, Black Jack, and me. Waiting one another out.

Thirty seconds passed like molasses dripping out of a small hole in the bottom of a can. Thirty more and nobody moved. Then, another sound, kind of like someone scraping a boot on a porch step. The wolf tensed, still not moving his head in my direction. No Más heard it, too, and gave a shake and a short stomp of his right iron shoe on the small rocks beside him. Black Jack wrenched his big belly, craning over in my direction. I was afraid he was going to try to get up, and thought about jacking a round into my carbine, just so he'd look over my way. But I didn't. I looked back the other way at the wolf.

Gone.

Not a sound, no sense of movement, no flutter of cold night air. Just gone. Now, I jacked a three-inch brass cartridge into the chamber, jumped up, and panned both sides on our little enclosure. Nothing. *Just us chickens*, I thought.

Breakfast was uneventful. The three of us spent the morning resting up from yesterday's long haul. I kept thinking about El Lobo. Was he really going to jump a sleeping mule? Never heard of such a thing, but he had my full attention for a short while. Bacon, bread, and sizzling-hot coffee for breakfast. Then, after four hours of sitting, followed by a lunch of jerky, cold beans, more coffee, and a can of grain for No Más and Black Jack, we headed down the mountain and on up the canyon toward Chama.

CHAPTER 4

Angus, No Más, & Black Jack
In the Toltec Gorge

NO MÁS LINED OUT NICELY on the ride through the gorge. Black Jack followed the lead rope like it was a magnet. We pulled up five miles from Chama just as the hazy winter sun signaled noon. My plan was to leave Black Jack with my old friend, Marse Johansen, at his livery stable in Chama. Marse would clean him up and feed him barn hay until I finished my job down in Albuquerque. I was looking forward to be shed of ponying a pack mule. But, before riding on into Chama, I had things to do. First off, I put on my only clean shirt, dug my holster and gun belt out of a canvas gun bag, and cleaned my pistol. Like most deputies, but unlike most working cowboys, I packed a single action Colt .45 in a cut-down holster. The cut was open at the top, for fast and easy access, but with a loop at the top. Folks called this a "Slim Jim" holster, on account of its slim design to fit the seven-and-a-half inch barrel on my percussion Colt. The trigger guard was exposed so a man could place his finger at the ready, if need be.

I removed and cleaned the thirty-odd .45 caliber lead bullets, and put each securely back in the leather loops on the gun belt before I strapped the rig on. I had not worn this rig for seven months. It wasn't something a cowboy needed in the high mountains where I'd been living. But, I was about to reenter a thriving town where I used to be known only as a cowboy. I held the silver badge to my mouth and gave it a mouthful of air before shining it up on my sleeve. Pinning that badge to my vest was another way of letting folks know that life was different now. For me. For them.

The Winchester Model 1873 lever-action rifle, which I'd had handy on the night the wolf visited us, was always clean. But, still, I broke the workings down, oiled everything, stroked the barrel whistle clean, and reloaded the brass. I did the same for the double-aught shotgun, then broke the barrel down off the stock, and put the pieces back into the hard leather case. I'd leave it in Chama, along with Black Jack and most of the stores. The high mountain kit would fit in one of the wood bins at Marse's livery stable, under lock and key. Sticking the lever-action rifle in its saddle scabbard, and tying my rope to a saddle ring on the off side, I oiled and smoothed out every inch of saddle, bridle, and tack I had. Hell, I thought, a US deputy marshal ought not to ride into town looking like a saddle tramp from Missouri.

Last thing I did before mounting up was to dip a gunny sack into the creek and wipe down my boots, and No Más.

Black Jack gave me the evil eye, so I decided he didn't need any cleaning up. I dusted off my hat, jumped on No Más, and we started off at a slow lope. Down the mountain and into Chama, a town I'd visited more than once in the last seven years.

CHAPTER 5

Angus Back in Chama

CHAMA HAD ONE RAILROAD TRACK, one street, three back alleys, and a dozen foot trails to the line of buildings west of the main street, which they'd named George. The east side of George belonged to the railroad and bordered the Rio Chama. The street's west side, including a boardwalk along all the stores on that side, was town property. The Denver & Rio Grande Railway was Chama's only real employer. But, everyone knew the fast-flowing, mountain river had been drawing people here for more than a hundred years. And, it was not George Street, Avenue, or Road. Just plain old George. Nobody asked why. Including me.

On George's north end, the railroad held sway with its station house, which contained the ticket booth, mail room, waiting room, and an indoors latrine. Outside, it boasted a sixty-foot long, engine roundabout, which allowed them to put the engine at the front of the cars for a turn-around trip back up into the Toltec Gorge to Colorado, and points north. If you were headed south, you'd have to take the stage, or make the trip on horseback. South of the roundabout was a ninety-foot long, tin shed used to fix equipment, and to store boxes and trade goods under roof, lock, and key. The middle part of George was home to two saloons, two brothels, a café, a big hotel, a small boarding house, three dry goods stores, and four clapboard houses with porches.

On the south end, where the road up from Espanola stopped, sat the post office, the livery stable, and the office, jail, and second-story living quarters of the Under-Sheriff of Rio Arriba County, Joe Pete. He was the second man I intended on visiting, after drinking a cup or two of Marse Johansen's scalding-hot coffee at his livery stable. Then, my plan was to get a room at the hotel, visit the Chinese bath house, the Mexican barber, and Big Dutch, who ran one of the saloons. Big Dutch's partner in both brothels was a tiny, little woman named Short Sal. Neither had any known enemies.

I tied up to the hitch rail on the shady side of the two-story livery barn and was surprised to see a new, freshly scored and painted sign:

GUNSMITH—BLACKSMITH—BOARDING—FEED—TACK
J. GARRISON, PROPRIETOR

Well, No Más, looks like you're gonna spend the night in a horse hotel. I thought. *That sign looks to be new. You don't suppose old Marse has sold out to Mr. J. Garrison, do you? Let's go see.* It was more 'n just a new sign. The west end now fancied two new 20' × 20' corrals, cut out of fresh pine, with an over-hang sticking out about ten feet. It held five geldings and two yearlings. A new side entryway had been cut into Marse's big barn. Marse's arrangement had been eight stalls, four on each side. But, now the front two had been rebuilt to accommodate a smithy stove, an anvil stand, and a tool bench for smithing tools. The opposite stall sported a new, double-hinged gate and a plank floor inside. It was good carpentry—one-inch fir with hammered iron hinges and a serious padlock.

The old, oversize, wood stove was still forty feet away in the back, fired up, with a pot of coffee puffing and siz-zling. I could not see far enough to the back of the big barn, where Marse's open kitchen had been. I remembered he had a bunk arrangement back there with a Mexican blanket for a cover. It was mostly open to the barn, so he could always keep track of his stock. Big change here. It was gone. In its place were a new knotty pine wall, with fresh unpainted boards, and a solid door leading out back. But, no more kitchen and bunking area. I went out the side door and could see that someone had knocked out the back wall and added another twenty-five feet to the rear, with an outside entrance, a good-sized porch with two chairs and a work table, and glass windows on the side I was looking at. Curtains, too. I asked myself who'd want to mess up a good barn by add-ing a house to the back wall.

I took No Más inside, felt the warmth from the stove, and stopped at the first stall.

"Anybody here? Marse?" I hollered, as I took the bridle and bit off No Más and started uncinching, taking down the breast collar, and releasing his back strap.

"No, he ain't," a girl's voice wafted down from the double door up on the hayloft, "you in need of boarding?"

"I am. Where's Marse?"

"Gone. I'll be down momentarily. Pick a stall inside, or out. Your choice."

I moved No Más and Black Jack into a double inside stall, swung my saddle and the mule pack rigging up onto the tack rail outside the stall gate, and was just starting to brush and curry No Más when the voice came back.

"You a friend of Marse's?"

Turning to face her, I was taken aback. She was about the size of a corn stalk, early in the season, with what looked to be yellow hair all stuffed up into a brown Derby hat. She wore overalls two sizes too big and boots with yesterday's mud caked on like paint. None of that fit her face. She had the face of—hell; I dunno—an angel, maybe.

"Yes, I am. I'm Angus."

"Jill," she wafted back at me. "Marse died last spring. In a horse wreck down river. His family put the whole kit and caboodle up for sale; all the stock, ten years of gathered up tack, tools, and a chance at a new life. My dad and I bought it, sight unseen. So, here I am, your new livery keeper. But, that's Marse's coffee you smell; he had twenty bags of it, unground, in the root cellar out back."

"Pleased to meet you," I said, continuing to brush No Más while Black Jack tried to stuff his entire head into the hay box.

"I can see by your badge and the gun rig that you're a lawman. Is Angus your first name or last?"

"Both. Angus will do in either direction. This badge is sort of a temporary thing. I knew Marse when I was younger, cowboying down around Espanola. Real sorry to hear about his passing."

"Well, Marshal, you're welcome. Will you be paying cash money, or by government warrant? I have my preferences, but I'll take either. Not too many strangers pass through Chama in the winter."

"I'll pay in cash. Where's your dad, or are you ramrodding this outfit?"

"Marshal, when you get your horse brushed, I'll be in the back. Coffee's always free. Livery services are a dollar a day per animal, plus fifty cents for grain—hay's free. Come on back and I'll tell you how J. Garrison, that's me, came to Chama by way of Topeka, Kansas."

Twenty minutes later, I went to the back of the barn and found that Marse's old office had become a home inside a barn. New floor, walls covered with brightly colored paper, and real furniture, all store bought. Over a half-hour's worth of coffee, I learned that Jill was the only child of John Wall Garrison, a gunsmith of some note in Topeka, Kansas. She came to Chama, New Mexico last summer. Her mother died when she was eight; she took over the household duties, and John, that's what she called her father, took her into the gunsmith and iron work trades. As she talked, I noted how different she was from any other livery keeper I'd ever heard about. Slender, with an erect carriage, which she accentuated by pushing her shoulders back like a Ute warrior astride a painted horse. She had quick eyes, a pointed, narrow nose, and rust-colored hair tied in a bob. Her hands were tapered and seemed inconsistent with the ragged sleeves on her canvas barn coat. Her grip was unusually strong for a woman, especially one so slightly built.

I guess she caught me staring at her hands after we shook because she gave me a mischievous smile. "What is it, Marshal Angus? Have you not ever shaken hands with a woman whose grip matched your own?"

"No, Miss. It's just that I've never met a woman who worked with horses before. Your hand grip sort of confirms your job here."

"It's Jill. Please. And I'm not just working here. I own the place, although Don Moya does a lot of the heavy work a barn operation requires. I do the iron work on the guns, and he handles the smithy and the anvil fairly well. If need be, I can do that part as well, but I so love working with fine weapons and teaching men of all ages to shoot. That love is my father's parting gift, may God rest his soul."

"I'm sorry. I misunderstood earlier. About you and your Dad moving here from Kansas."

"He bought this place for me and we both hoped he'd make the trip west. He sold out the Topeka livery business, but died two days before we were to board the train for Santa Fe. He was only fifty-three, but we'd known about his weak heart for two years before that. Now, let's talk about something else, shall we?"

I took the hint. "Iron is iron, is that it?"

"Working iron, whether steel in a gun or iron on a horse shoe, is pretty much the same trade. We fixed buggy wheels, Conestoga wagon rounds, and some of the best weaponry in Kansas. But, I wanted to go west, so five years ago, when I turned eighteen, John promised me we'd look for the right opportunity. It came up last summer, on my twenty-third birthday. This country's birthday and mine are both on the fourth of July. We bought this place, like I said sight unseen."

She had a voice that was mostly little girl, high with a squeak to it, but she smiled easy, laughed at everything, and seemed eager to talk to a stranger. I learned about her advancing the business in Kansas by adding leather work—holsters, scabbards, packs, cases, and the kind of tack needed for hauling buggies, carts, and people. She persuaded John to boost their Kansas business by buying iron-bending tools, including that big anvil now in the barn, from a man who died of an infected cut in his big toe, three winters ago. She handled the money, and John taught her the gun trade. Between the two, with the help of a young Negro boy, they manhandled horses, wagons, and harness work for rigs of all sizes.

For the last thirty years, Topeka had been a jumping off place for settlers and pilgrims of all kinds. Anyone headed west on the Santa Fe Trail. That's how they came to know of this "fine opportunity," as she called it.

"How did that happen?" I asked.

"A drummer selling iron pots, fireplace utensils, and second hand tools was here, in this barn, last June, when Marse passed on. Marse's wife had just got through hanging a big sign on the door an hour after the funeral—'EVERYTHING FOR SALE—CONTACT ILSA JOHANSEN—US POST OFFICE, CHAMA, NEW MEXICO.' She had little flyers printed up even before the funeral, describing the barn, the three-acre parcel it sits on, fixing a price of nine thousand dollars for it. Cash only."

"That's how you found out, from the drummer?"

"You betcha. He caught the train the next morning out of Lamy, so we learned about the offer from Mrs. Johansen's flyer three days after the funeral. John wired the sheriff's office here, and we bought the place by telegram. I could not believe our luck. Being in Topeka, we knew a lot about Santa Fe. Both names are on the side of every train that passes through our home town, you know. We thought Chama was closer to Santa Fe than it turned out to be. Everyone who goes to or from Santa Fe and the rest of America must pass through Topeka. Did you know that?"

Turns out, she knew a lot I didn't know about. Somehow, I guessed this little slip of a girl could teach me a lot. There was a certain sing-song about her voice and manner.

"I've got help, you know," she said, maybe because most men likely doubted her ability to run a business by herself. "Don Moya, a cousin of the man who owns the hotel, works here two days a week. He left early this morning for the Cross S to pick up two yearlings they want me to hold until the spring roundup. You staying long?"

"Just overnight. When's he coming back?

"Don Moya?"

"Yes."

"Probably a few days. He has a brother a year younger than him who rides for the Cross S. I'm new to the livery horse business," she said, flashing a smile.

"Well, I know Ernesto Garcia from past trips here. He's a hand and knows mules. I'm thinking about selling mine. You interested?"

"Maybe."

"Okay, I'll talk to you about it later. I need to talk to Joe Pete first. Nice to hear that the board is still a dollar a day."

"Well, that's the going price around here. Its two dollars in Topeka. Maybe in time I can inch the fee up to a buck-quarter. Think folks would stand for that?"

"Jill, I can tell you a little about riding the ridges and rivers around here, and a little about the law. But, the price of anything is something that I've never figured out."

I thanked her for the coffee, and went back to the double stall. No Más's winter coat was dirty and tangled after the five-day ride down from Denver. The mule could wait, but No Más needed work. So, I continued brushing, watching the little wisp of a girl. She said she was twenty-three, and I was willing to take her word on it. But, she looked sixteen and acted thirty. She looked at me head on, but was soft spoken. She could not have possibly known the effect she was having on me—she didn't look like Mazy. But, she had a confidence about her that shook me a little. Mazy had also been so sure of herself, and so eager to take on new challenges. Like leaving her comfortable life in the Espanola valley to chase up to the top of a mountain with me. Now, here was Jill, another wisp of a girl with her shoulders squared, and a firm grip on a new life after losing her dad. *Get a grip on your own life—you got a law job to do,* I thought.

"I'll settle up with you in a day or two. I'll send a boy for my gear from the hotel. Nice talking to you," I said, ducking down to pick No Más's feet and take a deep breath.

The Elliot Hotel had five rooms to let and only one customer, me. A bird-faced desk clerk said he'd send someone to fetch my gear, told me the room would be two-fifty, the Chinese Bathhouse was open, and the bar was not yet full. He slid a brass key across the desk before returning to the dime novel he held open to his chest. The room was musty, with a closed-in winter smell. There was a small wood stove in the corner, radiating a dry heat throughout the room. Don't know about the bed, but it was not gravel, and had three blankets. The wash basin was clean, more or less, and the towel rack held the same towel it did when I stayed here a year ago. I used the facilities down the hall, took a Chinese bath across the street, got my hair cut by a mute barber, and headed back up George to Under-Sheriff Joe Pete's office. It was nigh on to five o'clock. Be dark soon.

"Angus, by God. It's you! Ain't you a grand sight with that shiny bit of work on your chest," Joe Pete boomed, with his big hand stuck out, and a grin spreading out from one bony jawbone to the other. The lines in his forehead quivered and his gray eyes just could not help but squint at me.

"Yep. In the flesh."

We shook hands, he poured a cup for both of us, and we settled into the two cane-back chairs next to the stove. It'd been six months since I rode out of Santa Fe after the coroner's inquest conducted by Judge Blakey. That was the first time my undercover work as a US Marshal had been announced by anyone. There had been talk I was the law, or a lawbreaker; most didn't know for sure. Now, Joe Pete, wearing his own badge, beamed at mine.

"Eye god, Angus. You do take the cake. Deputy United States Marshal in the flesh! I heard the talk, but you lit out of Santa Fe after they dropped all the charges last year, based on what, no evidence, or you really were the law, or what? I never got the straight of it."

"It's a long story, Joe, but I got time if you do."

So I gave Joe the straight of it. I was working undercover for the federals in Denver looking into the cross-border train robberies. I reminded him about the posse he led to capture me, and we talked about me shooting Standard H. Plumb. I also told him about capturing Tom Emmett and then letting him go. He'd heard something about that, but since it did not involve Chama or Rio Arriba County, he let it go on past him like a dust devil on George. He filled me in on the no accounts that he'd dealt with here in Chama, and two cases of cattle rustling last summer. He also gave me the town talk about Jill Garrison, and what a surprise she was to everyone in town.

"She's just exactly what this town needs, Angus, a girl with spunk and a head for business. She's something this town has never seen, a young woman who looks like a princess from Norway or somewhere, with hair of gold, and a figure to match."

"To match what? All I saw was a pair of baggy overalls."

"Yes, and that's likely all you'll ever see, since you're only passing through. The town folk are protective about her, and she's smart. So, she don't show off none. But, we had a roundup party in town last October, when all the ranchers came to town, and Jill showed up in a dress. Oh boy! You should have seen the commotion she caused. The ranch boys stammered, the local girls took notice, and Mrs. Dorance, the preacher's wife, could not quit beaming. 'Ain't she something?' she kept saying. She was, everybody agreed."

"Yeah, well I'm glad for all of you here in Chama, but I need to ask what you know about the Santa Fe Ring, and the goings-on in Albuquerque with the Yarberry case."

"Sure, but let's do that over dinner—steak and whiskey sound good? At the Elliot?"

An hour later, I went downstairs to the dining room. It used to be a 20' × 20' cot room where two dozen Chinese railroad workers were housed between trips up the canyon laying track for the Denver & Rio Grande Railroad. Back then, the cots were lined up on both sides of the room, leaving a path to the latrine outside. There were no facilities on the first floor. They let the workers cook for themselves, on an oversize wood stove built up on a brick platform at the rear of the room. That had now been closed off for the kitchen, but they still had that old Cleveland Stove puffing a thin trail of smoke out the damper door.

There were four tables, with five chairs at each, and a bench cozied up to a waist-high shelf below the windows facing George. Joe Pete was settled into a chair at the table closest to the door and a little fresh air. The table was plain set, dark brown native pottery for dishes, railroad-style dinner settings, and little bottles of condiments, salt, pepper, chili sauce, and a jar of pickles. Everyone in town seemed to fancy pickles, including Joe Pete, who had two on his plate, alongside a double-size whiskey glass, half-full.

There was only one dining room employee in the winter, a tall Mexican with a drooping mustache, jiggling jowls, and a face that looked as if he'd been left outside in the sun all his life. But, his eyes seemed young, and they smiled at me when he hurried over.

"*Buenas tardes, Señor Angus, es un placer verte de Nuevo,*" he said, giving me a small nod as he pulled the chair out for me.

"It's a pleasure to see you again, too," I said, recognizing him from some years back. I couldn't remember his name, but recalled he'd worked across the street at the railroad station.

"I am Reyes, and I am working here now, and also at the Wall brothers' dry goods store three doors down. They don't need me over at the railroad station anymore."

"*Y así, viejo amigo*," I said, returning the nod. It made me feel good to be back in New Mexico, where manners counted.

"You remember I am called Reyes, but the regular customers here, including Undersheriff Pete, they all call me 'Hurry Up.' *Que no?*"

"Well, hungry customers are an impatient bunch. So, Hurry Up Reyes, I'll join in the sport of it."

"Sure, but my hurry up is not so fast. I'll try to get those steaks cooked; the dishes wiped clean, and be back here before that bottle is empty."

Joe Pete, snagged my glass with one hand, upended the whiskey bottle with the other, and poured me a double shot. The sharp aroma of whiskey, not yet six months, old seeped out of the open bottle. Pushing the glass back at me from his side of the table, he topped his glass off, raised it, tipped it toward me, and then up toward the tin ceiling.

"Here's to you, Marshal, and may the gods up there watch over you as you ride down the Rio Grande and away from the safety of these mountains."

"Joe, thanks for the toast, but I don't aim to put myself in harm's way in Albuquerque. I just need to sort out some facts that don't seem to add up."

We ordered steaks, rare for me, burnt for him, and whatever came with 'em. As usual, that meant two kinds of chili, a shared bowl of frijoles, a covered dish of tortillas, and a jug of well water to wash down the whiskey, quench the chili, and take a little sweat off your forehead. After we finished the steaks, Reyes served coffee and the only dessert on the menu, canned pumpkin pie. Joe Pete got back to our shared profession.

"Tell me again why the US Marshal in Colorado needs to send you to Albuquerque. There's a US Marshal for the Territory in Santa Fe, ain't there? Are they more federal up there in Colorado than us?"

"Nope. I guess it's because Colorado is a state. New Mexico is just a territory. And, there are some questions about this Yarberry fellow because he spent some time in questionable situations in Colorado. What I do know is that my boss wants to know what really happened in a shooting that seems justified by law, but not to a local jury. And, he wants some answers from Yarberry, which he might be willing to give now, seeing as how his time on this earth looks to be short."

"Ain't that the truth," Pete said, wiping a little ketchup from the corner of his mouth before pushing another forkful of carefully cut-up meat into it.

"Joe, how's it look to you? Pretty rare to find a lawman guilty of murder, ain't it? The territorial court has upheld it. The lawman, name of Milton Yarberry, is under lock and key in Santa Fe, waiting for the hangman to show up and drop him fifteen feet down a trap door to the end of an eight-foot rope."

"So, your boss thinks this Yarberry is innocent?"

"Don't know what he thinks. He got his facts from a judicial opinion that is about as clear as the Rio Chama at flood stage," I told Joe Pete.

"How come he's sending you?" Joe asked back.

"Dunno. Maybe because his orders come from the Justice Department in Washington City, District of Columbia, east coast."

"No, I meant why you? Why not just get it all squared away by the US Marshal in Santa Fe? Or from the Sheriff of

Bernalillo County—his name's Perfecto Armijo. I've done some business with him over the years. Straight shooter. Looks you in the eye."

I got up, took both coffee cups back to the big stove in the kitchen and asked Hurry Up for a refill. He obliged. I walked back and handed one to Joe Pete.

"Joe, you're causing me some heartburn. Hell fire, man, I don't know why he sent me down here. You ever heard of this Yarberry fella?"

"Yeah, I heard what the Santa Fe New Mexican said happened, back during his trial. Didn't follow it close. Ain't my jurisdiction."

"What do you remember?"

"Seems like Yarberry had a reputation up in Colorado before landing in Albuquerque. Got run out of Canon City, I think it was. There was something about him leaving Las Vegas in a cloud of dust behind a dead freighter's cold body, which had been cleaned out of whatever money he had in his pockets. Expect they hired him as constable in Albuquerque because they thought he was a gunman; I think the headline was 'Milton Yarberry, A Shootin' Fool.'"

"But, there was no connection between him and the victim? That right?"

"Beats me."

"Where's he now?"

"Santa Fe penitentiary, I expect. Waiting for his time to climb those twenty steps."

"Is there an execution date?"

"Dunno. But, it ain't legal without an execution warrant. You can look at that on your way down to Albuquerque. Gonna stop by Santa Fe anyhow, ain't you? The stage stops there for a half day to change horses and to take on new passengers."

"I ain't taking the stage. Gonna ride No Más, a new little pony I got up in Tierra Amarilla. But, I'm leaving my mule here for a while. You can use him anytime you need to pack something."

"How's he at packing dead bodies? Spring's coming in a month, and there's always a body somewhere needs hauling in to bury once the ice melts."

"Black Jack ain't never seen a body, far as I know. But, he's about as steady a hired mule as you've ever seen. He'd be fine."

"Speaking of riding south, with your new shiny badge on your chest, I'm wondering if you got the right kit for a lawman headed south to where they have real gunfights."

"Right kit? What do you mean?"

"Well, I can see from your holster that you've recently cleaned and oiled that Colt .45," he said, with a grin.

"Yep. Think you taught me that, some time back."

"Probably did, but maybe it's time you moved up in gun class, seeing as how you're the federal law, and headed down into places were federal law might not be all that welcome."

"What could be better than Colonel Colt's best gun?" I asked.

"Angus, come on back to my office. I have better coffee there than Reyes makes here. I got something to show you."

So, we walked back to his end of George. Full dark now, quarter moon coming up to the south. It was likely to drop the mercury down to well below freezing by morning. As always, I enjoyed the night and paid no mind to the cold. When we got back to his office, he stoked the fire and stirred the pot with some ground coffee out of a gunny sack. I waited him out. Don't work to hurry Joe Pete when he's building up to tell a story.

After a while, he said, "You don't read much, do you? And, you don't come to town all that much, either. So, you might not have heard of Colonel Colt's newest gun—it's called the Buntline Special. Want to see one?"

"Okay."

Joe Pete got up, went to the gun cabinet behind his desk, dug out a little brass key from the watch pocket in his vest, and opened the lock on the bottom drawer.

"Give this a gander," he said, as he came back and peeled back an oil-backed, canvas sheath holding the longest-barreled pistol I'd ever seen.

"Hell's that?" I asked.

"A Buntline Special. The story is that Ned Buntline, who was no shooter himself, but wrote a bunch of dime novels, and made a pile of cash for it, talked the Colt factory into making this special version of its Colt Frontier Special after it came out in 1878. That one, a double action in .44-40 caliber, is a damn fine piece especially because it uses the same cartridge as the Winchester Model 1873 lever-action rifle. I seem to remember you packing that in your saddle scabbard. Right?"

"Yep. It's still tied to my saddle, which is in J. Garrison's tack room down to the livery stable."

"Well, the thing about the Winchester rifle in your saddle scabbard and the Colt revolver on your belt is that you only need to lug around .44-40 bullets. No confusion and you get the same firepower in your handgun as your rifle."

"I suppose my mule would appreciate that, too. It'd be a lighter pack for him."

"True enough, but I ain't thinking of your mule. I'm thinking about you, in a fix with some bad hombres sighting in on you. The Buntline Special, in .44-40, has less hand kick, and a more accurate shooting range because of the barrel length. Hell, this ain't no small thing—the barrel is twelve inches long, and that gives the entire gun an eighteen-inch breadth. They say it's the most accurate handgun in the world."

"Yeah, but it's probably a chore to draw, especially if some fool is pulling leather on you at the time you need it."

"Suppose so," Joe Pete said. "You been in any of those situations lately?"

"Situations?"

"Gunfights, Angus. Wearing that badge sort of invites gunfights."

"No, not lately. Hell, not ever. I've arrested some outlaws, and shot two of 'em. Challenged a time or two, but always walked away from drawdown gunfights."

"Me, too, but men looking for reputations are itching to face a young lawman like you. Especially one with a big badge from the by-god United States of America. Federal ain't cow town, you know. This Buntline Special is dead-on accurate from fifty yards—puts some distance between you and a man with an itch to kill you."

"Could be. But my big badge comes with a small federal salary. It don't allow for buying a gun like this one; it's mighty fine to see and sure has a heft to it. Maybe I'll have to arrest somebody down Albuquerque way. But, maybe not. Either way, my Colt will do me just fine."

Joe Pete poured us another cup of what he called Law Coffee—a mix of scalding black root coffee, beet cane sugar,

and powdered milk. We sipped awhile. He was good at that—
sippin' and stayin' quiet. We shared a little recent history—river
riding, mountain game, interesting people on the trail, but
eventually he came back to the Buntline Special. Brought it
up when talking about gun hands with big reputations.

"You know why Ned Buntline had this model made?"

"No idea."

"So's he could give 'em away to his famous friends. Men
like Buffalo Bill Cody and Wyatt Earp. Buntline wrote about
them, and lots of other gun hands. 'Course, some say Buntline
never even hefted one of these. He just wrote about them and
cultivated real men of the gun for their stories by handing
over a few guns."

"So, if you don't mind me asking, how'd you come by
this one?"

"Bought it in Santa Fe off a homesteader. Seems he bought
it off a traveling circus man and neither one could shoot a short
barrel, much less a long one like this. I ain't got no real need
for it, but I'd kind of like to make you a trade for it."

I let that simmer. He went out back to use the facilities.
I hefted the Buntline and tried it in my holster. It fit, because my
holster narrowed down to a hole at the bottom for the barrel.
So, the extra length was OK. Joe Pete came back, cupped his
hands to the stove, and rocked back on his boot heels.

"Joe, it's mighty thoughtful of you to show me this, but
I'm investigating a past crime here, and not likely to run into
the kind of situations you're talking about."

"Maybe so, but you said you were interested in the Santa Fe
Ring, and whether those big boys had a hand in the shooting
case down in Albuquerque."

"I said my boss wondered whether the outcome of the case on appeal was their doing."

"Well, here's the thing about the Santa Fe Ring. They are not outlaws; they are in the law like ticks on a stray dog. They more or less control things at the upper reaches of law. They don't use guns; they do it with business dealings and elections. But, when someone gets in their way, they've been said to hire gun hands."

"Said to? What's that mean?"

"Well, just that—it's talk, not proof—no witnesses—just talk. But, if what you told me about the goings-on in Albuquerque with that town marshal, Yarberry, then maybe what you need is a gun that does two things—marks you as someone who knows his firearms, and someone to keep at a distance. Might make a man think twice before calling you out."

And, that's how I came to trade my Colt Peacemaker, with the shotgun thrown in, and no charge for using my mule for the next month or two, all for Joe Pete's Buntline Special.

"Good trade," he said.

I wondered whether he'd slicked me, or whether I'd just succumbed to a long barrel over a short one.

CHAPTER 6

Jill Garrison in Chama

I COULD HARDLY BELIEVE MY EYES when I stepped out of my office and saw US Deputy Marshal Angus Esperazza headed my way. He was one hundred feet up George headed south on foot toward my barn. He had heavy looking saddle bags slung over his left shoulder, two gunny sacks tied together by a leather strap over the other, a Winchester '73 crooked in one arm, and a near grin on his face. *What's he got to grin about on a morning this cold*? I thought. But, mostly, I thought he looked to be a man with a purpose. His canvas duster was layered over a felted wool coat with a big collar that stuck up high on his neck. His hat, a black 5x Beaver, was snugged down against the morning frost. His chaps were inside the barn with the rest of his kit, but it was plain to see he was about to head out. And, there was no doubt that this was a man who'd saddle his own horse, and took care in doing it.

"Good morning," I said, "north or south?"

"Pardon," he asked, as he lugged the bags and gun inside.

"North or south? Up Colorado way or down the Rio Chama?"

He narrowed his eyes, not in an unfriendly way, but the grin was gone. Somehow, I knew this was a man who grinned at life, not usually at other people, particularly girls, like me.

"South."

"Need anything from me, brushes, coffee, grain for the trail, anything?"

"No, but thanks."

That's the second thing I liked about him, now that I look back on it. He had manners, but did not use words loosely. He told me about leaving Black Jack here and that Undersheriff Pete was welcome to use him. He talked as much to No Más as to me, explaining in short, easy spurts that they'd be riding the Rio Chama to Espanola, then the Rio Grande to Albuquerque, with a stop in Santa Fe.

"No Más," he explained to me, "has never been out of Colorado before this."

A man who thinks his horse deserves to know where he's going before mounting up was a new notion to me. It was just a notch or two above freezing in the barn, but he took his duster, coat, and his second shirt off, and attended to the job of brushing, picking feet, and adjusting his saddle and bridle tack on No Más. That's when I saw the Buntline, holstered snug against his right hip.

"I see you're packing a Ned Buntline Special. That's a long piece of barrel fronting six lead messages, or so my father described it."

"You know guns?" he asked, giving me a half-grin from the far side of No Más, where he was adjusting the off-side Latigo leather, and tugging it to the heavy saddle bags.

"My father was a gunsmith, before he died. I used to help him some, and he taught me to shoot before I started school. He was unusual that way—thought women ought to do their own shooting. Would you mind giving me a look at that long barrel? I've only seen one other, on my father's work bench two years ago. He was helping the owner refigure the detachable shoulder stock."

"What say?"

"Well, Colt sold these as handguns, of course. But, they made detachable shoulder stocks for most of the other twelve-inch barrel guns in their inventory. Called 'em 'Buggy Guns,' as I remember my father's explanation. The .44-40 cartridge would fit rifle barrels, and this barrel. So, if the ammunition was interchangeable, why not the function of the weapon as well?"

"Not sure I take your meaning. Don't rifles and pistols serve the same function?" he asked me with a perplexed look on his face.

"Well, you know that the revolver was made for killing men. The rifle was for killing game. Liam, that was my dad's name, always said, remember what you're about when you strap on a revolver—it ain't gonna need skinning, just burying."

"I expect your father was right. Just never thought of it that way. I didn't know about the shoulder stock for a Buntline Special. I just traded my Peacemaker to Joe Pete last night."

"Why'd you trade?" I asked.

"Well, not sure myself. It just seemed like a good idea to be flexible in packing ammo—same bullets for my rifle and my handgun."

"You know how to shoot a handgun that's a foot and a half long?"

"Ain't fired this one yet, but I suppose it ain't all that different."

"It is. You'll see. Colonel Colt called the eighteen-inch handgun 'killing steel.'"

He let me see the piece. I hefted it and checked the load. Then, I showed him where he could take the black wood handgrip off—and the shoulder stock would slide into place. And, I showed him how to crook his left arm out in front of his body, lay the barrel over his forearm as a sighting stand, and fire from a standing position, just as though he were prone. He allowed as how it was a tricky maneuver, and he hoped he'd never have use for it. Then, he tied his chaps down, strapped the Buntline on, adjusted his spurs, and put on his duster. With a small smile, he mounted up, and walked No Más out the double barn doors.

"You've been kind, Miss, and I appreciate the gun lesson."

"It's Jill, not Miss. You're welcome. Stop by if you get back this way. Coffee's always at the boil."

He gave me the slightest little nod of a hat I ever saw, and tapped No Más lightly with one spur.

CHAPTER 7

Angus and No Más– Ridges and Rivers

"ALL RIGHT, NO MÁS," I said. "I know this is new ground for you, so here's the geography." There's those that think horses don't care where they are headed. Not true. At least it don't seem true for whichever horse I'm on. With that explanation, I spent the next few miles telling this new horse what *river* riding was about and how different it was from the *ridge* riding we'd done up in Colorado.

Rivers come from mountains where rain leaks out, trickles into little creeks, and in time grow up to become streams. Streams beget rivers. Rivers are powerful in spring when the runoff from melting snow cranks 'em up. But, they mellow out in summer and sometimes disappear underground. Then, they bubble up before reaching the closest ocean. The way I

47

think about it, rivers are like little kids. Kids become adults when they grow up, just like colts do. But rivers never grow up, they just become oceans.

"The headwaters of the Rio Chama are up north, just over the Colorado line in your home state, No Más, purtin' near where the West Fork and the East fork join up and become a dandy, little stream. Rambling south from there, it gets to where we are now, Rio Arriba County, where old Joe Pete is the by-god undersheriff. He's the only law in Chama, the town we just left. We'll fork up ahead, maybe five, six miles, and get ourselves over onto the east bank. That suit you?"

We forked in slow-moving, icy, water about two feet deep and thirty wide. No Más teased the water some, sticking his snout in and shaking the water off. But, I could tell he was having too much fun to take a real drink. Two miles downriver we came on a sight I was afraid would just plain disappear in a few years.

"Now, No Más, just you take a one-eyed gander at that," I said as I looked on the far side of the river, backed up into a little pond.

"That's where beavers live. It's a dam, and a hogan. It's also a fort. I know you must have seen some of these up higher in the Rockies. But, just you look at that one. See that still, deep water backed up into the draw? Beavers do that to protect against predators, like bears and men. They float their food to it, and chew up little logs to make it hold fast against ice and wind."

No Más paid no attention to the beaver dam, and seemed to have lost interest in my explanation of rivers and geography. But, big beaver dams like the one we were looking at, a good ten feet in diameter, are stuck up over three feet *above* the water line.

"See there, No Más," I said. "You're looking at five shades of green, all of 'em wet, and glistening in the midday sun. No beavers in sight, though. Smart little critters, beavers. Some say they're just overgrown rodents, but they aren't messy like rats, nor do they squeak like mice. And, I never saw beaver scat, so that puts 'em on top of the rodent food chain."

We made what I figured was more than twenty-five miles, mostly easy riding on the east bank of the Chama, following its meander, and letting it take the town feeling out of our bones. An hour before sundown, I forked the river again because I could see a bluff maybe a quarter mile up on the west side. Looked to be what the Utes would say is "good camp place."

Utes, and probably roaming Navajos, too, know better than to pitch a night camp within the sound of running water. They are raiders and always on the lookout for something to capture, or kill. Like them, I figured to scout that little ridge up off the flat of the river, in a thick stand of ponderosa pine. I'd have a distance to walk back down for water, but the view would be clear for five miles in three directions. Safer that way—I'd hear whatever man or beast was heading my way before they got wind of my smoke.

Unsaddling No Más in a little opening in the front stand of trees, I hacked a space for him, used my lariat to make a loose enclosure, brushed him down, and gave him a half-nose bag of grain. He'd eat that up in short order and then munch on the sweet grass around two aspen saplings that must have blown in last summer, but were leafless now.

I laid out my own sleeping pit six feet away, tucked under the overhanging branches of two, forty-foot tall pines. Then, I scooped out a circle in the hard, mushy moss, on the downslope.

The wind, soft now, would pick up some in the night. It was coming at me. Good, that'd blow the smoke from my little cook fire back into the trees. No sign of me from the east. Years of ridge riding and camping alone in pine tree country had given me a gift; I could separate the sound of a deer's footfall from a horse, or from the careful step of a man, red or white.

"No Más," I whispered, "you pay attention, too, but don't go to whinnying, or foot stomping, every time you hear something. Come nightfall, we need to be quieter than a Rocky Mountain lynx so's nobody sneaks up on us. But, before we get quiet, I believe it's time I tried Mr. Ned Buntline. Mind the noise now."

I walked No Más, now freshly brushed and without a bit in his mouth, down to the river. He drank a bellyful as I reloaded both water bags and my saddle canteen, and switchbacked up the ridge to our hideout for the night. Then, I checked the six rounds in ole Ned's chamber, checked to see the firing pin was tight, and looked through the open barrel at the orange sky to the west. Clean and ready.

I eyeballed a point about neck high on a big, solid pine about fifty yards away, stuck the pistol straight out at arm's length, breathed in, aimed, and fired. Swoosh, bang, splat, in that order. Two feet below where I'd aimed, and off to the right. I cocked the hammer back for my second shot. I adjusted for the drop in the shot by aiming an inch or so higher than what I hoped to hit—that splintery branch dead ahead of me on the tree. Missed by more than a foot. Too high because this time I didn't stiffen my elbow for the recoil. The next three shots more or less arrived in the general vicinity of the target. I thought about taking Jill's advice: using my left arm as a standing arch for the barrel. But I didn't. Figured I'd get better at this my own way. So, I shot another six rounds—got the same results.

Dinner that night was the same as every first night out— coffee hot, beans the same, hard tack hard, and one strip of slab bacon. It's a wonder what slab bacon can do for beans and hard tack. I nursed the fire to sleep a half-hour after sundown, and then turned in myself. My double canvas bedroll, with its felted wool liner, made me real toasty for about four hours. Then, asleep with one ear awake, I heard it.

Horse hooves, shod, iron clanking on shale; that probably made it a white man, not a Ute or a Navajo. Some soft squeaking, like leather pulling, and a little pat, maybe a rope off a saddle horn? Cowboy riding at night? Why?

Rolling out over the Winchester to my boots, I pulled them on slowly, breathing measured little breaths. No Más heard him, too; he didn't whinny, but padded both front feet down some. Inching up slowly, I pulled the pistol from its holster, slung it on the branch just above my bedroll, and cocked it to safety. Then, stepping slowly over to No Más, I laid my left hand on his nose. He settled. I just listened.

The horse got a little louder and closer, but still moved at a slow walk, so slow it was as if he were crawling. He seemed to take one step forward at a time. Guessing, I figured he was thirty, maybe forty feet away, but still ten feet down below me on the first switchback. I eased forward, and caught sight of him and his rider.

Big man, big hat, and coal black horse from what I could tell with a half-moon ebbing in the western sky. Fancy bridle rig, oversized horn, and a short-barrel shotgun crooked in the pit of his left arm, forearm held high, with long reins trailing out of his left hand. That left his right hand free to grasp the stock just behind the trigger guard. He wore what looked to be an elk-hide coat, with a sewed-on, sheepskin collar pulled up over his neck. His face was invisible under a flat-crowned sombrero. Here was a man with an outfit; wool pants, store bought, tucked into the tops of black boots, covered with mud and frost, with big heels dressed in shiny, big-roweled silver spurs. But, those rowels, which normally would have been audible for fifty feet, had been silenced by two, blue, bandana-style handkerchiefs wrapped around their backs. He was coming at me quiet as he could. Then he stopped and sat his horse for two minutes, listening. I knew he could not see me because he was looking ahead at the trail, and I was up above him to his right and slightly behind him. I just let him be. He finally broke the silence.

"Okay, señor, what I want to know is what you're doing on my land, *por favor*," he said to the trail above him.

"I'd like to know why a *vaquero* with a shotgun in his hand is sneakin' up on me in the middle of the night," I answered.

With that, he twisted in his saddle to peer up at me, but seemed to have trouble placing my voice. I lowered myself down behind the ridge and crawled a few feet to my right. Neither of us said anything for another minute or two.

"So, señor, we are standing still, in the middle of the night, waiting for what? I saw a small wisp of smoke just before sundown, that's what gave you away. But, I had a bull on my rope at the time, and had to take him back down to the pluma, two miles from here. Because I was not sure who or where you were, I had my supper first. Now I'm taking a ride up here. I like riding in the night, even in winter. You?"

"*Si*. Even in winter. Let's say you put your shotgun back in that empty scabbard, the one on the front of your saddle horn. I'll holster ole Ned, and you come on up here. Coffee?"

"*Si*, you got any brown cube sugar, señor?"

Over the course of the next day, I came to like Paco Armijo, his round, little *espousa*, and all six of their kids, stair-stepping down from fourteen to seven—four older boys and two younger girls.

"We had to keep trying," Luiza, his thirty-year old wife said.

The Armijo Ranch, branded with a slash A over a rocking bar, was a spread of about 10,000 acres, lifetime home to three Mexican *vaquero* families and probably fifteen hundred head of beef.

The next night, after I'd ridden back down the Rio Chama with him to his ranch, we spent the afternoon moving the bull he'd told me about on the switchback. Then, he explained that he knew me even before I rode across his ranch.

"Angus, I know you from something that happened maybe two years ago. I think you were being chased by the sheriff up in Chama and there was a big shoot-out up on Ten Shoes Up. Am I right?"

"Well, you got that right; do you know Joe Pete, the lawman leading that posse?"

"I never met him, but he hired a man who used to work here on this ranch for me. His name was Alfonso Ganado, and he was a good tracker and hunter. Someone shot him. Was that you?"

Wow, that took me aback.

"No, Paco. I did not shoot him. The man who shot him was called Bo String. I got to know him pretty well. Bo thought your hand, Alfonso, was an outlaw, and they pulled leather on one another. Alfonso got hit, but not killed. He still with you?"

"No, he moved on. He never talked much about that trip, except to say that the boss of the posse, I think his name was Captain Standard, or something like that, got himself shot, and that it turned out that you were not an outlaw. It was all very confusing. Now, you are a deputy US marshal. There must be some big story about you."

"Well, actually I was a deputy US marshal then, too. But, I was keeping the badge in my saddle bags. I was working on figuring out who was robbing the trains up north of here. Alfonso had no part in that. I hope he's okay, now."

"He was, last time I saw him—that was more than a year ago. I think he's leading pack trains over near Taos, and still hunting bear."

Eventually, over a shot of Mescal, the subject came up of why I was back in New Mexico. I told him that my boss was interested in a shooting by a lawman that happened down in Albuquerque two years ago.

"Oh, *si*, you are looking into the shooting of Milton Yarberry. Is that right?"

"Well, if that don't beat all. You know about that, all the way up here? Life's funny. But, I'd sure appreciate all you can tell me about it. Do you know the man?"

"I do not know Marshal Yarberry, but he works for the Sheriff of Bernalillo County, whose name, I'm proud to say, is also Armijo. He's my second cousin, as I think they say, only one time removed. His name is Perfecto Armijo, and he's the one who had to arrest this Yarberry, although he did not want to do it. Perfecto comes up here in the fall every year to hunt and fish with us. He brings all his kids, and they know all my kids. So, he told me about it—what was it?—maybe two years ago?"

"The shooting was in 1881, but the New Mexico Territorial Supreme Court just upheld the case, so I guess he is gonna be hung soon."

"Yes, and do you know who is the hangman?"

'No, can't say I do."

"It is my cousin, Perfecto. It falls to him to be the one up on the scaffold, and to tell them to drop the trap. Aiee, that's something he don't want to do. His friend and all."

I spent another full day with Paco because a winter storm moved in, dropping about three inches of fresh snow on the upper Espanola valley. It was nice to be inside, but the real reason for staying longer was listening to Paco's version of the Yarberry shooting. Well, maybe not actually Paco's version. I knew I was getting Perfecto's version, translated by Paco, watered down by the passage of two years.

Sunrise came to Paco's ranch at Tierra Amarilla sudden-like. Taos Mountain guards the predawn sun, and then throws it up into the sky all at once. I woke to a dusting of snow on the ground and a fine New Mexican breakfast in Luiza's kitchen.

Paco's directions were plain enough. "Just take the stage road from here down to Espanola, stop and see my cousins, then keep south to Santa Fe."

"I'm of a mind to ride the river bank, Amigo."

"Si, then you must ride west from here to the Rio Chama, cross over to the west bank, and go downriver to a very special place. It is the big 'Y' where the Rio Chama enters into the Rio

Grande. They are as one from there for more than a thousand miles all the way to the Gulf of Mexico. You know that's how we all got here; we came up that river to make a new life."

"Gracias, *amigo*. Maybe I'll stop by on my way back to Chama."

"You'll be welcome. But, don't forget. You can't ride the riverbank in many places from here to Espanola. There are deep canyons where the water hits both sides, and there is no trail past, only the water. And, it's too cold for you and No Más."

"Good advice. But, we've been wet before. *Hasta luego*."

CHAPTER 8
Angus at Tierra Amarilla

No Más and I headed due west, through the light snow on the ground, up and through muddy arroyos, climbing steadily to a blood orange mesa. Stopping at a small lake, I chewed down a hard tack biscuit and a stick of jerky. No Más chewed twenty minutes' worth of sweet grass in six inches of water at the edge of the lake. At high noon, when it should have been the warmest part of the day, we both felt the drop in air pressure. That's hard to explain, but you know it when you feel it. There was a noticeable shift in the wind from the southwest. The temperature sagged like a wet saddle blanket, dropping maybe five degrees in the last hour. We'd covered ten miles facing the southwesterly wind, and we'd be in the dark in another hour. Things were not looking good, so I pitched camp and stoked a good fire around a two-foot-diameter-sized ring of rocks. With my back to the wind, I fashioned a strong lean-to with one of my canvas tarps. The other would be under me when she hit.

"No Más," I said, "we got us a full Rocky Mountain blow. Put your butt to her."

Once the coals glowed inside the rock ring, I rolled over so that my back was to the pegged-down tarp with my belly facing the rocks around the fire of now-smoldering coals. The blow and the sound of the wind through the trees lulled me into a half-doze, half-alert state. Not cozy, but tolerable. No Más and I woke an hour before dawn to find two inches of new snow on my canvas tarp and an inch on his rump. He paid it no never mind.

"Used to that, ain't you, son?"

The day was heavy with clouds and a following wind. The ground was damp, but there was no falling snow as No Más broke a new trail through the brush. There are days when a cowboy can take credit for breaking trail, but this wasn't one of them. No Más paid close attention to his footing. I just enjoyed the carefulness he employed as we wound down the steep, granite shale to the riverbank. Late in the afternoon, the clouds gave us another hour of snow; a fine snow, wet enough to stick, but not affecting my view of the up-and-down country ahead. The snow whirled around us like a trick rider's lasso at a rodeo. I'd become accustomed to seeing what wet snow did to No Más's coat. It looked purtin' near a grizzly bear's hide with bits of ice hanging onto his mane and tail. I was dry as toast with three shirts and a leather vest under my well-oiled duster, but I could feel the cold seeping into my deerskin gloves.

With still about four hours to go before sundown, we hit the east bank of the Rio Chama. I scouted downriver a mile for a good fording place. Paco'd said we'd best cross over to the west bank for the ride down to Espanola. Figured he had a reason.

The spot I picked was a two-foot drop off into fast-moving water that looked about knee-deep. But, if there was a hole out there I couldn't see, we'd be belly deep. I swung down, loosened his front cinch, and moved the saddle pad up tight against his withers. He picked up his ears, knowing what it meant. Then I tugged up his back cinch one notch and swung back up. The fording was all up to No Más. He was courageous about fast-moving water. Removing both legs out of the stirrups, I gave him both knees, a double tap with my spurs, and he took the two-foot plunge off the bank. Grabbing ahold of the saddle hand with my left hand, I held the reins up high over his head with my right arm, but still looped to keep the bit loose in his mouth. There's a double trick to river crossings. Hang on to your saddle horn and remember that you can't cross a river by telling your horse where to go. Give him his head; he'll step or swim; either way you'll both reach the far bank.

"No Más—let's get 'er done."

We marched like a one-man army across to the west bank at a fast trot. I could feel No Más's big heart pumping blood up at me through his shoulder muscles. Every other step, he turned his big head slightly one way, then the other, making sure to move with the current, not against it. We drifted downriver maybe twenty yards, making the ford at about forty-five degrees. Then, with a mighty shake, he stomped two feet on the west bank and charged up the ten-foot bluff onto the Rio Chama's west bank. No Más like to shook me right off him when we reached a level spot atop the bluff. I tugged him back with the reins and gave him a loud whoa.

"Hoowee, No Más, you made that fine river behave, son. You're a keeper for sure."

About a half-mile down river, I found a wet limestone outcropping hiding a wind-carved, little cave dug in to its side. It was near covered by a stand of scrub oak and jack pine. "Perfect, don't you think, No Más?" I asked. And, it faced the northeast, which would deflect the onrushing wind behind us. I had a good three hours before sundown and some serious drying out to do.

I drug in enough downed timber to build a proper drying-out fire. Once the flames lapped up high enough, I hung my lariat on a nearby tree and strung my duster, chaps, coat, the two outer shirts, and boots. They all commenced to steam, with the fire lapping up and the water draining out. 'Course there was the danged smoke.

"No Más, don't be looking at me like that. You can't have one without the other."

In just over an hour's passing, everything was dry. I'd given No Más a long brushing, and rubbed him down with sage and a gunny sack. Couldn't tell whether he liked the sage, or just the rough feel of hemp in the gunny sack, but he whined what would have to do as a thank-you. I hobbled his front legs loose enough to let him move, but didn't tie him to the tree.

"Tied up horses and lightning strikes don't mix, do they, old son?"

Unrolling my tarp over both saddle blankets inside the little sandstone cave, I was pleased to find the back wall curved just right to fit my frame. I used my saddle bags as a pillow, my saddle as a wind buffer, and watched No Más settle in as I settled down. He spent the next two hours munching on tufted hair grass, sedges, and what my mother called pussytoes. "No, I do not know why they call them that," I muttered to No Más. I suppose he accepted my answer, because he turned his head away and continued to stomp the ground near the tree base with his hooves. I coffeed up, had a double dose of beans with two slices of bacon, and turned in before the sun went down. Figured I'd need all the rest and warmth I could store up for tomorrow. All night long, I heard trees cracking with frost. What looked like blue steam drifted off the river below us. At full dark, there were no stars visible, but I could sense a soft moonglow over the clouds. The pale blue, opaque sky comforted No Más and me. Not that he said as much, but I could tell—ears still, eyes half-lidded, and steady breath sounds. He might have gone to sleep before I did. Hard to tell with horses. They don't tell you in words what they're doing. But, they like to hear me talk. Most of 'em, anyhow.

I waited a full hour after sunrise, just lying snug in my bedroll, giving the day a chance to warm up.

"You have to be patient with winter days, No Más; you learned that up in Colorado, didn't you?"

The black ash in the fire pit covered up still warm coals six inches down. I used two handfuls of sage brush that I'd stuck under my tarp the night before to whisper the coals back to life. There was plenty of ponderosa pine cones and dead pine needles around, so I nursed a little fire into existence. Luiza'd given me two fresh biscuits wrapped in greased paper. I ate them slowly, sipped my coffee, and watched No Más. A near-starved horse will damn near inhale grain out of a nosebag. But, No Más, while always hungry, took his time. He'd given me four steady days of riding because I let him graze a few minutes out of every hour. He drank often and grabbed at tall shrubbery along the path. The grain in the sack was what they call supplementary, but No Más took it as dessert.

Thirty minutes after rolling out, I saddled up and headed downriver toward a cloudy sky on an uncertain trail. We rode against a steady headwind on uneven ground. No more snow. Just a beautiful river to ride along listening to the tweets, shrills, and occasional caws of birds along the way. We passed several cold, icy marshes, with snow-laden pines and firs stuck out into the flow. There were rocky crags to go around, but all in all, we made steady progress south toward Espanola. By nightfall, we'd ridden twenty-five miles downstream to a small bluff, twenty feet above the river with a nice stand of trees.

"No Más, there you have it. Level ground and not much visibility. You think this will do for a small, winter camp?"

The next day was heavy with clouds. No new snow; good, crisp, winter riding. No Más's heavy breathing fogged the air in front, and my own fog came around my bandana and whipped past me. We pushed harder, and made a good fifteen mile passage by early afternoon. By then, we'd been riding for two, maybe three hours on mostly level ground. By now, the river seemed to be dropping before my eyes, down into a steep canyon. That's when I first heard the roar.

The shadows from the canyon walls made the day darker, like a sheet thrown over No Más and me. The water to my left ran even faster, frothing and whipping up on the rocks and eroding the trail alongside. Of a sudden, even the rocks seemed to hear something angry, in front, but not yet visible. Corrugated slops of lava appeared, most likely from some far off volcanic blow. Now both canyon walls towered above me, narrowing my view downriver. This was a singular place, no longer at peace with the land. What had been a nice walk along a soft bank became a wild chaos of sharp rocks and stony levels cut about by vertical ravines. Thickets of thorny scrip replaced pine, aspens, and willows.

"No Más, hold up, old son. I'm going to dismount and put my ear to the ground."

Stepping off him on his right side, I settled on a ledge of flat stone. Here the roar was definite, but not yet a cause for alarm, either. Afoot, the rocks felt as though the trail had dissolved into gray and black vapors, moving downriver invisibly. No Más was picking his way carefully around a narrow ledge between the rock wall and the water's edge. What had been just minutes ago a roar of both wind and water now blustered into the full roar of a cataract.

"No Más, you ever ridden a river cataract before? I have, but only once, on Tucson. It like to drowned us both. You can't see it yet, but what you're hearing is tons of water dropping out of the river bed into a fall I don't know how deep."

No Más's ears picked up, his throat muscles tightened, and he started throwing his head back and up.

"I know, dammit, I know. It's a choice we need to make here, where we could turn around and find another way forward to Espanola. If we go much further, we'll likely be committed since there might be no safe way to turn around. Ain't no backing up from that point, old son."

As had become his custom with me, No Más eased at the sound of my voice. But, my spine was tingling, and I expect his was, too, as I pondered my choices. Over the roar of water crashing on rock, and something else, something I could

sense, but couldn't get my mind around, I decided to chance
the cataract. Still on the ground, I took off the heavy duster,
chaps, and my spurs. Leaning into No Más, I undid the heavy
wool scarf around my neck and tied everything down double
tight behind the cantle. Just to be safe, I left two long leather
straps loose on either side of the saddle. Turning to No Más,
I adjusted the chin strap and loosened the half breed roller
on the spade bit, so it was easy in his mouth. He knew. Can't
say he agreed, but he made no attempt to back up or get me
to change my mind.

Stepping back up onto him, I centered myself in the
saddle, and carefully took my boots clean out of the stirrups.
As though it were an invisible command to No Más, he started
twitching his ears this way and that, and pawed the ground.
We moved forward as I pressed knees into him. Seventy-five
feet ahead, and after a thirty-foot loss in elevation, the roar
became deafening. There was no longer a trail or any solid
ground between the walls of the canyon and the black water.
It was just water screaming up at us as No Más slid down into
the fast-moving pool.

Funny how color changes in a river from one section to
another. We'd been riding along dark blue water, with flashes
of color on the rock bottom. But, here, everything was black as
frozen coffee. The Rio Chama ain't all that wide on flat terrain,
ranging from twenty to fifty feet over the last ten miles. But
here, the deep flow narrowed to maybe twelve feet across. It
was like fording by going downstream instead of across. The
water traveled at the usual winter rate; a stick thrown in would
disappear in seconds, lost in the top water plunging downhill.
We twisted through a sharp turn to our left in water that was

up over the stirrups and onto the saddle bags on both sides. The boulders were taller than thirty-year-old ponderosa pines. What I'd sensed earlier, but couldn't place in my mind, turned out to be an undertow.

"Don't let it worry you none, No Más. That tug you're feeling is fast water," I said in a low voice. The Utes called it "fast-moving lake in river." Anytime the bottom of the river is moving faster that the top, a good horse is apt to be a mite confused. "Don't be. Just steady on; we are about to get to a waterfall."

We had moved forward another thirty feet when the bottom suddenly dropped out from under us. The freezing water hit my face and neck as it splashed up over the D-rings. We were chest high and pulled downriver. With a little more tension in my voice that I wanted him to hear, I said to No Más, "No backing out now, old son. Stay loose." I could only see twenty yards ahead where protruding boulders and a hard, left-hand turn in the channel blocked out whatever was ahead of us. He kept inching back, fighting the bit, as I tightened up so he would not turn on me, and try to buck his way back upstream. If he lost his footing here, it would be nigh onto impossible to keep any purchase on the slippery rock bottom. And, we had two other menaces to worry about. The swift current on top and the undertow, which would pull No Más's feet first down the rapids ahead. I could not guess at whether we were in a by-god gorge, or just a short draw in the river. If it was a gorge, then we'd be facing underwater boulders the size of outhouses. There'd be half-submerged tree trunks hidden under thousands of gallons of river water. No Más would be maneuvering in the middle of the river, with me, a heavy saddle, and a full kit lashed down on his back. Lots of things to snag. But, fretting wouldn't help. There was no going back.

Icy spray spewed up at me. Oddly, it felt warm. No Más made a deep, hallow gasp that horses make when they drop suddenly into cold water. But, the water just then became warmer than the air around us. The water was deep. We were floating, not swimming. Lagging the reins around the saddle horn, I leaned down and into No Más's neck. I put my left hand up onto his halter.

"Steady, No Más, steady now, don't panic on me. Just let's go on with the flow. Let the water carry us. Steady, son."

I gritted my teeth and held my breath as I forced myself to unlock my knees so that my legs could flow along No Más's back.

The sheer rock faces on both sides glistened in the wet sky. We hit a bend in the river, a little on our own motion, but mostly on the upper flow. Maneuvering No Más around the big, protruding boulders on my right with my knees, we swung to dead center in midchannel. That's when it got worse—white spew fifty yards ahead, climbing three or four feet over the over the top of the river in front of me.

"Rapids ahead, son. Steady now, stay with me."

Now the rumble was drowned out. I couldn't figure it. It felt like the water ought to be sucking us down, but instead there was a tamer descent. Debris on the top of the water parted for us, and the rocks sank beside us as we passed. And, No Más became his own rock—hard and invincible to whatever the river had in store for us. Now we were in the spray, the water hitting his face then mine, smacking ice into eyes, mouths, and ears. The roar became a howl, like a beast unchained. Now I knew the river was at its most fierce; screaming in a language I'd never heard before. The thunder of water crashing on rock sounded like army cannon fire. Boulders were crashing by us, and seemed actually moving up river. I knew that wasn't so, that it was the water going around them, but it was hard to make sense of it.

"Hang on to the river, No Más. Never mind the rocks, they ain't us. We're the river, son, we're the river."

No Más managed a turn seconds before we crashed into a giant boulder. It felt like the rock was trying to throw us up into the sky. Being in the full grip of rushing, white water is easy. Just float and you'll hit land soon enough. Ain't no use in fighting. I remember thinking about jumping from black water to white water without any effort. But, No Más was smarter than I was. Let the river do the damn work.

Then, white water turned black again, and the big boulders disappeared. A minute later, a new menace shot up. Dead ahead. A fifty-foot long captured western fir, with the roots and ball sticking up about chest level. No Más could have ducked under, but I was atop him, and had no play. I remember two things. First, twisting to my right to avoid an overhanging branch the size of a twelve-pound cannon, but not quite making it. Second, intense pain as my left arm fractured. I lost purchase on No Más's halter and my right-handed grip on the saddle horn. Torn from the saddle, I thrashed wildly with my good arm and swam, or maybe I crawled to where I thought I could see small rocks around a craggy pool of mostly still water, ten yards away.

Don't know how much time passed before I came around. Maybe just a few minutes, maybe longer. The roar was behind us. But, the roar in my head was a fierce pain, and the shock from the cold was so deep I couldn't open my mouth to stop my teeth from chattering. The duster I'd tied behind the cantle turned out to be a help; it had snagged on overhanging branches. And, somehow, I held onto it with my right hand. Together, we drifted over and onto the icy bank. I lost my hat, my seat on No Más. I thought I'd lost No Más, too.

I dragged my right leg out of the water and tried to roll over on my right side. Breath returned, the pain dwindled a little, and a trickle of blood from my nose brought taste back to my incredibly dry mouth. I was alive.

No Más was downstream, on the same side as me, about two hundred yards. I couldn't see him, but his whinny was unmistakable. I called out, but knew my voice could not carry that far. So, I half-crawled, half-walked down to him, along what had become a calm, settling stretch of river.

"Good horse," I said.

He just stood there, both rear feet still in the water, looking at me with hallowed eyes, covered in river slime and ice, dripping wet, but with my full kit intact, all lashed down, just like it was the end of a good day's ride on flat ground. Ten yards away, I spotted what looked like my hat. *Fancy that.*

The reins were hanging loose, his halter was half-off, but he still had the roller spade bit in his mouth. I motioned to him to follow, because I didn't have the energy to reach down and tug him. On flat ground, I could see a little piece of black sand and gravel. No Más followed, numb with cold, but no longer shaking with nerves. Unsaddling with one arm was messy. I just let his head stall, bridle, chest collar, cinch straps, and saddle fall like cut timber. No need to hobble, or tie him up. Neither of us was going anywhere today.

I spent the rest of that day, all of the next, and two full nights camped at the end of what I now knew was a half-mile long gorge, with no opening on either side. The rapids would have destroyed the best Indian canoe in the country. But, it didn't get me or No Más. My kit dried the second day, dirty as sin, curled up at every edge, but functional. My guns needed cleaning, a jigger of oil, and every piece of leather needed saddle soap and elbow grease.

My left arm took nicely to the splint I built out of two pieces of drift board. They were probably slats out of a buckboard, washed downriver. I tied my splinted arm to my chest with a canvas strip. Figured I could mount from No Más's off side by grabbing the horn with my right hand, and ride one-handed for as long as it took to get downriver to Espanola. My stores were played out, but the grain held, the coffee made the trip without damage, the bacon survived, and I was happy to feed the beans and soggy hard tack to the fish and birds. I saw no wildlife, none. Probably because I slept for the better part of two days.

"No Más," I asked, as I mounted from the off side, "can you get us to Espanola?"

He gave me a little bang with his head and pawed the ground. That's not horse talk. But, I took it as a signal. Espanola's just the next stop, but the job wouldn't be over until we got to Albuquerque.

CHAPTER 9

Angus Rides the Rio Chama to Espanola

IT WAS TWO HOURS AFTER SUNSET when No Más hauled me into Espanola, a hundred-year-old adobe village populated mostly by Mexicans. But, over the last three years new folks had moved in and the village became a town, more or less. Most of them worked on the Denver & Rio Grande railroad, and then just sort of stayed on. The D&RG laid its track through here in 1880, and then turned southwesterly to bend around Santa Fe, about forty miles down the Rio Grande. The town consisted mostly of old tents, new shacks, a dozen adobe buildings, and a two-story general store. The second floor over the general store, with an outside stairway entrance, invited anyone in need of a haircut, doctoring, or an undertaker. The sign said it all: *H. Schwartz—Barber—Undertaker—Surgery.* The barber,

Hector Schwartz, was a short, bald man with a mustache that wrapped around his lower face like a bank robber's mask. He cut hair, gave you a shave, and provided whatever kind of doctoring you might need. He was also the only undertaker for thirty miles in any direction. "My business," he told me an hour later, "calls for sharp blades and a steady hand in all three of my business offerings."

"Dr. Schwartz?" I asked when he came to the door carrying a lit oil lamp in one hand and a short, square-looking pistol in the other.

"My name is Angus and I'm in need of some doctoring."

"I'm not a doctor, but I am close. I went to the school in Germany where nurses are trained, but I'm no doctor. You can call me Hector, or Mr. Schwartz, but please, not Doctor."

"Your sign says, Barber, Undertaker, Surgery," I said, pointing with my good arm and hand.

"Yes, you're right, but it does not say doctor or imply that I'm trained in medicine. If you are here because of that home-made splint on your arm, I can replace it, or you can wait till it kills you and I'll handle your funeral. Take your hat off and I'll see if you need a haircut," he said, as he motioned me inside his upstairs house. The living room featured a large, chrome and leather barber's chair. The far end looked medical, what with the flat, sturdy table draped in white cloths, alongside several porcelain basins, towels, scissors, and a right-nasty-looking set of scalpels.

The thing about broke arms is you don't really know it's broke till they push it back together. That hurt some, but Mr. Schwartz handed me a thimble full of yellow liquid, "You will take this, please."

"What's in it?"

"It's called Laudanum here, but in Germany, when I was in school, they called it Tincture of Opium. And, because we were all good Germans, you know, we sometimes took it with a glass of German beer. I have some here, would you like a beer, also?"

"I heard of Laudanum. Chinese people use it, don't they?"

"The Chinese believe the best medicines are herbal—opiates are in that class. But, they use it to dull the sense of reality. I use it to dull pain. I'm going to have to realign your arm. It is quite painful, so do as I say, drink."

I can't say it worked. Or not. Maybe it'd hurt worse without the foul-tasting Chinese medicine. But, an hour later, feeling woozy, I walked out with my left arm encased in heavy plaster of Paris; that's what Mr. Schwartz called it. It ran from my wrist to a pinch below my elbow. He slung it in a canvas sack strapped to my chest and over my shoulder with two pieces of muleskinner reins.

"Keep it in this sling as much as you can, señor."

"For how long?" I asked.

"Depends on whether you heal like a kid or an old woman. A kid gets tired of slings faster than old women do. But, old women are smarter. Did you know that, Mr. Angus?"

I paid his fee and left without offering an opinion on old women. Five minutes later, I thought he ought to have given me two thimbles full of the foul stuff. I stumbled my way, in the weak light just after sundown, to the hitching rail out front where No Más was guarding my tack, and watching out for any more river crossings.

Espanola is pretty much the same as all the other little farm and ranch villages up and down the Rio Grande. It had a fair-sized livery stable. I bunked down in the livery stable barn, in a stall next to No Más. I took care during the night not to roll over onto my cast. It was so heavy I might have broken a rib. That would have put me back in Hector Schwartz's establishment.

When the sun crept in the next day, I woke up to the smell of fresh coffee and something frying on the cook stove in the shed next door. The livery keeper, who offered no name and spoke little English, served me coffee and fried goat. The coffee was good. I saddled up, rode through the little town, and came on a cantina, the last building at the south end of town.

The sign carved into the pitch pine door announced, *El Bonito*. But, once inside, the lie was given. Not lovely. Dark and dank—even though the early morning sun was low in the sky, and peeking inside from the east-facing front door. My arm was aching. Maybe, I thought, a pint of mescal would be good for the trip down the Rio Grande to Bernalillo. "Mescal," I said to No Más, "can be good medicine." Three tables, five hard-back chairs, and nothing on the tables except elbows and tin cups. A stout bar constructed out of heavy, two-inch planks nailed onto four oak casks took up most of the far side wall. Five or six bottles of whiskey, two mescal jugs, and something called port wine, with a fancy cork, stood upright on the bar. The bartender, a big Mexican, proud of his stout mustache, was wiping off his beer mug, and reaching for the tap on the keg when I walked in.

"I am called Jesús. Welcome to El Bonito, we are the only place opened to drink this early in the morning. ¿Cómo se llama, señor?" he asked, as he poured a tin mug of frothy beer.

"Angus. I broke my arm. Got any medicinal mescal for that?"

"Aiee, señor, you want the worm? You know the worm in the bottom of the bottle can cure many things, maybe even a broke arm."

The only light came in through the door behind me. What probably used to be a window on the west wall was boarded up, and the back door was padlocked on the inside. My eyes took a minute to adjust to the candles on both ends of the bar, and standing inside little holes carved into the adobe blocks on all four walls. And there was another surprise: customers, three of 'em, first thing in the morning. Drinking beer by candlelight.

"*Usted es bienvenido,* señor," Jesús said, probably to test my Spanish, as I leaned up against the makeshift bar.

"Well, Jesús, I'm happy to be here. I been over to the undertaker's office last night, and he put my arm in this little white coffin." I said trying to make light of the plaster cast, which had drawn the attention of all three customers.

"Ah, señor, I know Mr. Schwartz. He probably gave you some pain killer for your arm. It tastes like piss from a wounded cow, *qué no*? I have some mescal here which is better for you. I'll pour you one on the house."

A bartender who could read minds? No wonder he had three customers this early of a morning. It was a small room, maybe fifteen-foot square, with two doors; the one out back probably led to the facilities. A piñon fire was going in the kiva fireplace on the back wall. Two young men sat at the table in the back, wearing heavy, wool shirts, leather vests, and wide-brimmed black hats. At the front table, closest to the bar, sat an old man so hunched over his chin was no more than three inches from the table top. He had wild, white hair, mostly sticking straight up like a billy goat. His nearly black, gnarled hands held tight to a tin mug of beer, like he thought it was going to escape.

"Well, that's kind of you, bartender. I'll take you up on that mescal. And, I'd like a bottle for my saddle bag, if you've got one. While you're pouring, why don't you pour one for these gentlemen?" I said pointing to the three men.

"I'll take one, *si gracias,* señor," wheezed the old man, through a bullet-wide gap in his front teeth.

The two younger men didn't move, give me a howdy, or even a head-on look. They studied me, but didn't move a muscle or make a sound. The bartender poured three shots into smaller tin cups and took them around the bar to the tables. I turned my back to the room and sipped my mescal.

"So, señor, you are a lawman I see by your badge. Are you looking for some outlaws here in Espanola? We don't have so many these days, since the railroad came. But, the men you bought drinks could be your friends, *qué no?*"

"Seems a friendly place," I said, but sensing that the three behind me were not acting all that friendly. Maybe the bartender was trying to tell me something.

"So, señor, I introduce you, so that you will know there are no outlaws here. Those boys there are my nephews, Ignacio and Onchero Mendoza. And, the wild-hair man there is named Palmilla. He is not from here, but comes in to get out of the cold. Sometimes he stays here a week."

"Hey, Uncle, don't be calling us boys," said the larger of the two, throwing the shot of mescal back, and wiping his chin with the back of his leather shirt. "Besides, you ain't a Mendoza except by a marriage which is no more. You tend this bar, owned by the *Patron*, because our father decided you ain't worth piss as a *vaquero*."

Not looking at them, but smiling at me, the bartender said, "Ignacio Mendoza is right, señor. He and Onchero are no longer the little boys I used to ride with up and down this river. Now, they are men and carry big guns. But, forgive us our bad manners; I will say gracias for all of us."

Well, I don't believe the boys felt that cordial because they stood, gathered up sheepskin coats from the rack on the wall, and stomped out the front door.

"Don't give them no mind, señor. They are bored and headed to Bernalillo for some fun. The cantina down there is bigger, and they have upstairs women who can entertain you. They told me they are going there. You should avoid them, señor; they do not like gringos so much, and are not afraid of your badge."

"Ain't my business what they like or don't. I got no reason to bother them, and will expect the same from them. I'm on my way to Bernalillo myself, so thanks for the tip."

He busied himself with his bar wiping, and his tin-cup polishing. Now that I think about it, those were the cleanest tin cups I ever saw. Jesús poured a pint-size bottle of mescal for me out of one of the half-gallon jugs on the end of his bar. I could not help noticing that there was no worm in the bottle of the jug. I finished my drink, tipped my hat to the old man, and went outside to a bright, but cold morning. The sun was low in the eastern sky. We'd make Bernalillo just after dark. I figured six, maybe seven hours of steady riding along the river bank, weaving my way in and out of the cottonwoods along the Bosque. Mr. Schwartz had recommended the stage road which followed the river valley, but he said the valley was three or four miles wide and the river stuck to the far west mesa. He said the road would be easier on my horse. But, I had no hankering to ride a built road. No Más was a strong pony and did not need to follow wagon tracks. That kind of ridin' was fine for stage coaches and the Mendoza brothers. But not me. I tightened No Más's cinch, an awkward chore with only one good arm to work with. I stuck the mescal in the off-side saddle bag and swung up into the saddle using my right hand for a change. Felt good.

"Right, No Más? Any way I can board you is all right, ain't it?"

We headed on down to the river bank and off the damn road.

CHAPTER 10

Angus Draws Trouble in Bernalillo

MARSHAL RAMSEY'S INSTRUCTION WAS to bypass Santa Fe and get myself on down to Albuquerque where Yarberry was jailed waiting for the death warrant to be carried out. But, that's not exactly the way things turned out. I rode south out of Espanola down the Rio Grande's west bank, and rode on by Santa Fe in the midafternoon. It was just an hour or two short of midnight when I got to Bernalillo, some forty miles down the Rio Grande from Santa Fe. I was right proud of No Más for steppin' out like a war horse for over ten hours. We were fifteen miles shy of Albuquerque.

Bernalillo was near two hundred years old, and still small. Even so, the main street had ten buildings with lamp light showing in about half of them. The livery stable was on the north end of town, and No Más gave me a good shudder when we pulled up to the barn door. He could smell the grain from there. I stepped down, gathered my tack, and led him inside. I paid for a night's feed, arranged to lay out my bed roll in an empty stall, brushed No Más, and headed for the local cantina, named the Silva Saloon. My left arm was numb and my throat dry.

Even though it was long past the dinner hour, an old woman wearing a heavy, black-and-red serape offered me rolled tortillas to dip in a steaming bowl of chili and beans. There were three other customers, two at the bar and one passed out in the back, bent over a card table. There was noise coming down from the staircase. I could see a little vestibule up there through the stair rails. The bartender motioned up that direction when he served my dinner. Said I'd be welcome to go upstairs when I was done eating.

"You know, señor, there are women up there. A small bar, too, where Sustiana will serve you. She's better looking than me, señor."

"How come the ladies are upstairs? Is there a law against mingling with pretty ladies down here?"

He studied the badge on my vest before he answered. "Law? No, señor. But, since this is the only cantina in Bernalillo, the town marshal makes us separate downstairs eating from upstairs business. *Que no?*"

"Gracias, Mr. Bartender," I said, listening to what sounded like a banjo player plunking out notes.

"Since my arm is broke, and my butt sore, I think I'll just get on back to the livery and get some sleep."

That was my intent.

The Silva Saloon had an outside staircase, on the north side of the building. For privacy, I suppose. I paid the bar tab, thanked the man for the tortillas and chili, and walked outside. Turning south, I walked along a rough boardwalk toward the livery barn. When I got to the staircase, I was surprised to see Ignacio Mendoza and his little brother, Onchero, sitting on the bottom step. I passed them by. Can't say if they even saw me, but when I got fifty feet down the street, I heard a woman wail. I turned back and could see them boys cursing and stomping on the stairway.

Through the light of a full moon, I could see a woman. She was down on one knee with what looked like half her dress torn off. She was holding on to the bottom stairway post and the bigger Mendoza, Ignacio, was jerking on her arm and swinging his quirt at her. His little brother, Onchero, had her by the hair. The more she screamed, the more he giggled.

"All right now, you boys get off her. Let her go and walk on up here to me. This ain't right."

Now, fifty feet ain't too far to see faces or hear loud, spoken words. They quit their whippin' and turned to face me. They let her go and took three or four steps in my direction, with Ignacio in front and Onchero following a step behind. Both stopped, measured the situation, and studied me. I said nothing; neither did they. I ain't no gunfighter, but it was clear they were of a mind to smoke me. Except, they were *vaqueros* with guns, not men who'd ever faced a lawman head-on. And, they weren't all that sure about doing it from fifty feet away. So, after pausing for a minute, they began a slow walk toward me.

The thing about pistols is that you don't always hit what you're aiming at. Even when you're just plinking up on a mountainside to practice your aim. I expect a gunfight is a damn sight harder than dime novelists make it out to be. If a man's staring you down, itching for you to slap leather, your knees turn to lard. Mine did. But, I was not up to giving ground to those boys.

Seemed like neither of them wanted to draw from this distance, and I didn't want them to get much closer. I only knew one thing for certain. Whichever one of us got his courage up first would have the best chance of seeing sunrise tomorrow. Since there were two of them, I figured my chances at less than fifty-fifty. I remembered Jesús's warning to avoid these boys. But, there was no stopping the clock now. They aimed to kill me. I suppose they gave no thought to the opposite result. With boys like these, half-drunk, guns at the ready, blood up, and carrying a day-long grudge to boot, there's no half-way. All I wanted was to interrupt what they were doing to that woman. The town marshal could sort out who's right and who's wrong. But, as they paced slowly toward me, I figured more talk would be useless.

Ignacio, a barrel-chested man, had a long, horse-shaped face. His black, wide-brim sombrero was pulled down to his eyebrows, his dark skin looked charred, and his nose flat. He wore a fearsome beard, which made him seem more ghost than man. Some men wear beards because shaving don't suit 'em. Some are bearded as a mark of identity, like fire and brimstone preachers. And, some, like Ignacio, look like they've never shaved once in their whole lives. His beard and mustache were unmistakable marks of a fighting soul and a man who smiles only when he wins. My guess is no one had ever seen this man smile when his dander was up. What passed for eye sockets pushed out a glare toward me as black as a raccoon at midnight.

I didn't feel faint, exactly, as they sauntered toward me, but I suppose that was as close as I ever came to just turning my back and walking away from my duty to the law. I ain't proud to admit that. Those boys turned my eyes into magnets. I couldn't look away.

Onchero, was thin, maybe 125 pounds, no taller than the swinging doors in the downstairs bar, and nervous as a gnat. He couldn't seem to make up his mind—did he want to look at me, or his brother? His gaze darted back and forth like a sparrow on a fruit tree. He wore suspenders for no reason, and a sheepherder's vest. Unlike Ignacio, Onchero looked like he'd just come from a barber shop; face all shiny, hair slicked back with pomade, and a buttoned-up collar. No hat. But, what made him dangerous was the double-barreled shotgun he wore with a short, leather sling over his left shoulder. His hands, careless-like, hoisted the gun chest high, pointed straight up. He kept popping his slicked-back head side-to-side from his brother to me, to the sides of the street, back over his shoulder, as though he expected a parade to start any second now.

Most pistols are single action and have to be cocked as you pull, and then fired from instinct. They produce white smoke, the smell of burnt gun powder, and a thunder everybody recognizes. When you hear it, it's too late. A wad of lead about the size of your thumb is headed your way. Squeezing that trigger makes your eyes squint and your gun arm swings faster than a bronc inside a cyclone. Gunfighters call it going to sights on the first shot. Sometimes you only get one.

To get more than one shot, you've got to train your thumb. When you feel the gun rock in your hand, before the smoke pushes out ahead of the barrel, you've got to reach the hammer spur, ratchet it back, resettle your thumb on the frame, and squeeze the trigger to launch another round. And, you have to do all that without letting the barrel ride up even a fraction of an inch—that's where most missed shots come from. 'Course, none of this is in your brain at the time you're watching two men saunter toward you, bent on making this your last day on God's green earth. The full moon made the street visible even from fifty feet away.

Everything went quiet. They almost looked like they were tiptoeing down a slow-moving stream, one foot forward and planted before the other picks up, oblivious to the onlookers from doors and windows along the street. Their boots sloughed dust. Now, of a sudden, their arms quit swinging with the stride. I could see Ignacio's bent right elbow hanging loose only inches from the big iron on his hip. His left hand stuck out, palm down, as though he was feeling the air as he measured the distance between us. At what I took to be the forty foot mark between us, they seemed to agree without words that this was close enough. No smiles. No talk.

Ignacio looked like a bull elk sniffing and testing the air in my direction. Onchero no longer had that short man's swagger. They slowed to a dead stop, and squinted down the road at me.

I'd planted myself squarely at them, legs spread apart, right arm at the ready, gun hand to the ground, fingers flexed, and loose. Careful not to make an abrupt move, I stepped slowly back, two, maybe three feet. Picking up my left boot slowly, I turned to the right, showing them my left side. Then I swung my right leg back and planted my boot facing the side of the street—giving them a sideways look. Breathing out, I used my left thumb to push up the brim of my hat as though I was about to give them a cowboy's greeting. Then, as plainly as I could make it, I lifted my left arm, with the shiny white cast from elbow to the bottom of my wrist, aimed out toward the brothers, like a plaster shield. Sucking in two short breaths, and as slow as I could stand it, I made a pointed crook of my left elbow directly at those boys.

I couldn't hear their words, but my guess is Onchero asked Ignacio what 'n hell I was doing. What's that big, white thing on his arm? Why's he sideways? Is he funning us?

They stopped, facing me head on, but now only seeing my silhouette. This sideways view of me gave 'em pause. Something to think about. The bright white cast blocked the lower part of my face, with the crook of my elbow aimed dead center between the two approaching men. But, their eyeballs were fixed on the cast, my left arm, and hand. They could no longer see my gun holster, or my right arm, and hand. Deliberate as an Indian snake tamer, I inched my right hand behind my body to my holstered Colt Buntline Special, and slowly eased it up and out. Little by little, the twelve-inch barrel came straight up, but those boys couldn't see it happening. Not yet. When I knew I had it firmly in my right hand, thumb locked down on the hammer, I eased it back, hearing the tell-tale click signaling a turn of the chamber; a shell lined up. But, the Mendoza brothers were too far up the street to hear the sound of death, now just a split-second away.

"You boys stop where you are. Ain't no need to die on this street tonight. You're caught. I'm a United States Deputy Marshal."

They'd already stopped. But, somehow, they sensed they were facing a more complicated target than they were five seconds ago. Showing no visible emotion, the shotgun carrier's cocky smile disappeared. Both men now paused to reconnoiter the situation. With his face buried in his beard, Ignacio pondered my words and gave me a shout, loud but not as confident as he hoped. His voice was harsh, like the grating of the hinge on a seldom-used barn door.

"You ain't got no jurisdiction down here, you're federal. New Mexico don't pay no never mind to you. You interfered with us having a little fun with a whore; that's all you seen. Now she's gone, and we're calling you out. You can either slap leather or die where you stand, goddamned United States Marshal!"

Ignacio did the talking and stood his ground. But, Onchero, took a half-step backward and moved a little closer to his brother. The two men still faced me, but now too close for their own good. Ignacio seemed drawn to his big brother's back.

Seconds, maybe ten or fifteen, passed. Seemed a long silence. Couldn't tell whether they'd go to leather. My attention was on Ignacio's big right hand, inches away from his shiny black holster. Onchero's tightfisted grip on his double-barreled shotgun was a concern, except he had it pointed straight up. And, he was no longer alongside his brother, but now behind him.

The crisp winter air, not cold enough to show breath, and not warm enough to feel loose, was important to the moment. When your blood's up, pumping courage and slamming away at your brain, crisp air acts like a damper on a stove pipe. Shoot. Don't shoot. Draw or stand down. It gets all jumbled up in your mind. But, cool air unspools the tangling going on in your head. The dime-novel gunfight, where hands flash and guns jackhammer bolts of flame and smoke, takes no account of real men eyeing one another from forty feet in dead silence.

I'd only been in this situation once before, at my cabin on Ten Shoes Up. It flashed to me that killing decisions ain't made in the mind. They come from your gut. Fear ain't thinking, it's feeling. I needed to do something that might give them pause and not pull leather.

I shuffled sideways a little. I'd already pulled my gun and the blue steel of the barrel was clear in the light of the moon. But, instead of pointing it at them, I lifted it up to the moon as if I was going to give it a toss behind me. Ignacio and Onchero could see eighteen inches of blue steel now pointed straight up. Was I giving up? I was trying to position the Buntline Special without making the move look menacing. I moved slow like molasses dripping from a tree.

"I will not fire at you unless you draw down. But, I got five .44-40 cartridges headed your way if you so much as twitch your noses. Steady yourselves, boys, if you did no harm to that woman, as you say, then you'll be out of jail in the morning. Or, you can test my steel right here and now. Your call."

Then I slowly raised my left arm up and crooked my elbow straight at them. I layered my left hand on my right shoulder turning the plaster cast at the bent elbow into a human shooting stand. They steadied. I stopped. Then, slow as I could stand it, I started easing the Buntline from its straight up position down onto the crook of my left elbow. I intended to give those boys a head-on look no man wants to ever see: the open bore of a .44-40 revolver, cocked, and aimed.

Onchero panicked and spun to his right swinging both barrels of his shotgun in my direction. But, Onchero was a half-step behind Ignacio. Inexplicably, Ignacio moved his right hand away from his holster and seemed to raise his left arm up to the sky. But, Onchero's fear had got the better of him. I could see him fumbling with the hammer spurs and trying to cock both barrels before he got them swung to center. Both barrels swung toward his brother, rather than me.

Couldn't chance it. I took a bead on Onchero's left leg, hoping to mangle, but not kill the damn fool. Squeezing down, I busted the cap with a spurt of muzzle flame and a white cannonade of rocketing gas. The Buntline special launched a fat .44-40 on track forty feet away, with no wind to alter the trajectory.

The two-ounce lead ball hit Onchero mid-thigh. As it exploded through his thigh bone, the involuntary muscle reaction caused Onchero's finger to compress the right barrel trigger, now fully cocked. It exploded muzzle fire six inches away from Ignacio's left ear, likely shattering the big man's eardrum. The cartridge sent smoke, flame, and a biting gas into the side of Ignacio's face. He tried to clear leather, but in his pain and bewilderment, he checked the move at the last second. Then, instead of pulling his gun on me, he swung his big right fist over and down onto his little brother's slicked-back head, pummeling him to the ground. But, Onchero still had some purchase on the shotgun's arm. As he fell to the

88 *The Valles Caldera*

ground his trigger finger pulled, the left barrel exploded pellets into a horse trough ten feet away. Ignacio, looking furious and bewildered at the same time, had no gunplay left in him.

"Okay, boys, if neither of you moves, then everybody lives to see the sun come up in the morning," I hollered down at 'em.

It took two or three minutes to make the walk to them. Ignacio glared, not at me, but at his brother. He'd commenced to slapping and kicking Onchero, now screaming in pain and trying to crawl on one knee toward the now quickly draining horse trough. Two horses tied up to a hitching rail a foot from the trough broke their reins and nearly trampled both brothers as they bolted away. A cowboy, who had wisely taken no sides in the matter, darted out from an overhang and scooped up Onchero's shotgun. Ignacio's still-holstered gun was a concern, but he gave me no resistance. From five feet away, I was close enough to smell Onchero's blood and see blister marks on the left side of Ignacio's face. I took away their choices. My long-barreled Colt had done its job.

"Ignacio, just you reach over with your left hand, lift that pistolo out your holster, and drop it to the ground. Then you step over there with your brother. You're both under arrest for assaultin' a woman."

A skinny man with a shiny star on his chest ran past me hollering something fierce. When he got to the Mendoza brothers, he muttered something and took charge, more or less. He hollered at another bystander on a porch across the street to get help for Onchero. A cowboy came down the stairs from Silva's with a piggin' string in his belt. He used it to tie a tourniquet around Onchero's upper leg. Then a buckboard appeared and two burly men hauled him off. Somewhere.

When the dust settled, the town marshal turned to me with a big grin on his face. "Angus, we seem to meet in furious places, don't we?"

I was near bowled over.

"Bo String? Hellfire, Bo, if this don't take all!"

It had been near a year since I'd last seen Bo. He'd drug me off the water's edge on the south bank of the Rio Cimarron. I'd just arrested the outlaw Tom Emmett and was leading him across the river to jail when Jack Strong and his boys shot me out of the saddle. The time before that had been when Bo crossed my path up on Ten Shoes Up at my cabin just before the shoot-out with Captain Standard H. Plumb. Furious places all.

Marshal Bo, as it turned out, had heard me holler at the boys, from the porch of his office back down the street behind me. He had a brass badge on his coat and a revolver stuck in his belt. He told Ignacio that he'd be safe from me once he was on a bunk inside the Bernalillo jail.

"This must have come as a real surprise to you no-good Mendozas," Bo said to the brothers. "You called out the wrong man when you took on United States Deputy Marshal Angus Esparazza. You're lucky you lived to tell the story."

Turning to me, he said, "Angus, I'm going to lock Ignacio up for safekeeping and see to Onchero's leg wound. In the morning, I will get word sent out to his daddy's ranch. Their daddy is Mendoza Mendoza, a plenty tough hombre. You were in the right here, but that won't hold water with *El Patron* Mendoza. He's the boss bull hereabouts."

I followed Bo and Ignacio down the street to the jail. Bo put the sullen Ignacio in a cell, and poured me a cup of coffee, still hot, but tasting like yesterday's brew.

"Bo, I can't tell you how glad, and surprised, I am to see you here. Did you see the whole thing, or just the end of it?"

He grinned at me and said, "Angus, things don't change all that much, do they? You walked right by my office, but I didn't see you. I heard Ignacio hollering at you from down the street. By the time I got my coat and my carbine, you'd taken that sideways stance and the Mendoza boys were deciding whether to slap leather or turn tail. So, I just leaned on the post to steady my aim and took a bead on Ignacio. If he'd moved one more inch toward his holster, I would have dropped him. I was coverin' you. Again."

With Ignacio locked up for safekeeping, and Onchero bedded down in the little clinic run by the nuns at the church, he and I sat down close to the wood stove. We sprinkled a little sweetener in the coffee from a bottle under his desk. It improved the coffee some. I gave him the details about meeting those boys up in Espanola, and seeing them assaulting that woman at the Silva Saloon's back stairs. He wrote it up on butcher paper, had me sign it, and allowed as how that was the end of it.

"They called you out, not the other way around. You can't call the law out in my town—hell, I been the appointed town marshal here now for almost six months. This is the first time I even took aim at anyone, much less got involved in a shoot-out. Wouldn't you know that you'd be my first case? I'll give your statement to the circuit judge when he comes in next week. There won't be no follow-up."

We spent another hour jawboning about things, and then I took my leave, and went to the livery barn. By dawn, I was on horseback, headed south fifteen miles to Albuquerque. But, a complicated situation was waiting for me there. The man I'd ridden all this way to talk to, Mr. Milton J. Yarberry, was up in Santa Fe, where I'd rode by day before yesterday. The deputy in the Albuquerque jail said they took him up there for "safety's sake." So, I neck-reined No Más full circle, and we headed back up the Rio Grande to Santa Fe. This time, I took the stage road, and took care to give Bernalillo a wide berth as I trotted No Más up the hill to talk to Mr. Yarberry. I started to tell the shooting story to No Más, but he seemed intent on chewing as many chokeberry bushes along the side of the road as he could. So, I took the ride in silence.

CHAPTER 11

Angus Reaches Santa Fe

"WELL, NO MÁS," I said as we topped out on La Bahada hill, and looked down toward New Mexico's oldest occupied town—Santa Fe. "You being from Colorado probably don't know that Santa Fe was the boss town for Old Mexico. All this territory belonged to Mexico for more 'n three hundred years. Interesting, ain't it?"

No Más seemed more interested in catching his breath after the long pull up the stage road that wound back and forth on itself for the last four miles. Ahead we could see a line of snow-covered peaks and a long stretch of the Rio Grande. I'd intended on schooling No Más for the next hour it would take to reach the plaza in Santa Fe, when he bolted sharp to the right of the road. A gray fox, smaller than its cousin, the better-known red fox, popped out of a hole, realized how close we were to him, and skittered back.

"Whoa, old son, that's a skitter fox," I said, regaining my seat. "Pretty, though, wasn't he?" He had a grizzled, salt-and-pepper body with black fur lines around his neck.

We moved off the road to take advantage of some crabgrass sticking up. No Más was a continual muncher, and grazed every chance he got. I continued my education of him regarding New Mexico.

"The United States, my present employer, acquired this land in 1840-something. Long after the English sent those little ships to Plymouth's Rock, back east. 'Course, I've never been back east, but I'd bet a day's pay they have nothing to match this."

We long-trotted the rest of the way down into Santa Fe. I tied No Más up to the hitching rail in front of the huge, adobe building on the north side of the Plaza, dismounted, and leaned across my saddle to take in a helluva sight. The Palace of Governors was the biggest adobe building I'd ever seen. P'haps the biggest in the whole Territory of New Mexico. Whoever was in charge lived here, and everything worth spit was managed from here.

The territorial governor, the legislature, the courts, and all manner of lawmen all crammed into one building, trying their best to get along, I hoped. The US Marshal's office was two doors down on the morning side of the building, about a hundred feet away from the Santa Fe Town Marshal's office. In between was a courtroom, three jail cells, two of 'em crammed with what looked to be hungover *vaqueros*. This was a public jail—everyone could come and see if a loved one or a lost soul was among the guests behind bars. I took notice of a huge mountain man with a scar on one side of his face and a bloody bandage on the other. Numerous people were hanging around looking like they were waiting for something to happen, talking in little knots, smoking cigars, and looking all nervous-like. As you might expect, there were no women in the hallways. Just men waiting their turn to talk, or argue, or make something happen in New Mexico's boss town.

The door to the US Marshal's office was imposing; double doors, both with smoked glass windows proclaiming that the federal law was inside, open for business. The Chief Deputy Marshal, a man named Knop, was holed up inside another office guarded by a frizzy haired woman who sat her chair as if it was a throne, all three hundred pounds of her. She gave me a stare intended to put me in my place. I'd already introduced myself as a deputy US marshal from Colorado, and stated my intention to see Marshal Knop.

"But what about?" she asked with the corners of her mouth turned down. "We ain't got no Colorado federal prisoners here, and nobody here told me you're coming," she said, giving me a one-eyed cock of her big melon of a head.

There were half a dozen other people crowded into the little room. Some stood, two sat on hard-back, wooden chairs, and one leaned on a carved bench that somebody stole out of a church. Everybody seemed all-fired interested in my answer.

"It's business between my boss, the US Marshal in Denver, and your boss down here."

"Well, all right, then. Sit over there on the bench and I'll see…"

I did as I was told. She messed with some papers on her desk, then uplifted herself with noticeable difficulty, and made a little parade of walking the ten feet to the other smoked glass door with the gold lettering—"Chief Deputy Marshal Dave Knop." Not more than a minute had passed when she came back out, looking even more irritated with me.

"He says go on in."

I did.

"I hope Mrs. Kittering didn't make you wait too long," said the thin man in the black suit, as he walked toward me with his hand stuck out, and giving me a helluva of a good morning smile.

"Morning, Marshal Knop, I'm…"

"Yes," he interrupted, "you're Angus Esparazza, Deputy US Marshal. It's a pleasure to have you back in Santa Fe, sir. A real pleasure. I got the telegram from Marshal Ramsey up in Denver, so I know why you're here. And, you should also know, I had the pleasure of hearing a little about you from the Honorable A. Craig Blakey. You remember the judge, don't you?"

"Yes, sir. I do. Is he still judging down here?"

"Oh, by all means. We have two judges here now, he's senior and said he'd surely enjoy dining with you on your first night in town. I'll have Mrs. Kittering attend to that."

"Not sure that's going to be her pleasure," I said.

"Nonsense, it will do her good. She can be a tad protective of my time, and this will move you up a notch on her respectability chart. Now, tell me how we can help you with this hanging of the town marshal down in Albuquerque. While you're at it, gimme the short story on that broken arm and the long version of how you arrested those two pistoleros you locked up in Espanola. I believe that's a story I want to hear. Coffee, Marshal?"

So we coffeed up, thanks to Mrs. Kittering, and I told him about the Mendoza boys in Bernalillo assaulting a woman, me calling them out for arrest, and their resistance to that notion.

"Was she one of the upstairs women at the Silva Saloon?"

"Yes, I believe she was. Is that important?" I asked.

He clarified his belief that whores were entitled to the same law as any other woman assaulted on a public street, especially if it involved two armed men with no good intentions toward the lady in question. I explained the fool thing I'd done in chancing a cataract down the Rio Chama at near flood stage resulting in my broke arm.

"Well, all right, marshal," he said, "my compliments on your ability to haul yourself out of a swollen river and into a cast on your arm. But, the ingenious part was using the dang thing for a long-barreled Colt shootin' stand with the Mendoza brothers. I believe that's the talk of every bar in town. A plaster cast for a shooting stand! Whowee, they'll be buying you drinks tonight at the La Fonda bar, for sure."

"How's anybody know about it? It just happened two days ago."

"Well, there's the Rio Grande telegraph—anything interesting gets spread from mouth to ear all up and down the river. And, then there's the *Santa Fe New Mexican*. They ran the story this morning. Second page. Mrs. Kittering will send a copy for you over to the hotel. Gunfights are always news. If you'd killed one of those boys, you'd have made the front page. But, a leg wound barely makes page two. The Bernalillo town marshal did not seem all that bothered by it—his report to the circuit judge says you fired only in self-defense and in accordance with a lawful arrest."

"That already made it to your office? New Mexico is right prompt with news about shootings."

"Well, while that's true, I must caution you as well. Your interdiction of the Mendoza boys will be met with a fierceness out at the Mendoza Ranch. *El Patron* Mendoza Mendoza is a man of substance who's run things his way for decades up in the Espanola valley. He claims to have no truck with the law; makes his own, he says. Your good luck was that Bo String was an eyewitness. He saw the younger one, named Onchero, cock both barrels and aim his shotgun in your direction. You responded within the law, that's how he put it. Of course," he said, taking time to tamp down a wedge of tobacco in the bowl of his pipe. "I'll also file a report because you're a federal officer on official assignment here. I'll send a copy to Denver, with my recommendation you be thanked for a fine job."

"So, reports by town marshal in Bernalillo and your office here in Santa Fe. That's the end of it?"

"Well, I don't think you'll hear anything more about it from Sheriff Perfecto Armijo. Bernalillo is in his jurisdiction, and he is no man to coddle the likes of the Mendoza brothers. They got what they asked for."

"What about the woman? Was she hurt?"

"What woman? Report says you saw a woman being assaulted. Bo String saw a woman at the bottom of the staircase when he got there with her dress tore half-off. But, after he attended to the Mendozas, he went back to the Silva Saloon to talk to her. They told him she'd lit out. Smart woman, I expect."

"So, you think I'll hear from the Mendoza family? I hear they are numerous around these parts."

"They are, and you might well. They are an unruly bunch and there's lots of 'em. The ranch hands are mostly peaceable, 'cept when drinking, or carousing. El Patron Mendoza, who likes people to say his name twice, out of respect, can get their blood up. When that happens they can get mean and beat on women or strangers. They've spent time in my jail and most other lockups from Socorro to Chama. Keep those boys in mind while you're down in Albuquerque—they got family there, too."

"Hold grudges, do they?" I asked.

"Don't know as I'd call it that. It's more about their culture. Some call it Mexican machismo. You shot one before he could pull on you, and you made the other one appear right foolish. So, they will call you out next time they get the chance. Worse yet, their kin might take part."

I thought it best to change the subject.

"Marshal, did my boss up in Denver, Marshal Ramsey, tell you why I'm here?"

"Said it was about that fool Albuquerque town marshal, Milton J. Yarberry, but the telegram was short on details. I can tell you what I know, which ain't much, and ain't all that flattering, being he's a fellow lawman and all."

Knop told me that most other lawmen, except for Sheriff Perfecto Armijo, thought it was a mistake to turn a gunman into a lawman in the first place. Yarberry's reputation was that he's too quick to pull iron, too short on good judgment, and of a mean disposition when drunk, which he was most of the time. But, Marshal Knop's short explanation raised more questions than answers. He wanted to know just exactly what federal law enforcement in the state of Colorado might want with a shootin' fool like Yarberry in the New Mexico Territory.

"Well, there's a number of state crimes Yarberry's suspected of in Colorado, but one in particular is of interest to the federal government."

"Which one?"

"It's the killing of a teamster in Trinidad, the apparent theft of a federal payroll intended for troop payment, and an allocation to the Indian agent up there. Yarberry was the last one known to be with the deceased, and the first one out of town with money in his pocket the next morning. Makes him suspicious, but there was no real evidence to connect him up. That's what the US Department of Justice said, or so I was told."

"How'd anyone know he had money in his pocket?"

"On account of he paid his tab in the hotel, bar, general store, and the livery stable. He also bought two horses and a mule, gave generous tips to several nighttime women, and hosted everyone in the bar, at breakfast, to the best whiskey in the house; all in gold coin, freshly minted, in Denver."

"Are they saying Yarberry robbed the by-god US Mint in Denver? Whoee! I never heard of anyone robbing the Mint."

"No one told me he robbed the Mint. But, he had a pile of shiny coins from the Denver Mint. I expect there's some connection."

Marshal Knop excused himself to go to the facilities. When he came back, he gave me a copy of the report on Yarberry's case that he'd gotten from the Santa Fe County Sheriff. It more or less confirmed that Yarberry was a checkered man, and one with his share of important friends. Including Sheriff Perfecto Armijo. When he got back, he had a question that occurred to him while astride the privy, or so he said.

"Let's say your suspicions are right about Yarberry. What's the by-god Department of Justice intending to do about it? Hell, he's headed for the noose already. They ain't gonna charge him, are they?"

"Dunno. Doubt it. But, I'm hoping to talk to him before they stretch his neck. If he fesses up, then my boss can close some Colorado federal cases."

"Well, Angus, I'll send a boy over to the jail where they are keeping Yarberry safe till the execution next week. It's just on the other side of this building. They won't let you take him outside his cell. He's on close watch, you know. But, give 'em your gun, that helluva of a long barrel there hanging on your gun belt. You can spend the afternoon with him."

CHAPTER 12

Mendoza Mendoza, El Patron, At the M/ Hacienda

"IGNACIO, *MI HIJO,* you have let me down," I told my oldest son. He was standing looking down at his boots, taking my words seriously, as he should in such a situation as this. All of us were standing by the side of Onchero's bed, looking at him with pity. The other *vaqueros* were all behind us, making the room small. They shuffled their boots a little, but made no other sounds, hardly even breathing. They knew better to provoke their *El Patron,* at such times.

"You are the oldest and have the care of your little brother on your shoulders. You let him down. And me, also."

"Si, PaPa, I am sorry," he said.

It was good to hear him confess the sin of failure. But, I could not see in his bearded scowl the repentance he owes God, his brother, and me.

"Sorry? That's what you feel for making yourself the fool? For letting a gringo *cabrón* best you with only one shot! Tell me again his name, this *hijo de puta*, who you let dishonor this family, bringing shame to the brand on that door. Look over there, right now."

All heads turned to the door.

"See that! *M/.* That brand, my grandfather burned onto his first mule, *qué no?* That brand is our blood, *mi hijo.* It is on every door, every gate, and every animal on our hacienda. When did you forget that? Tell me his name!"

"Hees name was Angus, jus' Angus. That's what they said. I only saw him two times."

I hunched my shoulders together and lumbered out of the chair. Walking slowly to the door, I stopped and ran my fingers over the deep, charred lines of our brand.

"You men. You know this brand, do you not? It pays you—gives you food—*caballos*—a life of pride. By what name is this brand called? I ask you, Ignacio. Say the name of our brand to me, to our *vaqueros*, to your pitiful little brother who cannot walk now so good because of you. Say it!"

Ignacio was born with a stallion's fire, but this day he was like a pony, whimpering behind the barn door. He did not look at me, but he, too, came to the door and traced the brand with his fingers.

"PaPa, it is *M Slash.* It is respected everywhere in the valley and up into the Valles Caldera, too."

"And, what, my oldest son, what is the meaning of the brand? I have told you the meaning, and now I want you to tell our *vaqueros*. What is the meaning of the slash mark after the M?"

He pushed out his chest, like the man he should have been down in Bernalillo with the gringo Angus. I was happy to hear his words.

"*Vaqueros*, *El Patron* asks you to follow the meaning of our brand. The M is for Mendoza, now three generations riding for this brand. The slash mark is like a knife. We all carry a knife in our belts. It says what will happen if you disrespect the brand. We will cut you, slash you! Make you bend your head to our brand."

Ignacio hated me at this moment, I could see it in his eyes. But, he feared my rage more than he hated me.

"*Si, mi hijo*, that is so. The slash makes its mark on the M. My grandfather was a man of his word, but also a bandito. He was cruel, but proud of it. He never let no stinkin' Indian, gringo, or little shit of a man cross the land, or the family. You bear his name. Do you also bear his fierce honor? His protection of all his children, me, your brothers, all of us in this bunkhouse? Goddamn you, Ignacio! You will restore the family honor, I swear that. You will find this Angus, or I will put that brand on both your hands with a hot iron for all these men to see. Do you know I'll do that, Ignacio?"

"Si, PaPa, I know you will. But, you won't have to. I'm going to track this man down, as soon as Onchero can ride. And, we will shoot him, and bring his body here to you. You will see, Papa."

"No, *mi hijo tonto.* You will be with me, but this shame on the family is for all of us to wipe off the brand. All of us, you, me, Onchero, and also Chuches, our cousin who tracks the mountain lion, he will join us. And, some *vaqueros*, too. Together we will find this gringo *hijo de puta,* and he will know revenge of our brand."

"Si, PaPa," Onchero said, from his bunk. "When I can ride again, we will shoot the gringo Angus."

"NO! You did not listen to the lesson. None of you did. Think of what Ignacio just told you. Think of what I just told you. We will get revenge for the brand. By the brand! When we have this man, Ignacio will brand his forehead with the *M/.* Then I will cut off his head. That is the revenge of our brand."

CHAPTER 13

Angus Meets
Milton J. Yarberry

THE BORED GUARD LED ME back to the cells. Yarberry was in what they called an isolation cell—one bunk, in the middle of the big room, bars on four sides, and a privy hole in the floor with a pipe to the outside. He had a honey bucket next to the hole, and a small, wooden table with a wash basin, a tin pitcher, and one cup. There was a little stand in the corner with some books, and pen and paper. It was a sorry sight.

Milton J. Yarberry, the shootin' fool, didn't look to be a danger to anyone, including himself. The guard turned me over to a jailer, a man of lower rank. The jailer didn't take to conversation. He read the jail pass that Marshal Knop had written, and stored my gun in a wire box behind his little desk in the hallway.

"No knife, or rope or keys or nothing?" he asked.

"Nope," I said.

Pulling on the brass key ring hanging onto his gun belt, he fingered a key into the door to Yarberry's cell, then motioned me to go on in. Once I was safely locked in with him, I took a long, slow look at the man the papers called "a shootin' fool." At first, he took little notice I was even there. He was flat on his back, no pillow, or prop for his neck, with his eyes closed. He smelled like a stopped-up privy.

The jail log said he was thirty-three years of age, six feet three, and of a troublesome nature. It tagged him with brown hair, gray eyes, and given to drink. And, here he was, drunk, lying on a bunk atop filthy blankets, and an Indian saddle blanket tucked around his feet. There was a bottle of whiskey, but no glass close by. I stepped two feet toward him and caught the smell of a ten-day drunk. All gassy, with the stench of a hog stuck in the kill chute.

"Mr. Yarberry, I'm a deputy US marshal from Colorado. Name's Angus. Are you willing to talk to me?"

He opened his eyes, squinted, and rubbed them with his filthy hands. I got the sense that I was out of focus. He strained his head first one way and then the other, rubbing his fists around his eye sockets, and trying to swallow bile in his mouth. Kicking the Indian blanket to the floor, he rolled his legs off the side of the bunk and reached for the bottle a foot away.

"You want a drink, Marshal? I only talk to them as want to drink with me. I ain't got long on this earth, but I got time to drink and talk."

Can't say I've ever had a drink with a prisoner in jail before, but it struck me that the law ought to allow for whatever is necessary to get the job done.

"Mr. Yarberry, I'd enjoy a drink."

So, he passed the bottle, and I tilted it up and swallowed some down. Wasn't half bad.

"What you wanna talk to me about? The ladies in Canon City, Colorado send you down here? Is that it? They missing me?"

I'd read two long reports about the man, but the look of him didn't match up. He had a neck like a turkey that'd just swallowed a knot off a log; it was caught below the jaw and poked out fiercely. His mustache was more a gnat's nest than anything else. He hadn't shaved in some time, and his skin fairly crawled with grime. But, the most telling thing in the reports wasn't how he looked today. The official report confirmed that Yarberry could not read nor write. A lawman who couldn't read a wanted poster, an arrest warrant, or a telegram from higher-ups? What 'n hell were they thinking down there in Albuquerque giving this man a badge?

"Can't say you're missed up in Canon City. But, I've ridden all the way from Denver just to talk to you."

"Me? You rode five hundred goddamn miles to talk to me, on my death bed, waiting for a noose. Are you crazy?"

He didn't look like he wanted an answer, so I gave him none. I had no interrogation plan, but thought I'd best approach what I'd been sent to find in a backhanded way. I'd start with now, then work my way back up to the events in Colorado.

"I've read the court opinion upholding your conviction and was wondering what you thought about it."

"The court's bought and paid for. The Santa Fe Ring did it, you know about them rascals, don't you? I was acquitted by a court of killing that low-down bastard, Henry A. Brown. What'd the court do with that, maybe you can tell me since you say you read it?"

"The New Mexico Supreme Court upheld your conviction for killing Charles Campbell, not Henry Brown."

"Hell, Angus whatever-your-last-name-is, Henry Brown is the key to Charles Campbell. Didn't the report tell you that?"

"Mr. Yarberry, I only asked about the case that put you here, waiting for an execution which I'm told is next week. But, if you don't want to talk about the court's opinion, or what you feel about being here, I'll get to another point. I'd particularly like to talk to you about what you did up in Colorado. I'm less interested in the New Mexico goings-on."

That primed the pump some. No one'd asked him about Colorado for some time, and he seemed anxious to talk about it.

"I'm Arkansas-bred, by way of Walnut Ridge. You ever hear of it? The Arkansas River runs from Colorado to Arkansas, and so did I. Except I ran up river from Arkansas to Colorado. Followed the river all the way. You know much about riding along rivers?"

"Some," I answered.

I was to learn over the next three hours that Yarberry asked a lot of questions he didn't need answering. He just posed 'em as though they were interesting facts any man ought to know. He got up every ten minutes or so to belch, fart, or use the piss hole in the floor. He didn't use the honey pot. I bided my time.

"And, then I went and joined the Texas Ranger Frontier Battalion, stationed in Jack County. Shot a man in a duel. A duel that was supervised by the company commander himself, a man named Lieutenant Hamilton. Now that lieutenant was a clever bastard, I'll give him that. He loaded both guns with blank rounds. I fired first. The sound plumb scared the other fellow, so he pissed his pants, dropped his gun, and run off. They never found him and declared him to be absent without leave of the officer in charge. What you think of that?"

I decided it was time to take another fake swig of his bottle. It seemed answer enough. He finally got to Carson City, Colorado, when I reminded him that's why I was here.

"Yes, Mr. Yarberry, I can see how your gun hand kept you employed, but that wasn't the case up in Carson City, was it?"

"You got that right, young feller. I partnered up in 1878 with Tony Preston in Carson City. We had the best saloon in town, and the only one with a variety theater. You've heard tell of Eddie Foy, ain't you? He did vaudeville for us. Hell, I even played the violin for him one time, just to warm up the audience. I got it here, not right here, but here in the jail building. Maybe they'll let me play something for you; they do sometimes."

He hollered at the mute jailer to bring his violin. P'haps the man was deaf, also, because no violin appeared. There was a window in the empty cell, across the way. So the jailers left it open even in winter because ventilation was likely valued more than heat. I was glad they were of that mind, sitting here listening to and smelling Milton J. Yarberry. The man told me some of the most audacious lies I'd ever heard.

"But, the next year, the bartender at the Gem Saloon, across the street from us, shot my partner, Tony Preston. I mentioned him, didn't I? Well, the bullet busted Tony's spine. I drew my own piece and fired off three rounds at the bartender's ass as he jumped through a window into the alley. They formed a posse, which I joined, of course, and pursued the bastard. While we was out lookin' for him, he lost his nerve and surrendered to the Canon City marshal. He knew if our posse found him, I'd finish the job once and for good."

Sometimes a question helped: "What happened to your partner?"

"Pulled through. Never could walk well again, but he and Sadie, his wife, followed me down to San Marcial. We did some business there, and because of his injury, poor old Tony couldn't cut the mustard. Know what I mean? So, Sadie needed me for the physical comfort that Tony could no longer provide. I obliged her. That's what led to my lawful shooting of Henry A. Brown. 'Course you knew all along, didn't you?"

I did. The by-god US Justice Department reports that Marshal Ramsey gave me up in Denver covered that in some detail. Sadie Preston took up with Yarberry in several respects. Shortly after Yarberry showed up in Albuquerque, she and her four-year-old daughter arrived and took up quarters in the Gilbert Hotel. There she sported with Yarberry regularly, but also took a fancy to Henry A. Brown, who'd come west from Tennessee in 1876 as a guard for the Adams Express company's coach shipments. Brown was a hard drinker, a braggart, and quick to pull a gun. I hoped by talking about Brown that Yarberry might meander back and forth between Colorado and New Mexico, and I'd learn what I needed to know.

"Yes, I've read the reports about Mr. Brown. He admired the beautiful Sadie Preston, didn't he? Is that what sparked your quarrel with him back in 1881?"

"Hell, man, I didn't know she was two-timing me. I was babysittin' her daughter while she was having dinner with Brown at Girrard's Restaurant on Central Avenue in Albuquerque. I took the girl to see her mom and caught them. I was giving him a proper what for when he invited me to go to a vacant lot close by. There was some harsh talk between us, and he was insultin' and vile, and wanted to get the drop on me. We commenced to fist fight, then he drawed down on me, fired the first shot, and hit me on the thumb. I still got the scar, see?"

He had the bottle, which was by now getting low on liquid, in his right hand and tilted it to show me a yellowed scar below the grime.

"Yes, I see it, right there on your gun hand. So, what happened next?"

"Well, I had to defend myself, so I drawed my pistol and commenced firing."

"How many shots?"

"Two, drilled him directly in the chest, then two more in the body cavity as he was headed for the dirt."

"All with your right hand, right? You are right handed, aren't you? Leastways, that's what you've been using for the bottle."

Slamming down the bottle down on the three-legged stool, he spit at me and screamed, "n' hell's going on! You accusing me of something here? The jury and the judge believed me, now here you come in here with your shiny US marshal badge and call me a liar. You'd best get your ass out of here afore I take this bottle to you."

"Mr. Yarberry, you mistake me. I believe you were lawfully acquitted by reason of self-defense in the Henry Brown shooting. All I said was that it must have been difficult to get shot in your gun hand, and still have the physical stamina and courage to draw down with the injured hand and shoot your attacker. I'd say your gun work was first rate. That's all I have to say on the matter."

The noise of the bottle slamming on the stool drew the attention of the jailer, who apparently was neither deaf nor mute.

"OK, Yarberry," the guard said in a high-pitched voice, "don't you go a-banging on things again. What's the matter?"

Yarberry lay back on his bunk and seemed to gather himself. Then he said in a singsong voice, "Get me another bottle. That's what's the matter. I'm thirsty, and my guest is, too. How many bottles I got left before I hang?"

"Your friends in Albuquerque sent over a case from the La Fonda bar. You've drunk eight, maybe nine bottles, so I'll fetch you another. The sheriff says you're best off drunk because you ain't gonna cause him no trouble that way. I'll be back."

The case must have been close by because he came back in right quickly, handed me a bottle through the bars, and departed. I uncorked it with my teeth and handed it to Yarberry, who looked like he was about to fall asleep. He slugged down a big mouthful, and picked up the thread of his story. It was not what you'd call straight-out true, but his version was that the judge and jury believed a witness who said that Mr. Brown had publicly announced his intention to kill Yarberry for Sadie's attentions. Yarberry's lawyer, a man named S. M. Barnes, argued self-defense, plain and simple. It was just one month later that Yarberry killed his second man in Albuquerque, the unfortunate Charles Campbell. I didn't want to hear any more on it, but could not get him back to talking about Colorado till he had his say about Campbell.

"All I was doing, Marshal Angus, was sitting on a bench in front of my friend Elwood Maden's house with Mr. Monte Frank Boyd of a summer evening, when we heard a shot close by. Monte thought it came from the Greenleaf Restaurant a few doors up the street. Since I was the Albuquerque town marshal, it was my lawful duty to investigate. So I did."

"What'd you find?" I said, hoping for a short answer.

"Well, glad you asked," he said. "We got to the Greenleaf. A man in front saw my badge and pointed to a man headed the other way, in an awful hurry. 'He fired that shot,' he said. Me and Monte followed in haste, and I yelled out, 'Stop there, I want you!' That's fair warning under the law, ain't that right, Marshal Angus?"

"Fair warning by a lawman, right."

"The man was a stranger, never laid eyes on him before, but he stopped his running long enough to turn back and fire a shot at me. I returned fire only to save my life. That's all there was to it. Now, here I sit, convicted of self-defense."

"I don't mean to take up the other side, but the court papers say you and this Boyd feller both shot at Campbell, and that Campbell was hit three times in the back. No one could find a gun on him, or anywhere close by. And Mr. Boyd skedaddled. That left you. Do you suppose what the newspaper said about Campbell's funeral was an influence?"

"What'd they say? I don't read newspapers," Yarberry announced.

"They said the feller's funeral was the largest and most impressive funeral ever known in Albuquerque. Sounds like everyone knew him but you."

He kept on arguing his innocence, but eventually he ran out of talk and pulled longer slugs on the bottle. He also quit offering the bottle to me.

"Mr. Yarberry, I've been here awhile and got other business to attend to, but are you sure you don't want to clear up some of the Colorado business while I'm here? Might give you some peace of mind."

"Like what?"

"Well, like the woman named 'Steamboat.' Our understanding is that she was your partner 'n some brothels you and her ran up there. And, there's a matter about a freighter that got shot who might have had some gold coin, or something like that. That ring any bells?"

"Steamboat? What 'n hell you bringing her up for? She had a fine wiggle. I knew her, that's all. I run a good house, she worked there, but that's all I know about her."

"Thanks, that clears that up. What about the time you joined up with several other fellers following the construction gangs down from Colorado into New Mexico laying track for the Denver & Rio Grande railroad? There were some missing payroll shipments, for the construction gangs and for various mines up there and down in New Mexico."

"You accusin' me again?"

"No, I ain't. I'm just askin' is all. You see, someone spent a fair amount of money in Trinidad, Colorado, after a murder up there. And that someone used recently minted gold coin from the Denver Mint. And…"

Yarberry came up off the bunk like a snake was in his britches. He raised his arm back. I thought he was gonna throw the whiskey bottle at me. I backed up to the cell door, moved up my broke left arm up to cover my face, and clinched my right fist. But, he backed off as quickly as he started. "You been sittin' here drinking my whiskey and now you accuse me of what, stealing gold from the US Mint? You're a crazy man, that's what you are! Get out."

I called the jailer, who took two seconds to come, open the cell door, and escort me out of the jail into the front office. Neither of us said a word.

I gathered up No Más at the hitching rail and headed for the La Fonda Hotel. I'd had all the whiskey Milton J. Yarberry and I could take. Damn waste of time. I pondered my telegram to Marshal Ramsey on the way to the hotel. Telegrams were short for a reason. Mine would say, more or less:

REPORT—WASTE OF TIME—STOP—YARBERRY DENIES EVERYTHING—STOP.

CHAPTER 14

Angus At the La Fonda in Santa Fe

THE LA FONDA HOTEL is just across the plaza from the Palace of Governors. If you stand at the bar long enough, someone will likely tell you about the hotel. Truth be told, the southeast corner of the plaza in Santa Fe has been a road house or "fonda" since Santa Fe's earliest days. The bartender, a heavy man twenty years older than me, said that when Santa Fe was founded in 1607, this corner was the first "real business establishment."

"Any fake ones before that?" I asked.

He leaned toward me, and I could see yellowish eyes indicating a history of torments from skeptical customers like me. Maybe he could see I was just passing the time waiting for the line at the registration desk to go down. It was five in the afternoon, and I was tired of talking to bartenders and drunks like Yarberry. "Want another, or will you be moving on?"

"This one's fine," I answered, turning back to my newspaper. A man hoping to get a free drink from me chimed in.

"Sir, my own opinion differs. Before this was a hotel, it was a court. They held court right over where the hotel registration desk is now."

"Did not," the troubled bartender answered. "It was executions they held here, not court. How about you—want another?"

"Hangings in the lobby?" I asked.

"You betcha," they both said, one trying to outwit the other. *Evenly matched*, I thought.

I left the bar and walked back to the little knot of men at the registration desk lined up for rooms. Taking my place, fourth in line, I waited my turn. Some noticed my badge and said nothing. Most of them seemed more interested in my Buntline .44 long-barrel Colt.

"You here for a shooting lesson, or to get your long barrel worked over?" asked a big, grizzled man packing twin Colts.

"No," I said, "I'm here for a room."

"How's she shoot? Steady like they say, or does the extra four and a half inches of barrel weight force a lean-back from your regular shooting position?" he continued, pointing to my holstered gun.

"Steady enough," I said, moving up to second in line at the registration desk.

As I looked around the lobby, which faced the swinging half-doors to the bar on the east side, every man in the place seemed to hold or be fiddling with his sidearm. Half of the tables had guns laid out, with cleaning kits, and small cartridge pouches, or cans of ammo. But, none wore badges. No one looked like an outlaw or a railroad detective. It came slowly; these men were shooters.

The tall, elegant, Mexican woman behind the desk addressed me in Spanish and English, "*Buenas tardes,* señor, *¿desea una habitación?*; we have several up the stairs, but only one left on the ground floor with an outside entrance."

"*Si, señora,* I'd like a room. Downstairs is just fine with me."

I signed my name, took the key to room eight, and headed down the hallway on the opposite side of the room. I didn't get more than ten feet away when I heard rapid gunfire, four—then five more shots from the window outside the long bar. Two guns, I thought. No one but me seemed interested, as though it were just a flock of birds cackling at one another. They all just continued talking, smoking, sipping whiskey, and fiddling with their guns. The shots were measured, but could have been fired by one man, maybe. As I reached the door to the hallway where the downstairs rooms were located, the grizzled man, who'd followed me from the registration desk, announced, "That's likely Captain Zells. Sounds like his .38. Makes a whine, but he's got a knack for pacing, don't he?"

I turned to him; expect he could see the puzzlement on my face. "If you don't mind my asking, is there some sort of shooting competition going on behind the bar?"

"No, it's just the first day of the gunsmith's visit down here. She likes us to fire our weapons so she can make whatever adjustments seem necessary. Has she seen you shoot that Buntline Colt of yours?"

"She?"

"Yes, ain't that why you're here? To get your guns adjusted or your shooting stance figured out? She's one of the best most of us have ever seen. From up near Chama, they say."

I went on down the hallway to room eight, which had a partial view of the plaza. I unloaded my kit, and headed out to the rear of the La Fonda. Jill Garrison was giving what she called a stand-up shooting clinic.

"Captain Zells," she said to the young man in uniform, "you've got a good eye, but your focus on hitting the target center mass from this distance will only work if your right elbow is not cocked. If it's locked down, the strain on your forearm causes a slight waver of your gun hand, which makes it harder for you to get the front sight in steady perspective. Try again, but with a slightly looser grip and a little flex in your elbow."

He nodded slightly and turned back to the man-sized post with a bull's-eye paper target tacked to it fifty feet away. Taking a sidewise stance, he moved his piece up the sky, then slowly lowered it. When he had it parallel with the ground, he steadied himself, inhaled, and fired off two measured shots. I thought they were center-mass hits.

"Miss Garrison, that's a mighty fine tip. I sincerely appreciate the balance between what my mind is trying to do while my forearm is loose. Will you be available tomorrow afternoon as well?"

She said yes, looked over in my direction, smiled, and excused herself. As she walked toward me, I was reminded of that same awkward feeling I had when I first saw her in the barn. But, she made it easy.

"Afternoon, Marshal Angus. It's nice to see you again. That's a fine-looking cast on your left arm. I'd love to hear about your horse wreck in the Rio Chama, and if you don't mind, your shootout with the Mendoza brothers in Espanola. Can I buy you a drink inside?" she asked, pointing to the back door of the La Fonda.

"How'd you know?" I asked.

"The *New Mexican*, of course. Page two story, if you haven't read it. You're the most famous man in town today, more so than Captain Zells. Once the men inside learn you are *that* Marshal Angus, you'll be drinking free the rest of the night."

"Maybe you'd do me a favor? Don't tell 'em."

I had a glass of beer; she ordered wine. Asking her to dinner was a challenge, but she said, "why not?" We moved to a table in the dining room where I had a steak and fried potatoes. She picked at baked rainbow trout, green peas, and canned collard greens, while I filled her in on my horse wreck in the middle of the Rio Chama. Seems that everyone in Espanola knew about my broke arm because the undertaker that set it, Hector Schwartz, came to Santa Fe every Sunday morning and set up his barber's chair in the La Fonda lobby. That was yesterday, and he likely told every customer about my cast, not to mention how I had refused to let him cut my hair. Jill arrived two days after I left Espanola, but folks up and down the Rio Grande were buzzing with speculation and some accurate observations about my dust up with the Mendoza brothers in Bernalillo.

Jill's interest was not focused on the wreck itself; she wanted to know exactly how the cast on my left arm worked as a shooting stand for the Buntline, and whether it gave me enough purchase to fire one shot which ended what could have been a sustained shootout. Never asked a single thing about my horse, or my haircut.

"Yes, Angus, I understand you had no choice. But, before they came into effective range, did you just think up using your left arm cast as a steady gun stand? Did it help you sight-in your first target? I mean, did you plan to fire from a sideways stance, and how did it feel when you fired that way? Steady, calm, balanced, what? I'd really like to know."

I sipped on my coffee because my stomach was bubbling. Didn't seem natural for someone so small and beautiful to be so all-fired interested in the hows and whats of a gun fight. But, I was torn between changing the subject and having her stomp off mad.

"Don't think I planned it, but it seemed likely that standing sidewise made me a narrow target. Also, it hid my draw behind me. That's all I was thinking."

"Yes, but you lifted the Buntline up high over your head. Everybody saw that clear. When you lowered it down onto the crook of your arm onto the cast what did the men facing you do?"

"Well, that's it, you see. It's what they didn't do that counts. They did not draw on me. Their mistake, not mine."

"But, one of them did draw, didn't he? The one on your left, not the one with the shotgun."

"He was on my right, but no matter. It was too late, Jill. Too late. He hesitated. But, the boy with the shotgun was a second away from letting go with both barrels. Could not chance it. Gunfights come down to two things, a half-second jump ahead, and a steady aim out in front. That's all I can say on the matter."

"So, you're saying that by the time he reached for his gun, the fight was over?"

"I'm saying he ought to have figured out that I did not have to draw. I had a bead already on him before he twitched his hand. Hell, the man was a fool to draw. It was too late by that time, he should have just pointed to his leg and said shoot me here, right here."

She leaned back in her chair and gave me a squint. Then she took the last sip out of her wine glass and twirled it with her fingers by the stem. Pointing the open end at me, she said, "Whoosh."

"Whoosh?"

"Yes, Angus, that's it exactly. That's how being shot at feels before you even hear the boom of the bullet exiting the tip of the barrel. You feel it more than you hear it. The sight of a gun barrel pointed directly at you scares some men, but not others. It's the whoosh that gets their attention. Big brother Ignacio saw your gun barrel sighting in, but didn't really understand that you were steady as a fence pole dug in the ground. When he started his right hand toward his holster, he felt the whoosh. Hot damn! I wished I'd a been there."

Thinking back on it, I wish I'd asked her exactly why she wished she'd been there. To see me fire, or to see that damn fool get his leg near blowed off?

Next morning, as I hauled my kit downstairs to check out, she was sitting at a small table in the corner of the lobby with two midsize boxes of what looked to be ammo, a stack of paper targets, a list of names, and a cup of tea.

"Milk, no sugar, thank you," she said to the waitress.

Then she turned my way.

"Good morning, Angus. I was hoping I'd get a chance to see you before you left. Would it be too much for you to take a few minutes and help me out with something?"

She was decked out in leather britches, high-top boots, gun belt, but no gun, and a sheepskin vest over a red-checkered, wool shirt with ruffles on the sleeves. Near made me hold my breath. I more or less stammered, "Sure."

"Wonderful. I'm giving another clinic out back this morning. But, my list does not start until after ten, so I've got some time, and I've been thinking on that sideways stance you took up in Espanola with the Mendoza brothers."

"Well, I think I've told you all I can 'bout that."

"Yes, you were generous, and it was a lovely dinner we had last night. But, you see, there's something I need to know that we didn't talk about, and it would be better to see it than just talk about it."

I set my kit down beside the registration desk, told the lady there I'd be right back, and followed Jill out back. It was cold, but clear. She set up two targets up the little hill on two posts about a yard apart and fifty feet upwind. I did as she asked and took a sideways stance, laid the barrel of my Colt .44-40 across the crook of my left arm, and fired a shot at the right-hand target, like she wanted me to. No sooner than the blast sounded, she yelled, "Again, Angus! Fire again at the other target, quickly now."

I did. I missed the dang thing entirely.

"Right," she said. "Just as I thought. The second shot is always going to give you a problem with that stance. Have you thought about that?"

"No, Jill, it never occurred to me. It ain't like I'm a regular gun fighter. Hell, I didn't ask for the first shot, why 'n hell would I be all that worried about the second one?"

"Well, Angus, darling, you'd best be thinking about it. The Mendoza boys are thinking about it."

Darlin'? Is that what she called me? What's that mean? She's awful pretty of a morning, out in the cold, high air of Santa Fe in January. The air put a rush of red in her cheeks, sort of pushing up the freckles, and making her green eyes livelier than I'd noticed before.

"Well, I can't get a fix on those boys' minds. I suppose they can think all they want, but I got some business to attend to in Albuquerque."

As soon as I said it, I regretted it. Sure, I had business down the Rio Grande some sixty miles, but it could wait a few minutes, couldn't it?

"Angus," she said, scrunching her face all serious-like, "I am my father's daughter, and he taught me something about shooting. Could you take just a few more minutes and let me explain how muzzle movement affects trajectory, especially on the second shot in a sequence?"

"Sure," I mumbled, "Albuquerque can wait."

"Fine. Now here's what I see in that stance. And, it's probably the same even if you were facing two targets head on, with a normal draw from the right side of your body. That long-barreled Colt, in .44-40 caliber, has a recoil that the standard Colt does not have. You have to learn to shoot it a little differently."

"How's that?"

"I watched you go to the front sight on the first shot. Then when I hollered to fire again, you did, less than a second after the first muzzle blast. You missed, high and probably to the right. The reason was that the gun didn't set up in your hand correctly after the recoil. That happens because, especially with a twelve-inch barrel, the gun sets up a little higher in your hand. You gave that second shot less thought than the first—because I hollered at you."

"Thought? Don't know as I thought about it. I was just following your instructions."

"No, Angus, trust me on this. You were thinking in a split-second. We all do. It's instinctive thinking, and works just like the recoil of the barrel does. It pushes back into your hand, your hand signals your brain, and your brain reacts and tries to regain the same purchase you had when you squeezed off that first round. But, if your hand is set differently on the butt, just the tiniest bit, it affects the trajectory out of the barrel, twelve long inches away. In fact, with that Buntline Special, the butt plus revolver mechanism, plus barrel figures out to a little over seventeen-and-one-half inches."

I was trying to impress her. "Well, I'm told it's a flat eighteen inches, all told."

She smiled and countered, "Angus, their brochure says the Buntline Special is a foot and a half long. But, that's just marketing. I'm interested in trajectory and pounds per inch of muzzle blast, so I want accuracy, not sales talk."

"And, you think it's important enough to fix, is that what you're saying?"

"Let me put it this way. You fire once. Your recoil changes your grip, which determines trajectory—where the bullet you're about to fire next is headed. In those split-seconds, that post down there is not going to fire back at you. But, if you were to face those two Mendoza brothers again, the other one will be sighting you in while your brain's adjusting to the recoil muscle in your gun hand. While that's happening, you squeeze off the second round. It misses. Now what's happening?"

"Now that you put it that way, I guess I'm about to get shot by the post, or the second Mendoza. Is that it?"

"Precisely. You got it. Now, will you let me help you fix that little problem?"

I can't say the fix made much of a difference, but it was fun getting that close to her. She asked about my experience in such matters as gunfights. Two times, I told her.

"What do you know about the physics, muscle involvement, and eye-hand coordination on drawing, aiming, pulling triggers, and dealing with recoil and muzzle blast?" she asked.

"Nada," I said.

So, she ran me through some drills, explaining things in the same voice a fourth-grade teacher talks to her class. She said I needed work on my weak, right thumb to reach the hammer spur, ratchet it back, and then resettle thumb on frame before pulling easy on the trigger. More often than not, she said I was cranking the dang thing around so it was no longer aligned with my wrist. Which, she said, accounts for why you miss on the second or third shots. Eye is not lined up with hand, or something like that.

"Angus, we've made some progress," she said with a big grin, "but you will need to practice getting your piece to line up the same way each time you fire, or you won't hit what you aim at."

I assured her that I'd practice every chance I got. Then, quick as I could walk, I went to the livery stable, saddled No Más, and loped to the Rio Grande's east bank. Albuquerque was about seventy miles due south. We'd be there near lunchtime tomorrow. Just right.

CHAPTER 15

Angus Riding the Bosque To Albuquerque

"**N**o Más," I said, as we took a south-by-southeast bearing out of Santa Fe, "have you ever been this far south of Colorado in your life?" He picked up one ear at the sound of his name, but seemed more attentive to the sweet grasses growing beneath the giant cottonwoods bordering both sides of the Rio Grande. No Más liked the sound of my voice, especially when there was no one else around to comfort him. So, just to pass the time, I gave him a short lesson on his ancestry.

"Did you know," I said, patting him on the neck, "that the first horses to put a hoof print along the Rio Grande since the glacial age came up this way with the Coronado Expedition in 1540? There were exactly 556 horses mustered. One of them,

likely a blood stallion of some repute, was responsible for you."
No Más gave me an offhand look, twisting his neck back at
me, but otherwise didn't seem impressed.

"So, wadda you think so far?" I asked No Más, as we
moved to and fro in the Bosque along the east bank of the river
fifteen miles south of Santa Fe. As usual, he paid no mind to
my no-need-to-answer questions. Horses are social beings,
herd animals that live around other horses, including people,
without undue friction. They've singled out dogs, roosters, and
occasional saddle bums like me as inseparable companions.
But, so far, No Más had yet to give me any real sign I was all
that important to his daily existence.

Giving him more the sound of my spur than the actual feel
of it, I urged him over into the river itself without remember-
ing at the moment that he and I'd come near to drowning in
a cataract above this river a few weeks back. No Más pulled
up, backed up, and turned a newly stubborn head back to
the Bosque and the shield of forty-foot tall cottonwoods that
protected both banks from the ravages of a mostly quiet river.

By nightfall, we set camp a mile or two north of Cochiti
Pueblo, a peaceable farm village of Indians that'd been till-
ing the fields on both sides of the Rio Grande for hundreds
of years, bothering no one that passed by. When the wind
changed and started a little blow north by northeast, we
caught a drifting smell of piñon burning in a hundred fire-
places. And, when I settled down into my bedroll, five hours
before midnight, I could hear a distant sound of what sounded
like an Indian flute and a soft, slow drum beat. Comforting,
I thought. No Más, as usual, paid no attention to sounds that
meant no harm to him, or me.

We broke camp at sun up, without a fire, or coffee, and rode the east bank down toward Bernalillo. Having no interest in another visit there, and eyeing a giant slab of granite to the east, I nudged No Más up that direction. From the thick grass and cottonwoods along the river bank, we quickly came on a high desert area of juniper, then a mix of piñon and juniper. No Más was particularly interested in the thin cover of black grama grass. He avoided the prickly pear cactus and the spiny ocotillo. Higher up we could see large stands of ponderosa pine, and even a few stands of mixed aspen and oak. I told him they might even have some spruce and fir on the far side of the crest. He snorted.

"Hell," I said, "it's just like what you were used to in Colorado." He durn near fell asleep on me during my talk about trees and cactus. "Can't eat 'em," I told him, "but they bring comfort just the same."

By now I could read his mind—"if you can't eat it, it don't matter how pretty it is."

We saw prairie dog mounds mixed in with coyote dens, deer scat, but no sign of bear.

"Which was to be expected," I said. "They're hibernatin'. Smart thing to do in the winter." He likely agreed with that.

At the north end of the mountain, we skirted a nice, little Mexican village called Placitas. Seemed an agreeable place with lots of ditches and fields. There was some evidence of mining along the slope, but no recent activity I could see. An hour and a half later, I came to Albuquerque, which of recent had become the largest town in the territory. It had dozens of streets, an electric trolley system, the tallest building in a five-hundred mile circle, and the Sheriff of Bernalillo

County—Perfecto Armijo. Sheriff Armijo was the man who first befriended Yarberry when he settled in Albuquerque three years ago.

According to Marshal Knop, the friendship was an odd pairing. Armijo was a prominent citizen from an old and respected family. He was wel-educated and welcome in the highest circles of New Mexico society. Yarberry was uncouth and unknown by anyone of substance in New Mexico, except Armijo. Armijo hired Yarberry as a part-time sheriff's deputy out in the county, and helped him get the job of town marshal in boom-town Albuquerque.

Armijo had been notified of my interest in Yarberry by Marshal Knop. He welcomed me into his large, well-furnished office. That he was a wealthy man was obvious on this first visit to his office. It looked like a big, high-dollar board room. The adobe walls were adorned with fine paintings, the Saltillo tile floor with good, hand-woven rugs, from local weavers and old Mexico, and the furniture was handcrafted, leather-bound, and smelled of fresh oil and maybe a little incense.

"*Buenas tardes, mariscal Angus, ¿en qué puedo servirle a usted?*"

"*Su bienvenida, el Señor Armijo*, I hope you can help me. I'm interested in the case of Town Marshal Yarberry, and I'm told you may know him better than anyone in the territory."

"Whoever told you that overstates my influence and how many people I know. True, I was among the first to meet the unfortunate Mr. Yarberry, but there were many of us who at first thought he was a man of substance who was only a little down on his luck. He seemed to be a man who understood ledgers and guns. But, maybe he was too much a man of the gun and too little interested in how we do business in New Mexico. Can I offer you something to drink, something to eat, perhaps? Señora Armijo is an excellent cook, as you can probably guess from the size of my stomach, señor. Please, tell me what you'd like."

"I'm a little parched. The high, cold air makes you welcome a glass of water, if you don't mind."

"*Si, no es nada*, and maybe a galleta, *qué no?*"

"*Si, gracias.*"

My Spanish was passable, but I'd only talked to *vaqueros* working the Dos S brand up in the Espanola valley ten years ago. I didn't want to let this fellow think I was fluent or anything. His *espousa* came in, smiled politely at me, and listened to whatever he said to her. Three minutes later, she came back in with a pitcher of cool water, a Masonry cup with red and white painted figures on it, and a small plate of brown cookies with a little pot of honey in the center.

"So, Señor Angus, what is your history? You look to be a man from somewhere around here, am I right?"

"My family's ranched some up around Chama ," I said.

"And?" he asked, extending his arm with his palm up, like his bushy eyebrows went up, asking the question with his face.

"And that's 'bout it. My folks had a small spread that got gobbled up by the Dos S brand some years back."

"And, you, what happened to you in all that gobbling?"

"Hard to say. I did some ridge riding for the Chama railroad between there and Antonito. Packed some, did a little guiding for the railroad engineers, and some law work for the US marshal's office out of Denver. Nothing all that serious. I mostly do part-time assignments."

"A modest man, indeed, Señor Angus. I am well-known to some people, like Judge Blakey up in Santa Fe. I had dinner with him last night, and we talked a little about you. You don't mind that, do you?"

"No, Sheriff Armijo. Judge Blakey was right kind in helping me square away questions about how I shot a man named Standard H. Plumb, who was a double-dealing railroad detective for the AT&SF. In fact, I had dinner with him in Santa Fe night before last. That was arranged by Marshal Knop—they are friends. If you had dinner with him last night, I trust it was at the same restaurant in Santa Fe.

"No, Judge Blakey came down here yesterday to talk to the other judges about something, not the sheriff's business. But, he's an old friend, and we often dine when we go to one another's town. And, I knew you were coming today, so I was delighted to learn a little of you from him."

"Like what? What did you learn?" I said, trying my best to put on a smile.

"Only good things, Señor Angus. I learned from him your role in catching and releasing a bank robber named Tom Emmett up in Union County. And, also, I believe he mentioned the inquest some years ago in which you were involved with the AT&SF railroad's train robber and the man known as Standard H. Plumb. You are a man of accomplishment, but a man of mystery as well. Now you are here, on a mission, it seems. What is the mystery of this man Yarberry? I think you may know more about him than I do."

"Nah, I am down here on what is likely a goose track."

"A wild goose track? Like a chase, señor? Is that it?"

"Well, I do a bit of tracking, you see. This man Yarberry has tracks in three states and this territory. I know he's set to die in three days, and my assignment here won't interfere with that. All my boss, the US Marshal in Denver, Colorado, wants is some information about Yarberry's conduct in Colorado.

"You've talked to Yarberry, I understand."

"Yes, sir, I did. Dead end there. He didn't tell me much of anything we didn't already know."

"And, you are here because you believe I know something that will help you up in Colorado?"

"Well, honestly, I'm talking to you mostly because you are on the list of people that know Yarberry, and the only one that spoke up for him and who might think he's innocent. That's why I'm talking to you."

"Ah, I see. Innocence in the eyes of the sheriff, but guilty in the eyes of the jury. But, who told you I thought he was innocent?"

"Can't say for sure. It's in the report from the US Justice Department. And, I seem to recall the newspapers reporting that same thing."

"Do you know that innocence is presumed under the law, Marshal Angus?"

"I reckon."

"And, that unless guilt is proved beyond a reasonable doubt a man cannot be convicted of a serious crime?"

"Suppose so."

"Well, I initially hired Milton J. Yarberry as a part-time sheriff's deputy because I thought he was good with a gun, smart enough to do the job, and was a man of considerable substance. But, when he shot Mr. Brown, I arrested him and charged him—and the jury acquitted him. When he shot Mr. Campbell, I arrested him again. My comments about him in the paper were before the trial. They were arguments in favor of giving the man the benefit of presumed innocence. And, they were based on knowing that his only prior shooting was a justifiable shooting, according to a jury of his peers. Is that not our system, Marshal Angus?"

I was getting hot under my collar. I ain't used to being cross-examined. I know the law of arrests and crimes and such, but lawyering is not for me. I looked at him, but could not think of a good answer to his question.

"Marshal Angus, please accept my apology for making you uncomfortable. But, many people mistook my sense of justice. Instead, they took it as a personal belief in Yarberry's innocence. Frankly, I thought he might well have gunned down poor Mr. Campbell without just cause—no one saw a gun—there was no gun there—no one heard a shot once Yarberry chased Campbell down. So, speaking personally, had you asked me before the trial, I would have said that he was probably guilty as hell. But, I'm a man of the law, like you. So, I gave him the presumption of innocence. That's our job, isn't it? We investigate and arrest, but we don't judge, right?"

"Sheriff Armijo, I got to tell you I ain't never heard it put just that way before. But, I'll remember your position from now on. I'm sorry to have bothered you, and expect I'd best be on my way."

I got up, but the man across the desk from me raised his hand up and motioned for me to sit back down. He came around the desk and offered me his hand, "Marshal, don't let my lecture put you off. Everyone in my family thinks I talk too much and spent too many years in books and talking to lawyers. Did you know my own grandfather was an *abogado*, in Sonora Mexico, over fifty years ago? I studied law at university, but did not sit for the bar because my family's business required my presence. I ran for sheriff here because it's as close to the law as I will get. Please stay a little while, I have something else to talk to you about. Can you do this small thing for me?"

"Sure. I just don't want to be a nuisance."

"You're not, I assure you," he said, as he called for a little more coffee, and more galletas.

Settling himself back in his leather chair, he pulled a small, brass box lined in leather across the desk, selected a long, thin cigar and picked up a match box. "Cigarro, Marshal? I can assure you these are some of Mexico's best. I get them by mule train through Juarez."

"No, thanks. I never took up the habit."

When he got it going, he leaned back and blew a small circle of smoke in my direction, "Did you know that Bernalillo is in my jurisdiction, and that Town Marshal Bo String reports directly to me?"

"No, but I probably should have figured that."

"He does. I read his report about the Mendoza shooting, Onchero Mendoza, outside the Silva Saloon. He is quite competent, even though he's one of the least experienced deputies I have. And, he speaks well of you."

"Good to hear. I know him some, and I think he's a mighty fine man to have around, especially if you're in a scrape."

"What do you know of the Mendozas?"

"Never heard of 'em until I was in a cantina in Espanola two weeks ago. Hope I'm shed of 'em."

"*Si*, Señor, that's wise of you. But, that's precisely why I wanted to talk to you. Some people, whether Mexican, Anglo, or Asians, cannot abide an insult. Especially Asian people—when insulted they lose face. Have you heard that term, 'losing face'? Some of my people, those who still remember the old Hidalgo days in Mexico, are proud to a fault. We don't call it losing face. But, it is our machismo, just the same. Do you know about Mexican machismo, Señor Angus?"

"I guess you're talking about acting tough. I've known some very tough *vaqueros* up on the ranch."

"No, machismo is a little more than just being tough. Our mestizo culture places a high value on manliness. That's why it's different from losing face, because women lose face, too. But, mestizo culture is about how men must react to retain manly status."

"Yeah, I can see that. But, I can't exactly see how that culture affects me, or the Mendoza brothers. I shot one of them and arrested the other. But, they acted pretty manly, as far as I'm concerned."

"Well, you are not their father. Their father sees it through mestizo eyes—he thinks you made fools of his boys, in front of others, and especially in front of an upstairs woman, who had made a joke about Onchero's manliness. Did you know about that?"

"Hell fire, Sheriff, I was just giving them a warning not to go banging on that woman. And, they called me out, right there on the street. I don't get how I made a fool of either one of 'em."

"Well, of course, you are in the right. In the eyes of the law. And, in my eyes, too. But, Mendoza Mendoza is steeped in mestizo culture. As he sees it, you made Onchero the fool when he let you get a bead on him because he never saw you draw your big gun. And, then you made Ignacio the fool when you shot Onchero in the leg, and he misfired the shotgun injuring his own brother in the face. And, then when the shotgun went off into the horse trough, and all you did was walk up and disarm both of them without either firing a shot in your direction. Aiee, that's looking the fool mucho, mucho!"

"Well, dang it all to hell, they ought not to have been banging on that girl, and they ought to have listened to me. This was no big thing until they decided to show me who's boss in Bernalillo."

"Yes, Señor Angus, that's another thing. It was in Bernalillo. That's in your favor. Had it been in Espanola, a town the Mendoza boys think they own, it would be much worse. Their brand, the *M/* is part of their manliness, their machismo. But people in Bernalillo have relatives in Espanola. It's like that everywhere in New Mexico. Those from Bernalillo will tell those in Espanola that you, a stranger with a broken arm, bested the Mendoza boys. Maybe that's something *El Patron* Mendoza cannot walk away from."

"Hell, Sheriff, it was just a shot in the leg. He'll get over it."

"Onchero can take a shot in the leg, and it can be forgotten—that is what I think the man you shot, Onchero, will do—get well and forget you. But, his brother Ignacio is not the same. He knows that once people in Bernalillo get over the shock of a gunfight, they will smile when they think he lost his nerve, and laugh when they remember how foolish he looked falling down, without even drawing his gun."

"So, you're saying I ought to watch my back trail, is that it?"

"Yes, but there's more you should know."

"What's that?"

"Ignacio's father, you know he named himself twice—Mendoza Mendoza. He is a distant relative of a cousin of mine. And, he is a man who cannot live with what he will think is family shame. He will punish Ignacio for shaming the family in the street. If it had happened in Espanola, he would have beaten Ignacio. And, he would have not spoken to Onchero for a long time. Mendoza Mendoza is a man who will take his revenge. On you, Señor."

"I appreciate the head's up. I'll keep an eye out for him."

"No, Señor, that is not enough. Mendoza Mendoza will come after you, but you won't ever see him. He's not a man to duel, or face you down in the street. He's a man whose bullet you'll never hear. It will come from a high-powered rifle, a long ways off, and probably behind you. Or, if he gets as crazy as he sometimes does, he will use others, killers, to hunt you down like a panther. They will be wary, but he has dogs, time, and a hatred of you."

"So you're guessing he'll ambush me, is that it?"

The tip of his cigarro glowed red as he leaned back in his chair. He didn't talk for a minute. Finally, nodded his head at me.

"*Por forvor*, Señor Angus, this is no guess. Do you know why I'm so confident you are in danger?"

"No, can't say I do."

"Mendoza Mendoza tracked down a young man who lived on my ranch, the son of my cousin, ten years ago. It was something like this case, an insult on the family, the need for revenge. They found him in a canyon two months after he left the ranch one morning. He had more than a dozen rifle bullets in his back. And, they shot his horse in the head."

"I'm real sorry to hear that, Señor Armijo. How did they figure out Mendoza Mendoza did it?"

"They not only shot him and his horse. They branded both of them, on the head, Señor. The *M/*, or as Mendoza Mendoza calls it, the M slash. I knew it then, and I know it now. He is evil. Watch out for the brand, Señor."

"I'm leaving town as soon as the execution takes place, and I'll spin No Más in a tight circle every quarter-mile up the trail. He's a fine little pony, Sheriff, and he'll help me watch our back trail."

CHAPTER 16

Angus At the Hanging of Milton J. Yarberry

GETTING A HAND-DELIVERED, by-god official, invitation to the hanging of Milton Yarberry was a surprise. After the man was planted in the local Catholic cemetery, I learned that Yarberry's friend, Sheriff Perfecto Armijo, his official executioner, had sent out over a hundred of these printed invitations. *Come see the event of the year—hanging a lawman.* 'Course, it did not say that, but it turned out to be the first full-blown spectacle of my young life. Best thing I did was to leave No Más in the barn, five blocks away. Horses got better sense.

Marshal Knop got one hand-delivered, and he invited me. More than a dozen other lawmen got 'em; everybody showed up. Suppose it was a lawman's job to see one of our own get his neck stretched. Sheriff Armijo roped off a separate area just to the right-of-center scaffold for us lawmen, on what turned out to be a fairly warm winter day—February ninth, eighteen hundred and eighty three.

While waiting for them to bring the prisoner out into the jail yard at Second Street and Central, I got scrunched in next to a man named Colonel Max Frost. He said he was the commander of the New Mexico militia, called the *Governor's Rifles*. They had escorted Yarberry from his cell up in Santa Fe at the crack of dawn yesterday. He said they'd put him in an omnibus at the jail, conducted him to the Santa Fe Railway depot, and chained him in a seat on a special one-coach train bound for Albuquerque. The seventy mile trip took just three-hours-and-twenty-minutes train time. That got me to wondering how long a horse-drawn stage trip would have taken. Not wanting to talk about the hanging itself, I took advantage of being next to a man who knew more than anyone about moving men and horses from one place to another.

"Colonel, could you and your men have made the trip by stagecoach?"

"Young man, you have the look of a horseman about you, and I see a US Marshal badge on your coat. What would be your estimate of the time it would have taken by stagecoach? Any ideas on that?"

"Dunno. Ain't never made the trip in a coach, but I rode it twice of recent. When my horse is stretching out in a long trot, he'll carry me a good ten miles in an hour. But, with a four-up team, pulling a heavy wagon with, say, three men aboard, I doubt they'd cover that much ground every hour, even though it's mostly downhill on a fair to middling road."

"Well, sir, we got time before Sheriff Armijo drops the noose on his friend Yarberry, and the subject interests me. I'll say this. Travel time for moving a prisoner depends on the terrain, the condition of the stock and the equipment, the weather, and most importantly, whether there might be men around intent on impeding your progress. Had we elected stagecoach over the safety of the train, we would have taken care to post outriders watching for Yarberry's friends from Colorado. Now here's how I might plan it. We'd need one man inside the coach with the prisoner, two armed men up top, one handling the reins, the other keeping an eye out. Lemme see, now. A man on foot can easily walk thirty miles in a day, forty if he pushes it. Stonewall Jackson's 'foot cavalry' consistently did more than that. But, a man on the back of a well-rested, fit horse can gallop, depending on the ability of the animal and the terrain, at over thirty miles an hour."

Two other fellers got interested in our talk, and began nodding or shaking their heads depending on their own personal experience. One of them had trouble nodding because he had a chaw of tobacco in the side of his mouth.

I said, "No Más can push it as well as any horse I've ever rode, but, of course, he's only hauling me, not a heavy coach with four men on board."

"Well, sir, a US Cavalry horse can be pushed to carry a trooper seventy or eighty miles a day, but then will be pretty much spent for several days while he recuperates. Do you do much travel by horse, sir?"

"Most of my riding has been up high, on mountain ridges or alongside moving water. That'll slow you down some."

"Mighty fine," Colonel Frost said, before speculating on the question. "I'd estimate making the trip by coach, assuming seventy miles at about five-and-a-half hours. That would further assume a thirteen-mile-per-hour pace. Of course, it would exhaust the driver on top and would be damned uncomfortable for the passengers."

"Expect it would have lathered up Mr. Yarberry, too," quipped on of the men following the conversation.

Colonel Frost took exception to the attempt at humor and changed the subject to what he called the "logistics of transfer." He put his back to the man and posed a new question.

"You spent much time along the Rio Grande?"

"Some," I said.

"Well, then, you know it's one of the grandest rivers on the continent, more than 1,800 miles long from its headwaters in Colorado, covering the length of the New Mexico territory, across half of Texas, and right into the Gulf of Mexico."

"Was there much commotion up in Santa Fe, when you loaded a lawman into a train car headed for a hanging?" the other lawman asked.

"We guarded him extra special on account of the governor and the chief justice want this hanging to come off without a hitch."

"In the rope?"

"I did not mean a hitch in the rope. I meant trouble of any kind that might reflect adversely on the government of this territory. As a point of fact, I examined the actual rope last week when we came down to inspect the scaffold and the execution plan. The rope, you'll be happy to know, is new, one-and-a-half inches thick, although, of course, it's been soaked and stretched so that's it's half that diameter now."

I wasn't sure if he was looking for a response, but he paused, so I tried to make light of the conversation.

"So that's where the old saying comes from—they stretched his neck. It ain't really his neck; it's the rope around the neck, right?"

He went on as though I'd not said a word.

"You know that this hanging is a first in New Mexico for two reasons, don't you? It's the first lawman to be officially hung, and it's the first time we are using the jerk plan rather than the traditional trapdoor method. What do you think of that?"

I had no idea what 'n hell the jerk plan was, but didn't want to appear foolish, so I asked him a dumb question. "How many lawmen been unofficially hung?"

"Can't say for sure, but outlaws been doing their own hangings around here for a hundred years. Rustlers get hung and sometimes rustler's kin. Other times outlaws hang a lawman or his deputy, just for the hell of it."

The crowd was a whole lot bigger than I felt comfortable being around. Good thing I'd stabled No Más down at the end of Second Street at the public livery where Gold Street cuts across. There were horses tied to up to hitching rails both up and down the street. The conversation lulled as everyone stamped their boots on the frosted ground. This was as good a place as any to build old Yarberry's scaffold, I thought. It was a sturdy thing. The jail yard, usually open to the street, had been fenced off, but you could see right through the wire.

There were, as the *Albuquerque Morning Journal* said the next day, "more than fifteen hundred souls watching one soul make its way out of the human existence."

The hanging gallows, recently constructed just for this occasion, was done with freshly cut, split-pine beams. Two fifteen-foot uprights connected to a cross beam of considerable length. The rope, all shiny in the bright morning sun, ran from its noosed end up to a big iron pulley attached to the crossbeam. It hooked itself to another smaller pulley and trailed down to what looked like an outhouse right in back of the gallows.

Since Colonel Frost was so all-fired knowledgeable about these things, I asked him why they had an outhouse connected to a gallows.

"Not an outhouse, Marshal. That's the execution room, where Count Epur awaits. Fascinating fellow, the count. He's Polish, you know, and has done many executions. The law says that the local sheriff is also the executioner on a lawful death warrant, but Perfecto is close to Milton J. Yarberry, so he asked the Count to step up, so to speak, and do the deed himself."

"So, this Epur guy, he's the one that picked the jerk plan? Can't say I've heard of that."

"No, Sheriff Armijo himself decided that the jerk plan was preferable, given that the doomed man is a friend. It's more humane, you know."

"A more humane hanging; that's maybe why all these folks came to see it. No trap door, is that it?"

"Right, you see the execution booth, the one you thought was an outhouse, well that's where Colonel Epur will wait. That rope you see up there, from the second pulley, it goes down into that execution booth. It's tied to a four-hundred-pound lead weight. A smaller cord holds the weight suspended six-feet off the ground, right next to it, do you see that?"

"Yep."

He was pointing and speaking up because the rest of the crowd of lawmen seemed real interested now. One of them asked why the weight was suspended six feet off the ground.

"Is it because that's how tall Milton J. Yarberry is?"

"Don't know his exact height, but I personally commanded his escort down here on the train. I stood next to him the whole way. He was two-three inches taller than me and I'm just a finger shy of six foot. Anyhow, it makes no difference. It's plenty of height to do the job. You see, there is a cord that holds that weight up off the ground. When Colonel Epur cuts it, with a finely sharpened axe, it will plunge to the ground. The condemned prisoner will be snapped upward. By his neck. Rather suddenly, I should expect. Remember I told you it was the jerk-plan."

Another man, heavily mustachioed, and wearing a bigger badge than any of us, pondered a moment.

"Jerking the body up is more humane than dropping it down the chute, have I got that right?" he asked.

Colonel Frost was getting irritated with these skeptical comments.

"No, Sheriff, the whole method is more humane, and is, in fact, a model of scientific skill, being of the improved pattern used in all well-regulated hanging bees."

"Well, seems I read the same article in yesterday's *Santa Fe Mexican* you did. But, it brings up a question. Just what in tarnation is a hanging bee?"

Colonel Frost ignored the question, looked at his pocket watch, and said, "It's nearly three o'clock. The death warrant stipulates that the execution be carried out before three p.m. Perhaps there's been a reprieve."

Just to prove him wrong, for once, the militia he commanded formed up at the direction of a young man looking to be about fifteen, with a shiny gold bar on his epaulet. Colonel Frost stepped forward, called the squad to attention, and raised the first two fingers of his right hand to the lieutenant. They formed a double line from the jailhouse door.

First man out the door was Sheriff Armijo, dark felt hat pulled down; wearing what looked to be a black raincoat over a gun rig. There were two deputies and four men in black suits that I later learned were doctors. Then came Milton Yarberry, in a black suit which looked to be one size too small, followed by a parson in a black bowler, starched white shirt, and black collar.

Yarberry walked unsteadily on account of his leg shackles and looked miserable, perhaps on account of the oversized handcuffs, which were linked to a heavy belt snugged tight over his protruding belly. It made him look like he had two guts puffing out above and below the heavy belt rig. The deputies, both wearing black hats pulled down tight, nudged him at his own slow pace up the steps to the platform. The crowd just turned to stone—no one seemed to be even breathing hard. Puffs of light smoke curled up out of the jail chimney, and even the horses along the hitching rail quit stomping as the crowd went silent.

Soon's they got him atop, the deputies did their part; bound his thighs with belts, and closed his ankles tight with a piggin' string. Then they took off his hat and dropped that

big old noose around his neck. One of 'em tugged it in, just
below his Adam's apple, which seemed to protrude something
awful, from where I stood.

Sheriff Armijo stood like a statue in a graveyard; arms
folded, jaw clenched, not looking at the condemned. When the
tugging was done, he handed a paper to one of the deputies,
who boomed out the sparse sentences on the death warrant.
Then, without looking at the noosed man, he asked if Yarberry
had anything to say.

Yarberry seemed to take courage at this, can't say why, but
he twisted his head out toward Second Street, and the store
buildings on the other side, which had gawkers leaning out
the windows on the second floors. His voice probably didn't
carry that far, but we could hear distinctly from where we all
stood. He moaned something about killing Henry Brown, and
the dead man being the son of the governor of Tennessee. He
allowed as how he shot him in "defense of my life." After a
minute or two of yakking about how determined they were
to hang him, he brought up killing Charles D. Campbell. He
made it plain.

"He shot at me and I shot back, and…"

We all waited for him to finish his sentence. A minute
passed and the crowd milled around whispering to one another.
Someone yelled from a window across the street, "He's done."

Sheriff Armijo motioned to a deputy. A black cap or covering of some sort was produced. The deputy flopped it over
Yarberry's face, just as Yarberry screamed at the top of his lungs.

"Gentlemen, you are hanging an innocent man!"

Don't know about the innocent part, but those gentlemen sure hung him. Armijo nodded down into the open

part of what Colonel Frost had called the "execution booth,"
probably at Count Epur looking up. The Count must have
swung his axe hard, because we heard a big thud, then the
lead weight dropped. I can't say I saw it drop. But, Yarberry's
body shot up straight into the cross beam four feet above him.
Everybody within forty feet heard Yarberry's neck crack. It
was like a tree branch breaking off right in front of your nose.
Crack! Yarberry's head, black skull cap, and all were mashed
together—bone, blood, and split skin. His body dropped back
down almost to the platform and swung around, once, then
twice in the opposite direction.

Of a sudden, I lost my breath. Then like we was all out
of breath together, everybody let out a sigh. I know it's crazy,
but it sounded like a wail from a wounded horse trapped in a
mud bog. I expect he was dead, but Yarberry's body gave off
a big shudder. The doctors up on the platform cut him down,
laid him out, and put their fingers on both sides of his throat.
Then the one on the far side waved the other doc off and he
fingered both of Yarberry's wrists. Some minutes passed,
nine according to the paper next morning, and the officials
pronounced Milton J. Yarberry a dead man.

The thing that struck me as most inhumane was cutting
the noose about three feet from the body. It was free of the
hanging scaffold but still tied taut around Yarberry's neck.
I watched them carry him down off the scaffold and put him
in a plain, wooden coffin with the noose *still* attached to his
neck. They nailed the lid shut, lifted it up to a buckboard, and
hauled it off.

So we all hauled ourselves off, too. It struck me that calling one way humane and another way inhumane was plain

stupid. Colonel Frost was still explaining things out there in the hanging yard when I walked out by myself. I did not feel the need for any more palaver with other lawmen. Walking up to the livery barn to check on No Más, I thought about what I'd say to him on the matter of hanging men. I brushed No Más down and picked his feet. That done, it came clear to me. Horses are used in hangings out on the trail. Sometimes by outlaws and sometimes by lawmen who don't want to be bothered with what they call due process of law. What would a horse want to know about any of that? I kept it to myself and walked back to the La Posada Hotel. Bought a double glass of whiskey, but didn't drink it in the bar. Taking it to my room, I put it on the table beside the bed. It was empty the next morning, but I couldn't remember drinking it. I decided I'd seen my last hanging.

CHAPTER 17

Angus & No Más– Snowstorm

THE MORNING AFTER MILTON J. YARBERRY's hanging in Albuquerque, I had breakfast at Cole's café across from the La Posada Hotel. Then I walked down to the livery stable, hauling my kit. Took me a good half-hour to brush No Más, pick his feet again, and make an adjustment to his breast collar. He'd been gnawing some on the breast strap, and the cinch had been slipping a bit on the ride down.

I was in the saddle a half-hour after sunrise, headed up the east side of the Rio Grande, across the Sandia Pueblo lands. This gave me a mighty fine view of the river on my left, down about three miles, and the giant Sandia shale peak on my right, up about another three. This was wide-open country. A man could see forty miles both ahead and back, and at least two miles on either side. No one seemed to be interested in me. I could see no other horses up on the mesa, although I could clearly see the stage road, the rail track, and the Rio Grande off to my left. No train was scheduled today, and the cottonwoods did a fair job of hiding the river for long stretches. I thought about what Sheriff Armijo had told me about bad hombres on my trial. That Bosque would be handy for them if they were trailing me.

After an hour's ride, I was getting close to Bernalillo, and my thoughts were on the Mendoza boys. Well, truth be told, they were more on *El Patron*, Mendoza Mendoza. I've only got one name; he's got two, both the same. Ain't sure what to make of that.

I just could not get my mind around the notion that the old bastard would track me. But, careful ain't a bad thing to be if the sheriff was even half-right.

The air, clear but colder now, felt damp. I sat No Más for five minutes after that last, long draw uphill. This was scrub country now, scattered piñon and juniper, and sage broken by low, raw-backed mountains on my left and Sandia Peak on my right. And, the weather was changing fast.

The ground had been soft underfoot yesterday. Today it took on the hardness of a rocky shale. Felt like the ground was tightening up on me, to match the sky. It'd been cloudy and I had not seen the sun for two hours. The sky was looking like it was near nightfall, but it wasn't yet noon.

"Storm's coming up, No Más. Can you feel her startin' to blow?"

We rode on, a slow crawl up keeping the stage road between us and the river. Then, coming on a little shelf protected by two cabin-sized boulders, I dismounted and attended to nature's business. I unrolled my bedroll and took out the extra oilcloth I usually carried for winter riding, a pair of extra-long wool socks with the feet cut out and a felted wool scarf. I layered the oilcloth over my duster, snugged one of the socks over my left hand up to the cast, and the other on my right hand up under the thumb. This left my fingers free to thread the reins. The oil cloth would hang down from my shoulders and give me a little back and butt protection from the blow I figured was heading our way.

The first sprinkling of light snow commenced twenty minutes later, just as the wind quieted down some. It was wet and stuck to No Más's mane right off. The storm wrapped its giant arms around us as we picked our way down the side of a draw toward the river. I'd lost my sense of where the stage-coach road was because the heavy, almost liquid-wet snow covered the ground several inches deep. No Más's black hooves were slick and shiny, and icicles were forming on his tail and mane. It was one of those rare snows that began to freeze on the ground at the same time it was falling.

"Ain't no such thing as too cold to snow," I told No Más, as he gave me a mighty shake just as we stepped off a short embankment across one of the hundreds of arroyos running down from the mountain on my right to the river on my left.

This wasn't riding so much as it was just picking our way through the snow, forming ice, and in and out of the arroyos. I suppose we were making about the same time as a fat heifer cow does when grazing her way across a mesa in springtime. The oiled slicker over my duster was getting heavy with snow, and some had worked its way in under the scarf and below my hat. We just kept picking our way north. No way to tell time with a sky that looked gray headin' for black.

"Son, just you keep your head up, I ain't gonna be tugging on you."

The earth had loosed up some, and the crunch of gravel below the snow was comforting. But, No Más had to place his steps with care as we angled sort of sidewise down a draw into a sizeable arroyo. It would have been a little tricky in dry weather, but the slush and mud we were riding in now made this draw unsteady riding.

"There, up ahead of us, No Más, see that little overhang? Maybe we'll sort of saddle up alongside that and rest a little. You can blow and I can get this dang snow off my neck."

The arroyo was about to fifteen feet deep. This was mostly caliche, which was dusty as hell in summer, but turned to thick, cold mud in the middle of a blizzard. The overhang bent in under where the downslope had changed its course; from south by southwest to almost the opposite direction. At the top was a bent juniper tree, surrounded by sage brush. The twisted ends of the old juniper hung down like an umbrella over the bottom of the arroyo. I neck reined No Más so's that his big hind end would be between me and the blowing brace of wind and wet snow. Then of a sudden, something new. Hard ice, coming at us almost sideways, parallel to the ground.

"There," I said to No Más, reaching out across his neck with my right hand to tug on his head stall. "Just ease us on underneath the overhang, son. Nice and slow now."

No Más stutter-stepped sideways into the little crevice as I shifted my weight to the inside. As he was tucking us in, I laid myself over the saddle horn onto his neck, and began the slow lift of my right leg back over the cantle. I was right happy that no *vaquero* could see me now. Foolish lookin' way to dismount a horse. But, there was less than a foot between No Más's head and the underside of the twisted juniper above us. Somehow, I had to get off without pushing him back out into the arroyo. We were tucked in tight. I got both feet down on unstable ground, and leaned in hard up against No Más, tucking the dang cast up to my rib cage, and hanging on to a tie-down string from the cantle. My right spur was jammed up against a sizeable rock, but my left foot felt clear. It was too tight to look down, but No Más was steady and breathing even. He dropped his head down low, standing his ground. I laid my gun hand along his neck and could feel that big ole carotid pumping hard. It was a comforting feeling, given the fierceness of the wind. Between horse and overhang, I'd found me a hideaway from what was now a full blown sou' wester, comin' on like a bull elk after a cow in heat crashing down a mountainside.

"No Más, steady, son," I said as I shook off the heaped-up snow on my hat, shoulders, and arms. I cleared the snow and ice off my neck scarf, and tried to dry the top of my vest. My mule hide chaps had done their job—snow doesn't stick to mule hide. My feet were stuck frozen in the icy mud. No Más's body heat, and maybe mixed in with mine, kept both of us from freezing anything important, like fingers or ears. We waited it out for nearly an hour. Then, as a calm set down on us like the end of a day, the storm blew right past us, headed north up Santa Fe way.

"Come on now, son, easy as you can. Slippery here," I said as I leaned into No Más and pushed him slowly out from underneath the overhang.

The hideaway was layered with snow, icy sleet, and mud. Everywhere we stepped, we sunk down a few inches. Moving to the bottom of the arroyo, I leaned back and gandered at a whole different sky from the one that had driven us up against the side of the arroyo. No Más started nosing me, and twisting this way and that, trying to shake loose the heavy, wet hair off his mane and head. He shuddered mightily, and the snow and water fell off him like he was a five-foot-tall duck coming up out of a pond. He whinnied at the calm air.

"Yeah, you done good. Once we get to level ground, I'll dig a couple handfuls of sweet grain out of the saddle pack for you."

He stomped the ground just to tell me he was all for that. Like all New Mexico storms, this one cleared all sound out of the area. The quiet almost hurt my ears, except they were too cold to appreciate it. I banged my hands together and hugged myself a few times to shake the snow off. Then I cinched up, threw my leg over the saddle, and we climbed up the side of the arroyo at a fair trot. The view was out of some fairy land. White everywhere, as calm and peaceful as a cotton quilt laid over the ground as far as I could see. Nothing moving, no sounds; only a mountain-sized storm, black and gray headed north by northeast in front of us.

"Santa Fe will get it in another hour or so, No Más. Ain't you glad we're here, all white and cozy?" His answer, as usual, was physical. He dropped his head of a sudden and tried to rub the wet head stall and bit on his front left leg. "Quit, No Más, you're making me unsteady up here. Slogging through a half-foot of wet snow on a slope just ain't good for a stout horse, or a tuckered-out man."

"No Más, whadda you say we drop off to the east a little from the top of that rise up there, and see if we can reconnoiter the stage road?"

Stage roads all over New Mexico are mapped out to make it easy for a six-up team of horses to pull a two-thousand pound coach up a hill. So, instead of going straight on up the hill, like No Más would do with just me on his back, the engineers that lay out stage roads do everything gradual like, in switchbacks this way and that, to make it easier on the horses and safer for the passengers.

"Do you understand the thinking here, No Más?"

Just then two birds, likely scavengers of one type or another, came up toward us from the north, circled overhead, and moved on thinking we were too alive for their tastes. Stretching my neck felt good, so I unloosed the neck scarf and tied it to the offside saddle string. No Más was snortin' and blowing frosty air out in front of us. All in all, this was turning out to be a pretty winter day, now that the sou' westerner was a hundred miles north of us. The sun started playing hide and seek, peeking out over the horizon, and then ducking behind again. Temperature felt like it'd risen a bit. I reined No Más in a fifty-foot full circle, lookin' for tracks in the snow in all four directions. I zigzagged probably four miles to the north, one to the east, two or three westbound, and a good long way behind us. Nothing.

"No Más, we are unaccompanied out here. No beast, nor man is out here but us. Damn, that's a good feeling, ain't it?"

CHAPTER 18

Angus & Jill Ride Back To Santa Fe

N O MÁS SPOTTED THEM FIRST, coming to a halt of a sudden. Up ahead about a hundred yards and to our left, ruts
in the road—not fresh, but open to the air. Appears the snow
blowed off here, or maybe the ruts were too deep for a four-
inch snow. We rode on up to them, and I dismounted. From
fingering the wheel ruts in the snow, I knew these were old
ruts, probably dug in a light rain. They were cut by yesterday's
stage coach up the hill to Santa Fe from Albuquerque. I couldn't
see the Rio Grande, but I knew she was running over to the
west, probably four, five miles. We were on a slight upgrade.
I took the opportunity to let No Más blow without my bulk
in the saddle. I dug some jerky, a three-day old biscuit, and a
handful of grain out of the saddle bag. No Más chewed on it

while I washed the jerky and biscuit down with a long pull of my water bag. It was colder than the river itself; I could feel ice crystals down at the bottom as I squeezed the bag

It was while we were standing down that I heard the far-off crack of leather on a horse's back, followed by a not quite recognizable holler from a teamster or a stagecoach driver. Quick-like, I jumped back up on No Más, which gave me a sharp ache in my casted left arm. Touching my spurs to his sides, I urged No Más into a trot up to the top of the hill. And, there she was, down the other side, heading our way. The Santa Fe Stage Company. It was one of them Celerity wagons, four mules out in front, a driver atop, and no one riding shotgun. Her southbound wheel tracks behind her were plain to see for two, three miles. She was pulling a saddle horse on a twenty-foot lead rope.

No Más and I pulled off onto the upside of the snow-covered road, and I leaned back into a comfortable sit, crossed my arms, and watched her make the half-mile pull up to us.

Eyeing me careful-like, the driver gave me a howdy.

"Good afternoon, sir, see you must have overcome that big blow we had this morning. Are you and your horse okay?"

"We're fine. Yourself?"

"Takes more 'n a sou' westerner to put me off my feed," he said through his mountain-man mustache, and under the cover of a large, dirty cloth wrapped all the way around his head with a wool snow hat tugged down on top. "You headed Santa Fe way?"

"Yep."

"Well, you are likely to make better time going up the last fifteen miles than I did slogging down here through the storm.

We stopped nine miles back near the bottom of La Bajada Hill. Got so bad, I had to get inside the cab with the miss here. Mite embarrassin' it was."

"When did you leave Santa Fe?" I asked, just being sociable.

"An hour and thirty after sunup this morning. We'd be in Albuquerque along 'bout now, but for that storm. Gawd amighty, she was a blowin', weren't she?"

I didn't answer. The side canvas of the stage cab was being rolled up from the inside. Then the downslope door opened and a passenger stepped down; couldn't see who he was from my perch on the upside of the coach.

The driver turned backward to his passenger, revealing the snow-covered shotgun alongside him. "Might as well stretch your legs, miss; this stranger just came through the same storm as caused us a four-hour delay."

The miss he was referring to came around the far side of the coach causing me to take ahold of my saddle horn. The driver, a portly man with huge arms and short legs, climbed down and began checking the harness, tongue, and butt straps on his mules.

"Jill?"

"Angus!", she said looking flush from the cold, I suppose.

"I was looking for the stage road, thinking it'd be easier on No Más than slogging through the snow for another twenty miles."

"Well, kind sir, you're a welcome sight. I had a shooting clinic scheduled for this evening at the La Posada in Albuquerque, but the snow canceled that. We won't reach Albuquerque till long after dark."

"'Spect so, you ain't half-way down there, yet."

"I got the lunch packed that the La Fonda sends down with every stage, folks," he said looking at his mules, but intendin' the offer for Jill and me. "You're welcome to it. I can fetch the box down off the top."

Jill looked up to me and raised her arm up toward me in a questioning gesture.

"No Más and I had trail food an hour ago. Best we'd be moving on and 'spect you're anxious to get on down to Albuquerque."

"Well, I sure was five minutes ago," said Jill. "But, your happening to come along gives me an option. Would you mind?"

"Mind?"

"Well, you can see that saddle mare tied on behind. I rented her from my friend, Mr. Gallinas, the livery keeper in Santa Fe. This stage goes on down to Socorro and then to Las Cruces. My intention was to ride that mare back up to Santa Fe tomorrow morning. Could I ride back now, along with you?"

"Sure, I'll just check her cinch," I said, dismounting on the off side and protecting my cast.

No Más liked to take the lead if there was another horse along, and I had to tug him back a time or two in the first mile down the hill to the next draw. Jill's horse was a string horse and more comfortable following behind a lead horse. So, it was some awkward for us, trying to ride alongside one another. I wanted to talk *to* her, not over my shoulder *at* her.

"How's the arm? Don't imagine the storm made the bone crack any better, did it?"

"No, but it's mendin.' The undertaker in Espanola that casted me said it'd take three, four weeks. It's been three, as of today."

"Ah, the good German, Mr. Schwartz. He's purtin' near a doctor, isn't he? I've seen some of his fixing over the last year. He seems good at it; I hear his embalming is pitch perfect."

"Well, the river broke me up some, but didn't near kill me."

We rode through the next hour exchanging talk about the snow, the wind that kept changing directions on us, and how the wildlife seemed to appear in tracks in the snow, while slow ravens circled, and an occasional hawk glided by two hundred feet above us. She was more a conversationalist than me, but could keep still when the trail called for it.

We spotted a little clump of piñon wrapped in heavy juniper, nestled in some rocks up high on the next hill. This country is flat only between the hills, so the horses were either sucking in air on the long pulls, or stumbling a little on the down slopes.

"How about we dismount here and sit a minute?"

"Yes, Angus," she said, giving me another of those little girl smiles.

I squatted back on my haunches. She found a flat rock a few feet away and we sat. Didn't occur to me that we weren't talking until she said, "You don't talk much, do you?"

"Well, No Más would not admit to that. He's the one that don't talk, not me."

"Yes, I've heard you are in the lovely habit of explaining things to your horses."

"Who told you that? Musta been someone questioning my horses—that don't sound right," I said with a smile.

"Undersheriff Joe Pete. And, Bo String, too. They are good friends of yours, aren't they?"

"Yep. Fine men, both of 'em."

Four, five minutes of silence went by. For the life of me, I couldn't think of a single thing to talk about. Maybe because I was havin' a little trouble keeping my eyes off her. She'd shed the oiled duster and tied it behind the cantle. Underneath, she had a wool, thigh-length button coat, with tight-fitting, black leather pants tucked into knee-length riding boots. The outfit seemed right for the snow and rocks. And, she was definitely something pleasant to see as she mounted the mare. Sort of got my blood up, if you know what I mean.

"You went to the hanging of that Yarberry fellow, didn't you?"

"Yes."

"Come off all right, did it?"

"My first official execution hanging, but others there thought it did the job."

"The *Santa Fe New Mexican* had a gruesome article about it, the jerk upward part. That's something I never heard of before. They hung killers in Kansas, but I had not imagined that someone thought it more humane to break a man's neck by jerking him up rather than breaking it by dropping him down off a scaffold. Did they really break his head open somehow?"

"He cracked his head on the upswing, like a melon shot out of a cannon. The crowd went awful quiet. I don't expect they'll be jerking up the next poor soul they hang in the Albuquerque jail yard."

We rode quiet for a good stretch. The afternoon sky got a mite lighter, but still there was no sun to be seen. We crossed another sizeable hill, and came to a standstill at the top so's the horses could blow. Her rental mare was chugging pretty hard. I dismounted and scooped a small handful of grain for her. She nosed it some, tested it first, and then munched it out of my hand with a blank look in her eye. Took it as a thank you. Gave a bigger handful to No Más, who nudged my arm. Knew that was a thank you.

"Well," Jill said, just as we started the remount, "now I can see just where we are."

"We're heading north to Santa Fe, right?"

"Of course, Angus, but I mean exactly where we are. That long north-to-northeast pull you see up there is La Bajada Hill. From here, you can just start to make out the switchbacks. The stage driver told me this morning that the change in elevation, from the bottom of the switchbacks to the top, is more than one thousand feet. That's why it's so hard to pull going up, and so treacherous going down. It's safe enough in dry weather, but we came down it at the start of the storm, slipping and sliding from the inside to the edge. Not something I'd want to do every day."

"Better to ride the river bed," I said. "That's how I came down."

"So, what changed your mind coming back?"

Thought it best not to get into Sheriff Armijo's warnings about Mendoza Mendoza.

"How long is that pull?" I asked, pushing my cast out in the direction of the hill.

"It's an eight, nine mile pull, and then another ten miles or so down the other side before you reach Santa Fe. We cross the Santa Fe River and we're there. The Rio Grande is about six miles east of the Plaza. But, Angus darling, you didn't answer my question."

She said it again—darlin'. Dang, is she saying something, or just talking?

"Well, not that it's all that important, but Sheriff Armijo knows the Mendoza boys and their kin. The old man, *El Patron* he called him, is known for holding grudges and shooting from cover. The Rio Grande's banks, both sides, are fine cover, with fair stretches of open ground. Seemed a good place for one man to get the jump on another."

She pondered that. I felt another question coming on so I thought I'd head it off.

"And, besides, I already rode it coming down. Seemed sensible to try new ground, so I took the stage road up. It was a good plan till the sou' westerner hit this morning."

"Oh God, Angus. Did Sheriff Armijo really think that justifiable shooting in Bernalillo would put you in danger? I mean everyone saw the one you shot leveling a shotgun with both barrels cocked, right? You had no choice. Why would his father come after you for that?"

"Can't say, but Perfecto Armijo strikes me as a man who knows the difference. He seems all fire sure they'll come after me."

We rode down to the bottom of the stage road where a hundred-foot wide arroyo was already running with storm runoff. The muddy water, carrying bits of debris covered with ice, was less than maybe eight inches deep. The horses paid it no never mind. We let them take their heads and pick their own way across. The snow made the day quiet because the wind didn't kick up sand or debris in the high desert landscape. But, the arroyo carried a tell-tale sound of its own. Water rushing down a river sounds the same as water coursing down a dry arroyo. It was comforting to me, but not so to Jill.

"I'm never comfortable riding in a ditch like this. It sounds peaceful, like a farmland stream, but these arroyos can fill up in a heartbeat, can't they? I've heard of people being carried away by flash floods in these things, and this one is bigger than any I've ever seen."

"'Spect so. But, one this wide means the down rush is spread way out. It's the deep narrow ones you need to be mindful of."

We crossed without incident, and started the switchbacks up the other side. Riding side by side was easy here because the stage coming down had churned up the snow and made everything plain.

"Angus, I've been thinking a lot about the shooting lesson—well, it wasn't really a lesson, but I mean the half-hour you gave me about using your cast as a shooting stand. Can I ask you some more questions while we ride?"

"Yep."

"Do you know the technical difference between a carbine and a rifle?"

"Technical, no, can't say I do."

"A rifle has a longer barrel."

"That so?"

"Yes, it's so. And, that's why some gunmen like it over a rifle. Shorter barrel makes it easy to use in close quarters. Take that one there, in your saddle scabbard. That's a Winchester Carbine, Model 1973, chambered at .44-40. Same as that Buntline Special holstered on your belt, chambered at .44-40. We talked about that, remember?"

"Yep," I said, wondering where this conversation was headed.

"Here's the real question, Angus. Which has the longer barrel?"

"Jill, I'm wondering if you trained as a magic act, along with gunsmithing. Those magic acts that come to big towns always have fellers asking trick questions at the audience."

"Do I look like a feller to you, Angus?"

"No, Miss Garrison, there's no feller in you, thanks be the Lord."

"All right then, humor me. Which has the longer barrel, your pistol or your carbine?"

"The rifle."

"Well, that might be the case, but your Winchester 73 is a carbine, not a rifle. The tricky part of my question was which has the longer barrel, your pistol or your carbine."

"Oh. My carbine must be longer."

We came up on a hard twist in the road, around a house-sized boulder, and up against a stand of juniper sticking out into the trail. We worked the horses around it before she came back at me.

"If you laid your carbine and your pistol flat on a table, you'd be right. The Winchester carbine barrel, measured from back sight to front muzzle, is three inches longer than your Colt long barrel."

"So, I'm right, even though I ain't a gunsmith. Makes me feel right smart."

"Not so fast, marshal. You still have not figured out that it really was a trick question. Think of this. If you tuck the carbine into your right shoulder, lay your cheek on the back stock, notch the spur hammer back, and sight down the barrel, the muzzle tip will be about twenty-four inches out in front of your shooting eye. Right?"

"Ain't never measured it, but I'll take your word on it."

With a little uptick in her voice, she said, "Now, if you draw your pistol, hold it straight out in front of you, notch the hammer back, and sight down that barrel, how far out is the muzzle from your eyeball?"

"Tricked again. But, I'm going to guess, now that I know your way of thinking, that there ain't much difference, right?"

"Angus, I knew at that first lesson, that you are a right quick study. The difference is that the muzzle end of the barrel on your Buntline Special would actually be further out than the tip of your carbine would be."

Just then, No Más did one of his sideways jumps as a long-eared jack rabbit popped up behind a rock, and scampered right across in front of us, making a track you could see from forty foot away. I calmed him down with my right hand on his neck. The mare didn't seem to notice. Catching up with me on the inside of the switchback, Jill kept going.

"You see, the length of the barrel is a slight advantage if you're sighting in on something say, twenty-five feet away, or thereabouts. It's a distinct advantage when you're looking downrange at fifty yards. But, it's not really the barrel length, it's how your eye sees the back sight. With the carbine, that back sight is only a few inches away from your eyeball. But, with your arm extended, the back sight on the Colt is thirty odd inches away. The difference is that most shooters don't know how to compensate for the difference between eye and rear sight on the two weapons in the situation we're talking about."

"And you do? You know how to compensate?"

"Yes, it's something I teach in my clinic. And, given what the sheriff told you about Mendoza, I'd recommend we take the time to make sure you can do that."

"Well, I ain't against learning things that might save my life, but what's the likelihood of me needing to compensate with Mendoza Mendoza?"

"Might be considerable given what the sheriff said. Didn't he tell you that the man would likely come after you from behind, and under cover?"

"Yep."

"All right then, if that's how it starts, he's going to be behind you, probably with a rifle, and you might not be able to get to your Winchester fast enough. So, you'd be responding with the Colt Buntline."

I thought it best to chew on that awhile, so I spurred No Más a little. He responded by moving into a single- file position with the mare. We didn't pick up the conversation till we topped out and saw Santa Fe down in front of us, with less than an hour of daylight left. We talked about dinner, not gun barrels.

CHAPTER 19

Mendoza Mendoza in Espanola

ONCHERO COULD NOT YET WALK. So, I took Ignacio and Cruces with me from the Hacienda down to Espanola to talk to the German gringo doctor, Hector Schwartz. He was always a little scared when he saw me. I liked that. A man afraid is a man who will tell the truth so you don't shoot him. We came to find out where is the gringo Angus.

"Señor Doctor, you don't get my meaning here. I do not ask for your help to find this *hijo de puta*. You know him because you fixed his broken arm. With a cast. *Que no?* I'm telling you to do as I say, or you will be a sorry sack of shit tomorrow."

I could see the doctor's knees quivering as he stood before me. And, I could smell his fear—the live animal smell that pockets itself in barn corners and rafters. I liked making weak men feel lard in their knees.

"I already told you," Schwartz said, trying to sound more confident that he felt. "I'm not a doctor, but I know enough about medicine to set Onchero's leg. I did the same for that marshal from Colorado…"

"Angus, that was his name, *si?*"

"Yes, it is. But, all I did was to set his arm and apply a plaster of Paris cast to it. I have no idea where he is. He said, I think, he was on his way to Santa Fe, or maybe it was Albuquerque. Not my business. I don't know where he is."

"He came here from Chama?"

"Maybe, but…"

"I don't want no maybe from you, *pendejo!*"

I pushed him down into his own barber chair and unsheathed my grandfather's gelding knife from my belt. Grabbing his thin neck with my other hand, I let him feel the tip below his jaw bone. In my haste to make him cooperate, I bumped against Cruces, who hit a little medicine chest hanging on the wall. A glass door came open and some jars and little bottles crashed to the floor.

"*Pendejo*, I already tole you. You want me to cut you? Do you know what kind of knife is this, doctor man? It's what we use to geld horses, castrate calves, and slice up gringos who don't use their manners when a Mendoza is in the room. You better respect me, or you will learn the respect of a fine blade, curved to fit the huevos on an animal, and the throat of a man. *Que no?*"

"Okay, okay," Schwartz pleaded, keeping both arms stiff at his side. He told Mendoza Mendoza everything he knew.

"For now, I am going to pretend you are telling me the truth. But, I know this Angus man will ride through here again. He came here and you put the cast on. Maybe he's coming back to let you take it off, and give him some more of your go-to-sleep, Chinese dog piss. I want you to be my eyes in this town from now on. You will do that for me, won't you, Doctor?"

"Yes, Mr. Mendoza, I will do whatever you say."

"Better, Señor Doctor. We are going now, but you tell Jesús, at El Bonito, when this Angus comes back. He's my cousin; you tell him right away, and don't tell this Angus nothing. *Te entiendo?*"

"Yes, I understand."

CHAPTER 20

Angus & Jill Back At the La Fonda

I SLEPT LATER THE NEXT DAY than any other in the last ten years. Tuckered by the storm, the long pull through heavy snow, and thinking 'bout Jill, kept me in the bed at the La Fonda. I looked over at the little, wind-up clock on the nightstand—it was almost eight o'clock. Never kept a time piece of my own; never felt the need of one.

I got up, splashed my face in the wash basin, looked in the mirror over the dresser, and almost jumped back. My face looked blotchy, hair stickin' up, and my six-week old beard was nearing the disgraceful stage. I'd picked up the habit of shaving every other month for the last ten years, except during the dark months in winter. So, as soon as I came back from the facilities down the hall, I shaved, cold water style, with bar soap, and a straight razor from my kit that some uncle gave me when I was thirteen.

Digging out my other pair of pants from the kit bag, and the only clean shirt I owned, I dressed and went down to the lobby. The smell of breakfast lingered from the dining room next door.

The sight of Jill, sitting in one of the red, plush velvet chairs in the lobby almost took my breath away. Yesterday, in the snow and riding up the hill, all bundled up, she looked sort of secret. Now, she was out in the open, but there was a lot to take in with just one glance. Yellow blouse, with long sleeves, long, black riding pants flared at the bottom, and different boots than she wore yesterday. She wore a beaded necklace of blue and coral stone at her throat, and her face was all scrubbed clean so's her freckles sparkled and her hair looked—well, I can't say. It was just done up somehow.

"Good morning, Angus. Thought I'd wait and let you escort me into the dining room for breakfast."

"Well, sure," I stammered.

Yesterday, we talked for five hours. But, this morning, her looking like she did and all, I was mouth struck. She took my arm, and we went into the dining room where the last of the politicians and businessmen in black suits were finishing up plates of eggs, stacks of ham, and little silver pots of coffee at each table. They lit cigars, and began strolling out the door and toward the Palace of Governors. There were three empty tables, one by the window on the boardwalk side of the hotel. We took the window seat, and settled down on dark red upholstered chairs. I studied the menu.

"What will you folks have?" the waiter asked. He was probably seventeen but he looked fourteen.

"And, a good morning to you too, sir. What's your name, and how long have you been working for the La Fonda?" Jill asked, giving him that crinkle smile that made everyone want to talk to her.

Seemed it did him, too. "My name is Willford Simms, ma'am, and my father has been letting me wait tables at breakfast, on Saturdays and Sundays since I came into working age when I turned fifteen. We have, that is the hotel has, a fine breakfast ready for whatever you want, well, not everything, but..."

"Well, you have fine manners, young man. I'll have coffee, three slices of sourdough toast with butter and jam, and a glass of buttermilk, to go with my coffee. My friend will order for himself, but don't be surprised if he orders more than one breakfast. He's starved, aren't you, Angus?"

I gave him my order, but he wasn't ready. He just stood there looking at Jill. That bothered me some, so I gave him a loud ahem, cleared my throat, and said, "Willford, I'll have flapjacks, extra butter, hot syrup, and coffee while I'm waiting for you to bring out four fried eggs shining up at me from the plate, a stack of ham, cooked through, some tortillas, a bowl of beans, and your best chili. Got that?"

He didn't. But, he had enough presence of mind to reach into his back pocket and pull out a pad and a short pencil. "Coffee, then flapjacks, then eggs to start, then I forgot. What was next, Mister?"

We sorted out the order and he backed away from our table, nearly falling down over something in between our table and the one closest by. It looked to be a traveling salesman's double-latched bag, which was blocking the space between the tables.

"Do you know what I liked best about young Willford Simms, Angus?"

"No."

"He had a shiny face, just like you do this morning. I don't believe I've ever seen you freshly shaven. It makes you look not much older than Willford."

The coffee came quick, brought by an old woman less than five feet tall, with vertical wrinkles in her brown face that made her look like a short, near dead, cottonwood stump down in the Bosque. She served the coffee and poured Jill's buttermilk from a blue-and-white porcelain pitcher. She took her time pouring. We waited for her to finish, then sipped our coffee in unison. Well, maybe not in unison. I dropped in four lumps of sugar, and she took two teaspoons of thickened cream from a fist-sized bowl in the center of the table.

"Strong coffee. How's the buttermilk?"

She smiled, nodded, and leaned back in her chair, looking out the window at the light snow still on the boardwalk.

"Angus, is your assignment down here at an end?"

"Well, I need to write up a report, and send it off to the chief of the US Marshal's Service in Denver, and see if he needs anything more from me. I expect not, but he sometimes surprises me."

"What's that mean? Are you done marshaling or not?"

"Jill, I'm not a full-time anything. The federal department of justice calls on me every once in a while. Otherwise, I just do what comes natural."

"Which is? You don't have to answer if it's too personal."

Now I don't know how she did it, but once started, I was like a gully washer, pouring out things I'd not talked about in years. I covered pretty near ever piece of ground in my adult life. I talked through her toast and my flapjacks, eggs, tortillas, beans, and chili. I gave her the nutshell version of my life. The death of Mazy, my wife on Ten Shoes Up, eleven years ago. How that came to a near hermit addiction—riding alone—along high mountain ridges, down alongside wild river banks, and spending my time hushed up except for talking to my horses. Even as I spit it all out, I knew it sounded like places no one except me would ever want to go. She probed a little, but I felt no intrusion. Somehow, I thought she had, well, almost a right to know. She asked about chasing outlaws. Did they mistake me for one of their own kind? She dug down into the secret pride of both wearing and hiding my US marshal's badge. And, more deeply than I felt comfortable about, she circled the outer edges of gun work. What did I feel when I had to shoot the man at my cabin on Ten Shoes Up? Did I regret shooting the young Mexican *vaquero* in Bernalillo? Was it perfectly clear in my mind that I had no other choice? Without even thinking about it, I volunteered the notion that shooting another man was something I took no pleasure in, even if he needed killing. All of this took purtin' near two hours, long after they cleared the breakfast plates and set all the other tables for lunch.

"Angus, can we continue this lovely exchange this evening? I've got a make-up clinic to give after lunch, and there are two men here from Las Cruces I promised to talk to about modifying their long guns. But, can we spend some time late this afternoon? We need to talk more about adjusting the eye to the rear sight, when your gun is at full extension from your body.

"Sure."

"Wonderful. Then, there's my story, if you are at all interested."

"I am."

"How about we meet, say around four this afternoon, out behind the hotel in that little shooting range they set up for me? Okay with you?"

"Yes, I'm going to go over to Marshal Knop's office this afternoon. I'll pencil my report out this morning, and give it to him after lunch. He'll have someone write it up. It'll go in the US Mail bag tomorrow on the Las Vegas-to-Trinidad run, and be in Denver in three days. Expect I'll hear back by telegram later in the week."

CHAPTER 21
Angus In Santa Fe: Job Done

"**M**ARSHAL ANGUS, good to see you back. How's the arm?"
Knop said, motioning at me from the hallway outside his
office. I gave him a nod with my hat, and took a seat in a deer-hide
seat in front of his little desk. He poured us each a glass of cool
well water from a pitcher he kept on a side table. He asked if I'd
mind if Mrs. Kittering came in and took notes while we talked.

"She's good at writing up reports for the US Department
of Justice and meeting their exactin' standards when it comes
to the nits and nats of official communication."

"Sure, suits me. I got the main points penciled, but that'd
shorten it considerable."

Mrs. Kittering smiled at me when she came in. Sort of.
Not a big ole smile; more like a little upturn of her gigantic
cheeks. I asked her if those little squiggles on her pad were in
English or what. She said government.

Marshal Knop summed it up when I finished.

"So, Angus, you're satisfied that there is no reason for the DOJ to look into Milton J. Yarberry any further. Whatever he might have known, or did for that matter, died with him and is in his casket down in the Catholic cemetery in Albuquerque."

"Yes, sir, along with the rope that put him in the casket."

Mrs. Kittering asked if that addition were necessary for the report. I said no. Knop allowed as how you never knew what would interest the government.

"Go on and include the location of the rope; maybe it ought to be a footnote."

"Or maybe an asterisk," he added.

She scribbled something on her pad.

"Angus," he said, motioning that Mrs. Kittering could go and type up the report, "I have two telegrams here for you, one from Joe Pete in Chama and the other from Marshal Ramsey in Denver. Both were delivered to me with the instruction that I was to give them to you upon your return from Albuquerque at the completion of your report. I'll give you some privacy while you read them if you like."

"Don't need that, Marshal, they look short enough."

The one from Ramsey was an inquiry into my health, and an assurance that my salary would continue for however long it took for the arm to heal up.

"Marshal Ramsey says I'm on the payroll even after my final report is in, on account of I got a broke arm in the line of duty. How'd he hear about that?"

"I telegrammed him, the day you first came in here. Gave him a short brief on what you'd found out by then, and mentioned your arm. Hope you didn't mind. Guess it was not official by-god Department of Justice business, now that I think on it."

"No, don't worry about that. He's a fine man, Marshal Ramsey is. I'm glad you told him I was on the job, broke arm and all."

"So, how is your arm? Should be about time to take the cast off, isn't it?"

"'Spect so. The undertaker in Espanola said three, four weeks. That's up on Friday. He thought it was a small break, but I've no idea how he could tell. You can't see inside an arm."

"Well, undertakers see a lot of damage to human bodies once they're dead. Maybe that gives him an edge on what might be below the skin on a live deputy."

"Well, he was good to see me late at night, and I figure to stay here a few days; or maybe only one. Not sure where I'm headed next."

Marshal Knop motioned me to the other telegram. "Best you'd read what Joe Pete says. I already know part of it because he wrote to me two days before yours came in last week."

WESTERN UNION TELEGRAPH COMPANY
FEBRUARY 7, 1883
TO: UNITED STATES DEPUTY MARSHAL ANGUS
FROM: UNDERSHERIFF JOE PETE, CHAMA NEW MEXICO

HOPE YOUR ARM IS MENDING—STOP—I AM NOW SHERIFF—STOP—VALLESTO DIED LAST WEEK—STOP—THEY WANT ME TO COVER WHOLE COUNTY WITH THREE FIELD OFFICES—NEED YOU TO BE UNDERSHERIFF CHAMA—STOP—JOB STARTS YOUR SOONEST OPPORTUNITY—STOP—INCLUDES OFFICE PLUS ROOM IN BACK PLUS

PAID LIVERY FEES PLUS EXPENSE ALLOWANCE—STOP—SAME SALARY
AS ME—STOP—BUT YOU ARE NEEDED—REPLY SOONEST—STOP

"So," Marshal Knop said with a wide grin across his face, "life in the federal service might be a good step. Hell, Angus, you could make law enforcement your full-time occupation up in Chama. If you take it, there's some federal and territorial law enforcement we could work on up in the north part of the territory. If you don't mind a personal comment, I think you're the perfect man for the job."

CHAPTER 22

Angus Aiming a Buntline Special

THE AFTERNOON WAS clear and sunny, temperature in the low fifties out in the plaza. There was still a light dusting of snow on the ground, but nobody was bustling about. I spied a stout, little bench under an acorn tree with bare branches. Seemed a reasonable thing to do, so I took a seat. *What about the ridges and the rivers and talking to a fine horse every day?* After a while, with my mind still unsettled, I walked around the side of the hotel to the back porch. Jill was there, saying good afternoon to a tall, bony man carrying two rifles. Maybe one was a carbine; not sure.

"Angus," she said, her face flushed in crisp Santa Fe air.

"I see you been earning your living. Lemme see, that feller had one rifle and one carbine, right?"

"You're a good guesser. The Henry was a repeating carbine and the Springfield was a rifle. At .50 caliber, you need the extra length, unless you got an iron shoulder to take the recoil. Which was which, can you tell me now that the man's gone?"

"Well, I've seen a Springfield, even fired one once. But, the other gun, a Henry, you said, is a mystery. It just looked shorter, that's all."

"There's other big differences in those two, but both are percussion weapons. That older gentleman carrying them off paid me to improve his odds of hitting what he aims at. Mostly deer and elk. He's a game hunter and guides Eastern gents who come out here on the train to hunt."

"Improve his odds, how's that?"

"He's been shooting since he was twelve, and he's in his midsixties now. His strength is different now and his breathing is wheezy; smoking five cigars a day will do your lungs a good deal of harm. So, I honed and polished the internal metal faces on both trigger and hammer. Now, he's got a smoother trigger pull. I also modified the main spring to reduce the strength required to pull back on the hammer. Little things, but it's all about odds. I improved his."

"But, he ain't a gunfighter."

"No, wild animals don't shoot back. Sometimes I think that's too bad. I'm not in favor of sport hunting. My family always ate what they shot. If you like, this evening over dinner, when I tell you my story, I'll tell you about hunting in Kansas. For now, let's work on improving your aim with that eighteen-inch barrel on the Buntline Special."

"Truth be told, I'm more interested in your story than in getting my eye to match up with my front sight."

She walked away, talking back at me over her shoulder, "After dinner. Now, we got important work to do, darlin'."

Taking my gun in her right hand, she told me to assume a normal, extended-arm shooting position. "Just stick your arm out in front natural-like."

Feeling a mite silly, I did as she asked. She just stood there, six inches from my right side. After a minute, I dropped my arm.

"Heavy, right? A fully extended arm weighs whatever it weighs, less what your gun weighs. This long-barreled Colt weighs just over four pounds with five shells in the cylinder. If you have a sixth shell, it's less safe, and heavier. I recommend five rounds in a six-round revolver at all times. Lighter and safer. Now, extend your arm again. I'll place the gun in your hand. I want you to feel the difference the gun makes in the tension on your arm."

I stuck it out there again. She moved up close, put her left hand on my waist, leaned a little into me, and lifted the gun up into my hand from the outside. God, she felt and smelled good. I liked these lessons. Then she stepped away. I held the gun out there longer this time, but still had to flex my arm as it was stiffening up.

"That's because you are locking your elbow to make a straight arm hold. Don't do that. Keep your elbow a little cocked, and it'll give you more blood circulation, and your forearm won't cramp up on you."

"Got it. Could you check the arm for me up a little closer?"

"Angus, this is serious business we're at here. Don't be getting all personal on me."

I jiggled my wrist some and moved the Colt around in a small, figure-eight motion.

"All right, now let's get to sighting with iron sights. They're barely accurate; so far there's just plain, no good, optical sights for handguns. The industry will come up with them in time. But, you have what you have now. We're going to start with matching up your shooting eye with your iron sights, both of them, at short distances for the moment. Longer distances magnify errors, in both you and that Colt. We're going to dial you in at twenty-five yards. That's actually a long way for a gunfight, but right now, I'm thinking about an ambush, not a man-to-man gunfight. You won't see the shooter. He'll fire from cover. And, I'm making two other assumptions. Want to hear 'em?"

"All right."

"First, I'm assuming that because he's some distance away, he'll be likely to miss on the first shot. That first one is what we call dialing in. Second assumption is this happens when you cannot get to your Winchester. It's a fight you are forced into with that eighteen-inch barrel chambered at .44-40. Lots of firepower, and a long enough barrel, if you extend your arm. That's your advantage.

"Those are grim assumptions. Maybe I ought to go to Kansas, where it's peaceful and Mendoza Mendoza will be noticeable in a crowd."

She ignored me, took the Colt, and removed two rounds from the cylinder. Then she put the gun back in my hand.

"We're going to fire in three-shot groups. I'm looking for the average point of impact from the three rounds. We'll use that as the point of impact; we can measure from there. Then, we'll adjust your sights according to this average. That fresh target down there is exactly twenty-five yards from that stick on the ground in front of you. Move up a little and lift up the muzzle over the stick. Fire three rounds when ready."

She stepped back behind me. I fired off three rounds hoping I wouldn't miss the whole damn target. Then, when I lowered my weapon, she headed off down range with a fresh target in her hand.

"Not bad, considering you know almost nothing about that weapon," she said. "You hit within the second circle once, the outer circle once and the white no-shot area once. All three high and to the right. Let's dial that in. This time remember that whatever way you adjust your rear sight, the point of impact moves in the same direction."

She took the gun to a little work bench she'd set up against the rear wall of the hotel. Laying it on a white cloth, she took out her tool kit and reworked the rear sight. Then she handed it back.

"Try again. Same stance, three new rounds."

I reloaded, sucked in a long breath, lowered my arm full, careful not to lock my elbow, and loosened three more. She waited till I dropped the barrel to the ground, and walked the twenty-five yards to the target. I was thinking this was the best part of the lesson. She had a walk.

"Better, we fixed the rear high and to the right trajectory. Let's pay attention to the front sight now. Just fire as usual, but try to get your eye aligned as best you can over the rear sight, without losing it, and onto that front sight. When you think it's dead on, give me three rounds."

I did. She got the target and showed me the three holes, a little low, and a few inches to the left of the bull's eye.

"See, Angus? If the target tells you to adjust the front sight, to adjust point of impact, your point of impact moves in the opposite direction from your front sight. That's a little different fix. Let's work on this." She took the gun back to the table and did whatever it was she did.

"Round three," she said.

I fired off three more and felt good about it.

"One bull's eye out of three," she said walking back with the third target. "Let's hope Mendoza Mendoza can't shoot any better than you can."

Jill gathered up her tools, targets, and me. She said we'd covered part of the problem, but one more lesson was needed.

"Why's that?" I asked.

"Because now that your gun's sighted in, you need to work on stabilizing the long barrel on the Colt when the muzzle is three feet out in front of you. If it was a rifle, you'd use a gun rest."

"A gun rest? Jill, gunfights ain't the time to rest."

She turned, frowned, and then saw me grinnin' at her; she grinned back. Maybe she was warming up to my humor.

"Dinner about seven? I'm going to take a bath. Meet me in the lobby, and let's have a bottle of wine, shall we?"

CHAPTER 23

Mendoza Mendoza– an Impatient Man

THE *M/* BRAND ON THE CROSSBAR over the corral was
burnt deep into the wood, jus' like it was on everything
else in my haciendia. Ever since the gringo Angus dishonored
our brand, I was thinking about my *abuelo*, the father of my
papa, when was he was only five years old in Mexico. His
mother, who we don't talk about, gave him to a blacksmith in
Sonora. She could not feed him and his two younger sisters
at the same time. That's what the family story said, anyhow.
Maybe she didn't want him, I thought. Some women don't
like strong men, or little boys who they think will grow up
strong. So, anyhow, he knew, my *abuelo*, some things about
making steel and bending iron to do what you want. And, he

knew, as a young man, how to brand everything—and bend it to your will. It was burnt deep into his nature.

My father, who was killed by an Indian twenty-three years ago, nailed a big, wooden chair down to the narrow, little porch that fronted the hacienda. No one could sit there but him while he was alive. Now I sit there. I can see all the barns, corrals, the bunkhouse, the blacksmith shop, and some cutting and branding chutes. The only thing different now from my papa's time is that bell. PaPa had a bell on the floor next to the chair. He would ring the bell when he didn't like something out there. Someone would come running. They would change it so he was happy. I threw the bell away. If I don't like it, I chop it down. Or cut it. Sometimes I shoot it from this porch. But, not so much anymore. Now everyone knows what I like. Nothing to cut or shoot from here, these days. But, I wish that gringo *pendejo* was here. I would ring PaPa's bell for that.

Ignacio was a hundred feet away at the blacksmith's hutch when he heard me holler. He didn't know what I wanted, but he ran up here anyhow.

"Ignacio, *venir aquí*, I want to talk to you."

"Si, PaPa," Ignacio said, when he got close enough to hear my words.

"I am getting tired of waiting for the gringo with the foreign badge. Go to town and send a telegram to our cousin at the La Fonda in Santa Fe. He works sometimes in the kitchen. He'll know if the man we want is there."

"Si, Papa, I'll ride into town this afternoon. We are near done on the buckboard, so Onchero can ride with us when we go to shoot the gringo Angus. Like you told us, we fixed the back of the wagon so his leg will swing in a leather harness, so it won't hurt him when the buckboard bounces."

"I don't care about him hurting. Onchero jus' has to be with us when we catch the gringo. And, I don't like you to use the gringo's name. Jus' say the gringo. I want two big mules on the buckboard and one more to pack supplies, *qué no*?

CHAPTER 24

Angus And the Lady in the Blue Dress

THIS TIME I INTENDED ON being in that plush chair myself when she came down the stairway to the lobby. I was all prepared to act like a gentleman. I'd brushed my other pair of pants, tried to press out my clean shirt with a wet towel, and used some boot black on my boots. The fireplace in the corner made the room comfy, and the folks coming in and out of the dining room didn't pay any mind to me. But, when she started down the staircase, everyone took notice.

I hadn't seen her in a dress before. Hadn't ever seen any woman in a dress like this one before. She sort of tiptoed down the stairs because the dress was so long she might have tripped. You know how light blue the sky is of an early morning, before the sun's full up? Well, that's the color of her dress, 'cept it shimmered as she moved. Somehow, probably a trick only women know, she had stuck herself entirely inside a dress that's hard to describe. An S-shaped silhouette is 'bout all I can say. Jill was a small woman, just over five foot, but she had strong forearms, which barely showed below a frilled cuff sort of thing where the elbow bends. Her ankles showed above what looked to be slippers. She held her chin high as she came down the last few steps, and the men in the lobby gasped as her dress was open enough at the neck to show a hint of creme-colored flesh. That caused some of the men to choke on their coffee. She was full there, if you know what I mean. Just as she looked over at me, I tried to avert my eyes to her hands. She was wearing gloves, inside kind of gloves, made of gray leather that looked to be finer than sheet cloth.

"Evening, Angus. You look handsome with your boots all shined."

I started to tell her how she looked, but the words disappeared in my throat. I figured the gentlemanly thing to do was to extend my good arm to her. But, she came to the other side of me, took hold of my elbow at the top of my cast, and sort of aimed me at the door to the dining room. We walked slow, because of the way the dress fit. Both waiters stopped what they were doing and nearly run over one another trying to get to us.

"Angus," she said no sooner than we'd been seated and the waiter was headed for the menu rack, "no wine is served in either of the cafes in Chama; do you suppose we could split the cost on one here? I looked at the wine menu after breakfast this morning. They have two in red and one in white. Haven't been in a restaurant with that many choices since St. Louis."

Stupidly, I said, "I only drank wine with dinner once, up in Denver at the St. Francis, with Marshal Ramsey, a lawyer friend of his, and a bootlegger. The bootlegger ordered red table wine for all of us, without asking for preferences. It was different than what the monks up at Jemez Springs make; not as sweet. You name it, and I'll buy it. Looks like I got a steady job coming up, so I can afford it on my own."

"Steady?"

"Yep."

"Are you going to make me cross-examine you, or might you just volunteer it?"

I told her about the telegram from Joe Pete, and the fact that my federal salary was going to continue until my arm healed. She sipped her wine. So did I. She didn't ask for more details except about where I'd live.

"Joe Pete fixed up the back room in the jail real nice. An iron springs bed, Indian rugs on the floor, a rocking chair in front of a little wood stove, and a gun rack. What more would a man need?"

"What more, indeed. Depends on the man's situation, doesn't it, Angus darlin'?"

I was not going to let this go on one more damn minute.

"Jill, can I ask you what you might consider a personal question?"

"You may," she said, putting the wine glass down, and folding her hands on her lap.

"More 'n once, you called me darlin'. Is that just something you say, sort of a matter of common speech? Or do you mean it like...?"

"Like what, darlin'?"

"Well, there you go. I'm just going to say it. My wife died nine years ago. I am a lot more than smitten by you. I think I love you."

Her eyes were all ablaze.

"Angus, I meant darling in exactly the way you took it all three times. When you say you think you love me, are you sure, or are you just thinking about it?"

"I'd like to marry you, if you'll have me."

"I will, and I've more to say on the matter. Let's just enjoy this wine, and those little biscuits they serve. No dinner. Then, darling, let's go upstairs and see just how much we love one another."

CHAPTER 25

Angus Talks About Aiming True and a Monster

W E ORDERED BREAKFAST sent up to her room. I gathered up my clothes and headed for the facilities down the hall while the waiter brought up two trays. As I was coming back down the hall, he was just backing out the door to her room. He smiled at me, "*Buenos días, Señor. El amor es bello, no es?*"

"*Si*, beautiful. I'm a lucky hombre, *qué no?*"

As we ate, I reminded her that last night was supposed to be when she told me her story.

"Well, you put that off my dear, didn't you? So, now that you've seen me both in my best dress and in my birthday suit, what part of my story don't you already know?"

We talked till noon, and she told me about her folks, the little farm that didn't work, and the gun smithing and horse selling that did. She cried a little when she got to the part about her mother dying when she was thirteen. But, she was lock-jawed about her dad dying of stomach cancer when he was only fifty. It changed her view on eating sausage every morning, she said.

"So, we'll eat healthy, in my house, and you can give that little room behind the jail back to the government once we're properly married. Besides, the children will need their own room, won't they? And, No Más will be close by in case you get tired of talking to me."

Jill could pack more into a question than a judge could pack into a long jail sentence. But judges just laid it on you simple. Jill answered her own questions and laid the future out at the same time.

"Now," she said, standing up and walking to the quarter-sawn oak armoire in the corner, "enough of me. You are in need of that final shooting lesson. But, before we go out back and use live fire, let's talk it through up here. It's about the thinking part of shooting, which unlike love is more important than the doing of it. Sometimes."

"Suits me."

"How much do you know about what happens to a bullet when it leaves the end of the barrel?"

"It goes where you aim it, right?"

"Yes, if your aim is true. But, what is it that makes the bullet go to one side or the other? Too high or too low? That's the final lesson you need. You've got an instinct for shooting, more or less, but it doesn't seem like you've practiced very much, right?"

"Truth be told, I guess I ain't never really practiced. I never planned on getting in a gun fight. I've only been in three. Two of those came up sudden-like, and the third was when Ignacio and Onchero came at me slow- and deliberate-like. That was the only one where I had time to think about things like where the damn bullet might go when it left my pistol."

Jill gathered up the tin trays and put them out in the hall. She walked back to the mirror behind the dressing table, picked up a large-handled brush, and stroked it down her hair. I could see her reflection in the mirror from where I sat beside the bed at the little table.

She talked through the mirror. "Here's why shots miss the bull's eye. The tip of the barrel in any hand gun, or even a rifle, is a line between the bullet and the target. If the target is stationary, the odds of hitting it are good, but only if the shooter has the muzzle perfectly lined out the whole distance. Even when the shooter has drawn the line perfectly, shots miss when the shooter flinches at the trigger pull, moving the muzzle off the line. You can cure that most of the time by shooting from a gun stand, a log, a sack of sand, anything that makes that little flinch of no consequence."

She paused, turned, and fastened the top button on her flannel shirt. I watched carefully. Continuing, she said, "Flinching at the trigger pull is always a problem. You already know the importance of a steady pull on the trigger, a squeeze really, rather than a pull. Remember yesterday afternoon. We had to extend your shooting arm to get maximum barrel length. But, that stance always means muscle tension, head pressure, and distractions that might cause a little flinch. That's what we have to fix."

"How?"

"The same way you fixed it when you stopped two gun hands facing you down with one shot. You used your left arm as a gun rest, actually the outside shaft of your left elbow. Then you took your time to lower the gun down onto your elbow-stand, took in a breath, picked the right target, and let fly a .44-40 slug."

"So, I did it without thinking, is that what you're saying?"

"No, not exactly. You needed to get a fix on those boys before they even knew you had a gun in your shooting hand. You hid your gun draw; when they finally did see it, it was pointing up. No danger to them. Lowering it onto your cast was a surprise. Not like a draw from your holster. Those boys had enough courage to face you down, and would have pulled on you if you'd given them more distance. But, they knew they were too far for handgun accuracy. The important thing is you acquired a gun stand, your cast, which turned your pistol into the equivalent of a carbine. I'm trying to replicate that situation, and give you an advantage over a back-shooter."

"Jill, there's another thing about missing shots. It ain't very technical."

"What's that?"

"Paper targets don't move while you're aiming at 'em."

"True. And they don't make you think about marriage, kids, and love, either. That's what I'm thinking about, so let's go outside, where the air is cold. We can focus on what we have to get by before we get to Chama."

The makeshift shooting range was cold, but clear, with a bright New Mexico sun high in the sky. A breeze from left to right made the targets flutter some as Jill tacked them up fifty yards down range.

"Why fifty yards?" I asked when she came back up.

"It's a middle distance. One too far for normal handgun shooting, but perfect for a well-sighted-in rifle, shooting .45 caliber or higher. It's what might make a bushwhacker over-confident. Of course, nothing's predictable here. I don't even know if this Mendoza monster will actually come after you."

"Monster? Maybe he's just mad at me for shootin' his boy. Maybe he'll get over it."

"No, he's a monster. I can feel it. But, let's talk about the one thing we haven't yet. There's another reason rifles and carbines are more accurate at distance shooting. You use both hands on them, one on the stock and the other closer up to the muzzle. When you're firing from a prone position, you use your elbow to support the gun, and if you're lucky, you also have a rest of some sort to add a second layer of support to steady the tip of the barrel. That's what your cast did; it steadied your barrel for the one shot you fired at Ignacio. Let's see if we can replicate that."

We tried several standing positions, but the barrel length still wobbled some, like it did just before I let loose on Ignacio. Looking back, it seemed a wonder I hit him.

"What about this, Angus? What if every time you were faced with a gunfight, you hit the dirt, drew your Buntline Colt, and fired prone, using your left elbow as a stand for the barrel?"

"But how'd that look? Might make me a laughing stock in the gun world," I said hoping she'd catch the pun and my pitiful attempt at humor.

"Darling, I'd just love to see you diving for position. Wouldn't be such a bad thing if you came to be laughed right out of the gun world. But, seriously, remember that the monster will think he owns the high ground behind you. He's probably lying down behind a bedroll propping up his long-barreled rifle, chambered with a big .50 caliber. Let's try this, drop to the dirt, but instead of laying your left arm out flat on the ground, dig both elbows into the dirt, lift up your chest, and fire from a semi-prone position on the ground. That might give the long barrel more stability, and you better flinch control. It will be awkward with the cast, but better when we get it off in Espanola."

So, on command, I practiced dropping to my belly in the dirt, and then using my still broke left arm as a two-handed hold on the gun. We did a dozen sets of three rounds each, at five targets. The last two were sixty-five yards away. I didn't always hit the black, but most of 'em were within one of the three circles.

"Okay, Angus, I think we got something here. The best shots you take are the second and third shells out of the chamber. And, that's probably because I'm asking you to move from one target to another. The lesson I think we're getting here is to hold fast to your Colt with two hands, both elbows dug in the dirt, fire as many shots as you can reload, and keep it up till the monster dies. Got it?"

We packed up her gear, and I headed to the general store to buy ten more boxes of .44-40 shells. We gave ourselves two more days at the La Fonda, and then headed back up to Chama by way of Espanola to get the undertaker to crack the cast on my arm.

CHAPTER 26

Angus & Jill At the Confluence of the Rio Chama and the Rio Grande

WE REACHED THE CONFLUENCE of the Rio Chama into the Rio Grande north of Espanola late in the day. We'd ridden twenty miles yesterday from Santa Fe to Espanola, then spent last night camped three miles out of Espanola. That was a normal day's ride for me, but Jill had very tender knees when we stepped down after almost seven hours in the saddle. So, we just let the horses and the pack mule graze until late morning. This was one of those rare places in the whole West where two big rivers shake hands and agree to live as one; from here all the way down to the Gulf of Mexico. That's two months' riding time, but the water that mingles together right here makes the trip in just a few days. 'Course the time of year makes some difference. This February, there's no snow melt. In June, damn little rain. But, rivers, both wild and tame, are alive every moment and never the same. And, they always flow downhill.

"You love these wild rivers, don't you?" Jill said as much to the fast-running water as to me.

"Yep."

"What draws you to them, the clear water, the lack of people, what?"

"It ain't easy to place, but something like this. Two rivers melding into one another is nature's way of saying we ought to be unharnessed. That's what I think about every time I come on something like this, even if it's just a creek catching up with its mother, a river somewhere."

"Unharnessed? How so? It's free to move wherever gravity dictates, right? Downhill all the time?"

"No, it's not that simple. Most moving things have harnesses; rivers have dams and drop-offs, and tributaries that drain off to one side or the other. Even when raging over rocks, spitting foam, and creating swirls that sink down into the river itself, the white caps come at you with their hands up. They are at peace with everything around them."

Jill and I stood there awhile, taking in the notion that two rivers can be one. From here to all points south, no one can tell one from the other. That's the way I wanted us to be, from now on. But, something held me back from putting it into words. We could have forded the combined river a mile south, but Jill wanted to see where the Rio Grande went before the Rio Chama cut into it. We were on the east bank when we saw it the first time—a flash of light on the gray rocks. Something bright and shiny up ahead of us. Then it disappeared.

"What's that?" she asked.

"Dunno. Binoculars, maybe. All the hunters carry 'em nowadays. Maybe there's a hunting party."

"Could they be Indians? Would they carry binoculars?"

"No, there's been no hostiles around these parts now for more than a dozen years. The Utes are mostly subdued, and the Navajo, over to the west, no longer raid the pueblos up and down this river. If it is a hunting party, they are ranchers, or maybe someone from the village, lookin' to eat fresh venison instead of smoked beef."

It flashed again—this time it hovered a mile northwest, upwind and maybe nestled in a rocky upshift, what is sometimes called a hogback.

"Maybe we'd best mount up," I said, not wanting to spook her.

Jill turned and tightened the cinch on the Appy mare, mounted, and settled herself in the saddle. I gathered up the pack mule's lead rope and mounted No Más from the offside. As I did, No Más did one of his little half-spins, just to make sure I was paying attention. As he turned me around, he gave me a south look, at another flash behind us. I snugged my hat down trying to get a clear look against the late afternoon glare of the sun. The flash disappeared, but within three seconds, flashed again. Off then on, off then on, for a half-minute.

"Somebody downriver is trying to get the attention of somebody upriver. That's not glare off a looking glass, that's a signal mirror. I think we'd best get on our way, and out of theirs."

"Angus," Jill said, "that could be, but maybe not. We've been here enjoying this confluence for a while. Maybe it's somebody trying to make us move on."

"Why? Who? Not sure what you mean."

"Well, what if it's the Mendozas? If so, maybe going upriver on the Chama is where they want us to go. And, soon, before good shooting light is gone. And, since I'm from Chama—and now, so are you—maybe there's a gun waiting up the Chama River."

I pondered that a minute. "Could be, but if it's the Mendozas and they're tracking me, one place's as good as another, don't you think?"

"Well, this place isn't. The distances are too spread out, there are at least three open escape routes visible to us, and flat country like this does not lend itself to shooting from high ground. That's what I know 'bout shooting, whether it's game or humans. You can hit an antelope from a perch better than you can from the same level."

"Makes sense. Let's take the Rio Grande up, but on the east bank. That takes us away from a long canyon I know up the Rio Chama, the one where I broke my arm. Mendozas might know that canyon, too, from talk in Espanola."

"And," Jill mused, "they might know you got your cast off yesterday in Espanola. We told your friendly undertaker we were going up to Chama on the river, remember?"

"Well, if we follow the Rio Grande on a northeasterly track, I know where we can turn off and head west. It's called Tres Piedras. Ten miles out to the west, there's an awful big stand of ponderosa pine sheltering tall grass in the valleys. Not too much out of our way. Let's head up that direction and make a safe camp; more 'n a mile off the noisy river."

"Tres Piedras?"

"Yep, it means three stones. It's nestled in-between two look-alike canyons on the eastern side of a mountain range I've guided in for years. There's a mountain road for mining wagons from there on over to Tierra Amarilla, a place where a new friend, name of Chaco, lives. I'd like you to meet him. We could stop by his place, rest up, and then make the last little push up to Chama, maybe day after tomorrow."

CHAPTER 27

Mendoza Mendoza On the Hunt

"**W**ATCH YOU MEAN, BOY? The hell you do to scare 'em off like that! I oughta strap you." Ignacio looked wide-eyed at me. Like a child hiding a stolen apple behind his back, he shoved the little signal mirror down into his saddle bag. Goddamned boys and their tricks. They'd practiced this way of talking to one another for years, ever since they were kids trying to escape my discipline.

"You were talking to your brother with the mirror? *Peor que estúpido!*"

"No, PaPa. It is not stupid. I was only telling Onchero that we were close behind, and to watch for the gringo."

I had sent Postino, a good man for small tasks, ahead driving the buckboard with Onchero in the back. He got that name not from his mother, but from the *vaqueros* in the bunk house. He was *estupido* as a post, they said. Now my own sons were also *estupido*. Postino only rode or drove mules; he was more than sixty years old. He did not like pistols because he never hit where he aimed. But, a shotgun, he said, always hit something. His was an old, single-barrel model that the blacksmith had cut six inches off the barrel. So, it was two feet long. He had a rope strap for it, which he wore around his neck to keep the gun in front.

The mule we used to pull the small buckboard over rough terrain was called *bastante grande*—big enough. He was in his prime, ten years old. Everyone knew this mule was big enough for any job. He would die in the traces rather than stop. We used him to haul elk out of the big ponderosa pines when we went on hunting trips to the Valles Caldera.

Ignacio and Chuches, the tracker, were riding with me about two miles behind the gringo and the lady. Chuches had picked up the gringo's trail just a little north of Espanola, after the doctor told Jesús that the gringo came to get the cast off his arm. Chuches could track a Navajo on foot over a rock shelf. So, it was easy for him to track Angus's horse, pack mule, and the little mare the lady rode. The track was distinctive, and Chuches knew it well by this time—by the time, that is, that the *estupido* boys warned the gringo with their game of sending signals by mirror flashes.

"Well, Chuches, what you sitting your horse for? My sons played their foolish games with those little mirrors. They spooked the gringo. He's not crossing over the Rio Grande to the Rio Chama. He's taking the east fork up the Rio Grande. Go. Follow him. Ignacio will go get his *estupido* brother. We'll follow your track behind the gringo. I want to know where he camps tonight before the sun sets. *Vaya con la velocidad.*"

"*Si, Patron,* as quickly as I can. If they leave the river bank, I'll leave you a mark at that place. You will know it."

CHAPTER 28

Angus Taking the Right Fork North

JILL'S HORSE, A FIVE-YEAR-OLD appy mare she'd named Darlene, was steady in rocky river beds, and could move uphill at a quick pace. But, she'd been in a warm stall in the barn for two months. That'd sour even a mountain horse. I let Jill take the lead as we moved north up the Rio Grande, so I could watch her horse and maybe give her some tips. Jill bought her three geldings last summer. She treated the mare differently, feeding her a little too much sweet grain, brushing twice a day, and cooing to her softly every morning. Some old cowboys think spurs is the way to fix a barn-sour horse, but I don't.

I watched her from thirty foot back as she kept looking at No Más and me, dipping her head down to the left, and two or three times just whirling around halfway in the trail. Sulky, I thought. After a mile or so, I rode up alongside them and let No Más's reins fall loose in a big loop from saddle to bit.

"Ask her to do this," I said to Jill, who turned to see me sideways on the trail. She tried it, but soon's she dropped the reins a little, the mare began to speed up and move away from No Más and me.

"Let's rig a tie-down, and maybe shorten the chin chain some; might help your little mare remember her trail manners."

I rigged a tie-down from the iron circle on the bottom of her bosal, ran it down through the heel knot, and then down through the breast collar. I tied it to the mecate running down under the little mare's chest to the three-inch front cinch. She was using a single-rig saddle, with no back cinch. Good thing we didn't have to rope anything with this saddle.

"When we get home to Chama, you might ought to switch to a double-rig saddle, one that's not too heavy, don't you think?"

"Angus, I like the way you say 'home to Chama.' I confess there's a lot I don't know about horses and tack, even though I'm in the business of selling both. 'Course I know the difference between a single-rig and a double-rig by sight, but I am not sure why saddle makers rig them differently."

"You ever roped a calf?"

"Me? Absolutely not."

"Well, when you do, you'll understand why you only rope off a double-rig saddle."

"Anything you can do about this little horse bossing me around all the way back home to Chama?" she asked.

"If the tack ain't right, neither is the horse. This tie-down will keep her from throwin' her head back at you and make her think twice about the tricks she's playing on the trail. And, we need to get you outfitted for the trail a little better. Kicking that mare's ribs is uncomfortable for her and a lot of work for you. Using a light spur, tapping your horse just right, will cure both of those problems. Don't suppose you got spurs in your saddle bags, do you?"

"No, I don't. I thought spurs were for herding cows. I can see a deal at work here. You teach me about horses, and I'll teach you about guns."

"Let's hope we do lots of riding and no shooting at all."

Just then, I saw a crook in the river where the land dropped off to the west, and there was a considerable bluff on the east side.

"Why don't we stop here while I take a better look at that bluff up ahead. It might make a good night camp, but I don't want to turn off this trail just yet."

Dismounting, and letting No Más drop his head to graze with the reins looped up loose over the saddle, I slow-like picked my way up the rocks, leaving no obvious boot tracks. Jill had asked if she should come along. I suggested she stay mounted so's our trail would not look like we'd stopped here. The rocks gave way to ledges. They spiraled upward some three hundred feet to a stand of big juniper and scrub oak. It looked passable, so I stepped from rock to rock back down.

"It'll do just fine. I'll lead out from here, and we'll go up alongside the river for a half-mile and find us a way to get into the river for another half-mile."

Jill looked puzzled. So, I explained the advantage of riding in the middle of the river—"no one can track our horses out there. Then we'll come back up the bank and circle back to that little camp spot right up there."

"We can't just go up there from here? I think the mare can make it all right."

"Ain't the mare that's troubling me. It's whoever was doing the mirror signaling down at the confluence. If suspicions pan out, they might be following us. We'll give 'em some confusion."

"Confusion?"

"Yep, I'll hear them from up there, once it's dark and the day settles down. They won't know we've left the trail. You'll see how hard it is to ride quiet at night."

"Angus, darling, does this mean we won't have a campfire? No coffee."

"No fire, but I'll keep you warm."

We found a shallow river up ahead a quarter-mile, dropped down into the cold water, but it was only a few inches over No Más's hock. He seemed unconcerned, and he led us without giving it any concern for another quarter-mile. Once there, I spotted a rocky ledge, with not much of an incline, leading directly down into the river's flow. We used that as a bridge up out of the river onto dry shale. No tracks. No way to tell we left the river here. We rode up a couple hundred feet, turned back the way we'd just come, and pulled into the little stand of trees from the top side. I picketed the stock and built us a lean-to out of downed tree growth.

"That's it?" Jill asked, looking at the little tree hut I'd made.

"Yep, it'll be all comfy once we're inside, sittin' quiet."

And, that's what we did, whispering small talk, but mostly listening to the night sounds; an owl behind us, the soft rustle of the river below, and the usual cawing and wind rushes in the trees. While we waited, sitting on our saddle pads, we nibbled on jerky and biscuits.

No Más heard it first, or maybe he smelled something in the low breeze coming up at us from the river, five hundred feet below us. He snorted, sniffed the air, and pawed the ground with one hoof. The mule turned toward him, and the mare picked up her ears.

A few seconds later, it came; the steady, slow click and clack of horse shoes on gravel, then stones, then nothing. Just the still of the night.

"Is it them?" Jill whispered into my ear.

"It's a man, just one, horseback, down there along the trail, moving might slow, like he was studying something. Don't move. I'm only going to crawl out to take a quick look over the ledge. It's probably too dark to see anything, but I might pick up branches or stones moving. Stay here."

As I unfolded myself from the ground cloth, she tucked her knees up under her chin and leaned forward, cupping her hand to her right ear. I brushed some loose gravel trying to crawl out onto the ledge and froze. The click-clack stopped. The usual noises of a winter night were there, limbs creaking, a different hoot owl far up across the river, and as always, the soft sound of the river hitting rocks, sucking up and away from the edge, and an occasional thump as a floating branch or log came up against something. But, for two or three minutes, no click-clack. Then, it started up, even slower than before and somehow different. It took a few more minutes for me to get it. A spur jingle, almost not there, but once I recognized it, I knew. A man on foot. Leading his horse. Looking for a sign by the light of the moon, broken twigs, boot prints, anything different. But, the quarter moon was not yet high in the sky. More light up here, and likely less down there. He could not know what I did. He could look alongside that trail in full daylight and not see a thing. That's why I rode the middle of the river up and then circled back to where I was laying, trying to get a fix on him.

Then, louder and without trying to cover himself, I heard him say something unintelligible to his horse, mounting noisily, banging a canteen or something against metal, saying "get" or something like that, and the click-clacks much closer together.

"He's mounted, turned back, and heading down river," I told Jill when I stood up and walked fifteen feet back to our little hut.

"So, it was just one man, you think, and he's turned around? Are you sure?"

"Just one, moving slow afoot, looking for sign. When he could not find any he concluded that we'd probably dropped off down into the river, or maybe turned upslope and he missed our sign earlier. Either way, there's nothing he can do pressing on, except maybe run head on into my gun. In the dark. He ain't a fool. He's a man who knows sign."

"So, where will he go? Will he ride down into the river and look for where we came out?"

"Not in the dark. He's got to wait for sunup, and even then, he might figure it'd be best to put some distance between him and us. He's a tracker, not the man who's hunting me. Mendoza Mendoza is down river from us, waiting for his man to figure out the sign."

I told her we'd best get three hours' sleep, and then head on out two hours before dawn.

CHAPTER 29

Mendoza Mendoza Changes the Plan

"**Y**OU ARE *ESTUPIDO*, CHUCHES. I tole you to find their camp. Now you say you lost them in the dark! I don't know what to do with you. How come you let them get so far ahead you don't know where they turned off, and what? Camped in the middle of the river? Are you saying this to me?"

Chuches knew better than to argue with me, but still, he tried.

"*Por forvor, Patron,* this gringo, *Patron,* he's a *muy inteligente hombre.* We won't catch him from behind. I can pick up his track tomorrow morning, but he probably don't sleep much. He'll be ahead of us, and we got the buckboard to wait for. He's going to Chama. We could go there and get him when he comes into town."

Instead of answering Chuches, who was making my stomach hurt, I looked at Onchero, whose fault all this was.

"What you looking at, Onchero? We are being made the fool again, because of you. First, you get scared and piss your pants when the gringo jus' points his gun at you and your brother. Ignacio—he's worse than you. Instead of shooting the gringo, he hits you and then you shoot the horse trough. Aiee, you two are the laughing stock! But, people are not laughing at you, are they? No, they are laughing at me, as a man. And for what? For raising sons without *los testículos?*"

Postino brought his little cooking pan around with hot roasted chiles, sausage pads, and tortillas. Nobody wanted to eat before me, but they were all hungry. Now they had a fire, but not last night. Ignacio was thinking maybe the gringo was coming down river after us because he didn't like us crowding him. He wished I would forget about this man. Nobody ate. Postino went back to the little fire beside his little buckboard—to eat by himself.

"PaPa, maybe Chuches is right," Ignacio said. "You can't ride to Chama if you go up the Rio Grande in only one day. He will go west at Tres Piedras, but it will take him close to two days. And, the buckboard jus' slows us down. If we leave now, we can be in Chama tonight, and the buckboard maybe a little later. We will get someone to watch for him, and then call him out and kill him."

"We not going to call him out. And, we will do no shooting in Chama. The gringo has to die somewhere nobody can know, jus' us. In time, some words will be spread that Mendoza Mendoza did it, but the law won't come after us on words. We need to kill him someplace that's not a town. We will bury him with no grave marker. Under the law if there's no body, there's no crime. That's what my asshole cousin Perfecto Armijo would say. I'm sure of it."

Chuches listened and then ate Postino's little breakfast while he waited for me to settle my stomach. He knew there was pain in my gut from something, not just this gringo. Sometimes in the night, he saw me bent in half, holding onto my stomach, and pushing down so hard it might bust a gut. But, I did not believe in gringo doctors, or Mexican priests, neither.

"*Patron*," Chuches said to me in a low tone. "Maybe you can get the gringo to come to you. In a place you choose. There is the lady with him; why I don't know. But, the undertaker said she was very pretty, and the gringo was holding her hand. If you had her at the ranch, then the gringo, I think, would come anywhere to get her back. *Qué no?*"

Nobody talked. Postino rubbed his little cooking pan with dirt, and wiped his knife off on his pants. He knew a decision had been made, not one he liked to hear, but still they would go soon, he thought.

"Her, the gringa," Ignacio scoffed. "Who knows who she is? I think Chuches is right, maybe. But, if he is right, the gringo will not let us just ride up and take her away."

"Maybe we could steal her in the night, when he's asleep," Onchero offered in a quiet stutter.

Nobody wanted to think about this problem.

"Chuches," I said jumping up. "Goddamn, *mi amigo*—you have it. Let's not steal her. Let's shoot her!"

"PaPa, I don't understand," Ignacio said. "We don't know her, but she was not in Bernalillo. Why do you want to shoot her?"

I was disappointed. Am I the only one who can think in this family? "Ignacio, *mi hijo*, then the gringo, he will come for us at the ranch. That is where we will kill him."

"*Si*, PaPa, but he will bring a posse with him."

"No, not this man. I don't think he would wait. Like me, he's a man who can taste his own revenge. This is a good plan. Chuches, get back on your *caballo*. Chase them and shoot her, then ride the wind to my hacienda. We will go now to there. We will wait for you, with the gringo following behind. Then we will kill him, and I will cut off his head."

Chuches just sat on his rock, eating peaches out of a can with his pocket knife. Then, after he drank the juice and threw the can in the fire pit, he looked at me.

"I could do it if I did not have to worry about him. But, I don't think killing her will be so easy with him around. Maybe he won't leave her side. If he did, I could shoot her, spin my horse, and ride like the wind. He will not chase me right away. He will wait to give up her body to God. Then he will track me just like I've tracked him."

"Chuches, my friend of more than twenty years. You will do this for me. Go find them, Chuches. Shoot the woman and leave our brand behind. The gringo will know where to go. He won't have to track you."

I walked over to the buckboard, where we have a tool box and things strapped to the side. Grabbing the shovel, I said, "Here, leave this at the place you choose to shoot her."

The long-handled shovel had a big *M*/ burned into it. And, I gave him my Knops .50 caliber, with a Civil War brass rifle scope fitted down almost two-thirds of the thirty-six-inch barrel.

"You know I killed that bull elk last year up on Redondo Peak from five hundred yards away with this gun. The bullet is so big, when it hits her, she will explode. Aiee, this gun is longer than her whole body! Her man, the gringo, if that's what he is, will grieve, but not for long. He'll bury her first; take some time. He'll find the shovel stuck in the ground where you take the shot. Leave the brass cartridge there, with the shovel. It will tell him we did it, and he'll wear out his saddle getting to us."

Postino got the Knops out of the scabbard in the buckboard and ten .50 caliber cartridges. He tied the shovel on Chuches's horse, with no more words passing.

"But, PaPa," Ignacio said, as Onchero started using his crutch to get back into the wagon, "what if Chuches misses the woman? He will need our guns then."

"Ignacio, do not insult Chuches; he is a better shot even than me. Chuches, take the gun. Shoot her, and I'll make you a rich man. We will go back to the ranch and wait for you to come, with the gringo riding his horse to death to catch you. Take Ignacio's horse with you so you have a remount. *Paseo rápido!* Ignacio deserves to ride the buckboard with his piss-in-the-pants little brother. Go, now. We will wait at the ranch for you to come. And him to follow."

CHAPTER 30
Angus & Jill
Facing Black Hat

JILL TRIED, BUT COULDN'T SLEEP. I dozed off a time or two. It seemed only a few minutes before she nudged me. "Look," she said, pointing to the horizon in the eastern sky, "morning's heading our way."

There were only two stars left in what'd been a black sky just a minute ago. Now the black was fading to gray, and I could see well enough to brush the horses, straighten the pack on the mule, and saddle No Más. Jill saddled the little mare, and snugged the tie-down. We took a long pull from our water bags, and I gave a handful of grain to each horse.

I followed our trail from last evening back to the north, then down to the river bed. We forded it half-way, and turned up river. We had ridden about a hundred yards when we came to a rock formation that narrowed the river channel down to no more than a dozen yards wide. That made it too deep for the horses and a pack mule, under a load, to manage.

"We'll have to come out here. But, let's go up the west side of the river, and find another place to cross back over once we've gone ahead a mile or so. It'll be a little slower on that side. Looks to be narrowing as we climb north."

"I'm right behind you," she said.

We rode four, maybe five hours, till the sun was straight up. I'd turned off the trail a few times, and we'd circled back along low ridges and tree stands, watching our back trail. I saw no one following, and there was no sign of anyone else traveling the river's edge.

"Let's stop over there in that little saddle. These horses need a break, maybe an hour's stop with a double-handful of grain, with the saddles off."

"Sure," Jill said, "I'm doing fine."

I knew she wasn't. She'd been bending down rubbing her knees for the last ten miles, and she'd been taking lots of small sips from her water bag. We'd gained elevation, probably riding now at something over seven thousand feet. The peaks off to the east, the Taos Mountains, were snowcapped, and the gray clouds hovering around them showed signs of more on the way. But, there was no frost on the ground. Jill favored gloves, but the sun felt good on my bare hands. My left arm was happy to swing free without that damn cast. No pain, and my elbow movement was free and easy.

I slid the saddles off, gave both horses a brushing down, and hobbled them to graze after I'd taken them to the river's edge for water. No need to hobble the mule; mules stick to horses. Standing the saddles up against a low rock ledge, we sat down with our backs into the sheepskin, and breathed in the high mountain air. Jill fell asleep in under a minute.

Can't say what it was for sure, just a feeling, I guess. Couldn't see or hear anything, but the natural sounds of the river and the wind blowing in the trees, but it was something. So, I let Jill get a few minutes more shut-eye, and I walked around the big rock, and found a way to skinny up a little crevice to the top. When I got to the top, I realized I was forty feet above Jill and the horses. I laid down on my stomach and squinted at our back trail for as far as I could see along the river.

There he was. On foot. Just standing and looking down at the ground, maybe a quarter-mile back. That's where we'd stopped to let the horses take a deep drink, and Jill had dismounted and gone back behind the trees upslope.

At that distance, I couldn't tell much about him. Black hat, long, heavy dark coat, buttoned to the waist, but open down to his chaps. He crooked a long rifle across his left elbow, and used his hand to push something on the ground at his feet. He looked up my way, but as I was on my belly, I knew he couldn't tell me from a rock at this distance. He must have felt the same thing I did, because he whirled around, jumped on his horse, and spurred it upslope into the rocks and out of sight.

I eased backward down the big rock, skinned my left hand in doing it, and dropped to the ground. When I got around to the front, Jill had just stood up and was stretching her arms above her head.

"They're here," I whispered.

She froze tight, with her hand over mouth. She instantly went pale.

"What are we going to do, Angus?" she mumbled, heading for the mare. She was pulling the saddle blanket over, trying to brush the dead twigs; I reached her and took hold of both arms.

"Stay still. I don't think they know we are just a quarter mile from them. But, those boys are nervous, and they have the low ground. We cannot outrun them. Get that pistol out of your bag. I'm going to take the Winchester up top of this rock again. There's a fine view from up there, more than a quarter-mile back behind us. I need to know their number and their intentions."

She said something, but I shushed her putting my finger to her lips. I motioned her over to the side of the big rock and mouthed, "stay there." Then I fished the Winchester out of the saddle scabbard, and jacked a .44-40 into the firing chamber.

"What are you going to do?" she asked through tightly pressed lips.

"If they come in range, I'm gonna light those boys up."

Five minutes later, I'd shinnied up the crevice again, and snuck out low and quiet as I could. When I got to where I'd seen the big man in the black hat, I eased down from my hands-and-knees crawl to flat out on my gut. Easing the Winchester out in front of me, I noticed a sage brush root stuck in the crevice on my right. I eased it out of its hold, laid the gun barrel down on it, and tried to measure my breathing. Jill would be pleased, I thought, because I had remembered to pick a stable barrel rest for a better shooting position.

From behind, I heard the rustling of small gravel . Leaning up on my elbows, I could see Jill—not sitting still like I told her to. Half bent over, she was moving down river toward a rock ledge about half as high as the one I was on. I watched her creep down toward the edge of the water. I had told her to stay put, but there she was, crab-hopping her way downslope. With her father's well-oiled Henry rifle held in both hands, chest high, and at the ready!

Then I watched as she crept down. She moved the rifle sort of inside her coat, muffling the trigger guard, and jacked a shell into position. Without looking up at me, she continued on down. My God, the woman was flanking Black Hat, I thought. Now he was facing two guns, head on, but with fifty feet of separation between Jill and me. If he was alone, he was in an unfavorable position. But, if he had more behind him, well, I thought, let's just see.

A hawk circled overhead, and the river kept gurgling and sloshing water on the rocks. The wind was still blowing some, but in little gusts, not a strong blow. Tree branches moved, and the day sort of stood still. But, there was no sound downriver. No Más and the mare were hobbled, but they'd followed the grass up river about fifty feet, and the mare got herself tangled a little bit. She snorted loud, and let what sounded like a bray, and then she stomped her feet on the loose gravel upslope about five feet from the river. I knew the sound would carry downriver, so I locked my eyes on the trail looking for sign of any movement.

Five or ten minutes passed. Not sure how long. But, a slow, odd sound wafted over on a wisp of wind. At first, it sounded like rock rubbing on rock. But, it seemed to come not up at me from the river, but down at me from above. There was a rock ledge above me about thirty feet higher and fifty yards over. It was Black Hat, afoot, coming around a little turn on the rock ledge. Off his horse, with that long barrel aimed down toward the river, he was a ways off, I guessed maybe a hundred yards. But, my gut spit the message up my throat to my brain. He was sighting Jill in. He had not seen me yet, prone and still. Scrambling to move the Winchester from its little stand, I pointed it straight up and pulled the trigger.

The .44-40 crack wasn't aimed at him, but he heard it. That took his attention off Jill and on me. As I jacked another round into the chamber, he swung that long gun my way. The muzzle flashed. I heard the boom, like it was a thunderbolt in my right ear. The unmistakable sound of lead ricocheting off the rock an arm's length in front of me. Bits of limestone spat back at my face. I turned to him; he was kneeling down, and pushing another round down with his thumb into the firing chamber. It was the last thing he did in this life.

Jill's shot was dead center, cracking his sternum wide open, and knocking him backward onto a chamisa patch. He sprawled, one leg over the bush, the other bent backward behind him. I could see him plain. He never twitched or moved a single muscle. I kept him in my gun sights for three, four minutes. Nothing. I heard his horse whinny. But, it was plain enough. The rider, Black Hat, was dead.

CHAPTER 31
Angus Gets His Blood Up

WHEN I SCRAMBLED BACK DOWN to Jill, she was sitting cross-legged staring at the flow of the river. Her chin was nestled in her hands with her elbows on her knees. I dropped to my knees behind her and wrapped my arms around her. There was no cry in her. She melted back into me like a rag doll.

"Sometimes, Jill darlin', you come on a fork in the trail no one's ever seen before. You just stay here; there ain't no need to go up there. I'll take care of him. You don't need to look at him or…"

She shook me off like an overcoat. Springing up, she picked up the Henry repeating rifle, brushed the dirt off, and carefully slid the hammer down. Then she quickly jacked three shiny brass cartridges out and leaned the gun against the rock.

"I'll clean the barrel and oil the works when we get back. I want to see him," she said, with a set to her jaw I'd never seen before.

By the time we reached him, he'd bled out. His chest wall was black with mottled blood, and the hole in his spine was clean through and through.

"All right now, you've seen all of this you need to…"

Looking up into the trees, she said, "I'll go get his horse. I heard him thrashing about just a bit ago. Angus, that long gun of his is branded on the stock. See that *M/*. Do you recognize it?"

"Maybe. Let's get his horse. It's likely carrying the same brand. I'm thinking this is *El Patron* Mendoza's tracker. He'd have drilled me for sure if I hadn't had you…"

"Angus, if I had not been here, neither would you have. He would not have been following us. None of this makes any sense if you think about it from our side of things. For sure, this man was going to kill you. That's all there is to it. It's, like you said, a fork in the road for me, but I know I took the right one. Teaching shooting is one thing, but, Angus, there's no lesson here today. I'm not sure I'll ever understand it, but I do not for damn sure regret killing him to protect you."

I was out of words. So, I held on tight to her, and turned her back around toward the river, away from the body. We just sat there for a while until his horse began to paw the ground somewhere up above us. She pulled away from me, and set out to fetch his horse.

"You're right," she said, as she led the stout gray horse back down to where I was standing, "look at the *M/* brand. In a way I don't understand, this brand clarifies things for me.

Now I can see why I killed him. But, I don't remember pulling the trigger. I can remember the boom and the muzzle flare—I think he was shooting a fifty caliber at you. I can see the long barrel, the shooting tube, and the stance he took aiming at you. But, I can't remember squeezing the trigger on the Henry, or even jacking a round into my rifle."

I took the reins and stroked the gray's neck. He was calm and accepting. When I moved him to a little clearing, I saw the shovel tied to the off-side of his saddle, with another *M/* burnt into the handle. Slowly, looking at the shovel, then him, then back again, something started to bother me. Why would Black Hat take all the trouble to pack a heavy, long-handled shovel with him? Men like Black Hat don't bother burying dead bodies. But, they do follow orders. What could Mendoza Mendoza have had in mind for me? What 'n hell was it?"

"Why was he packing a short-handled shovel, Angus?"

"Can't say for sure, I was just trying to piece it out myself."

With her help, I got him up off the ground and laid out over his saddle. I strapped him down as tight as I could. That made the gray twirl some. It's a rare horse that will pack a lifeless, human body without getting a nervous sweat up. By the time we led him down to where No Más was, the gray was wet and prancing up on his toes.

Before we mounted up, Jill asked me to sit with her for a minute, "I need to know something," she said.

I was afraid she would.

"When I first saw the man on that ledge, he was not aiming at you. Now that I refocus on it, I don't think he'd seen you yet. I was out in the open, and I thought he was sort of spanning his rifle in my direction because it had a high-power optical sight on it. Now that I see the gun, I am sure that's what he was doing. But, then I heard your gun go off. You shot and missed him. And then…"

Her voice trailed off, and she reached out and took hold of my forearms. "Oh God, Angus. You didn't miss. Did you? You fired just to move his attention toward you, but why? What's the sense of it if he was here to kill you? Why alert him to where you were lying flat?"

"Jill, I fired straight up into the air because I had no time to reset. I could not swing around in time to keep him from firing—he had a bead directly on you."

"On me? Why would he do that?"

"I ain't thought it through yet, but I remember what Perfecto Armijo said about the man—a back shooter, but a man that does his own killing, even if it is in the back. Maybe he sent this tracker to shoot you, knowing that I would come after him with my blood up. The shovel was a message—he's waiting on the *Ml*, if I'm man enough to come there."

"That's a wild guess, Angus."

"No, it ain't, Jill, I saw him clearly. He settled his frame, sighted you in, and was starting to squeeze down. I had no time to reposition and aim his way. So, I just pointed the Winchester up and fired. It caused him to miss. You nailed him on the rebound. You and that shovel were supposed to get me to meet him on his ground. And it worked. I'll see him soon."

We gathered our gear, mounted, and sat our horses.

"Which way, Angus? Up to Tres Piedras, or back down to Espanola?"

"Well, it's a Hobson's choice, either way. This man tried to kill us, and we need to explain his death to the closest law.

We're halfway between the two, best as I can figure. But this man, whatever his name was, worked for Mendoza Mendoza, on his ranch some distance to the west of Espanola. He might have had family there. We'd best backtrack to Espanola."

CHAPTER 32

Angus Back At Espanola

SOON AS WE REINED IN our horses in front of the small adobe building with the sign ESPANOLA TOWN MARSHAL on it, a young man in baggy pants wearing a dull badge in need of soap and water came hurrying out. "Chuches, that's his name," the deputy told me, as he helped me untie and lower Black Hat's body down off the big gray.

I'd tied his hat to our pack mule, and I handed it to the deputy. He seemed unsure about what to do with it. A boy in a big soft hat and a heavy serape was walking by. He told him to fetch Mr. Schwartz. That took care of the body, but the hat seemed to him to present some difficulty.

"You saved his hat? You say he tried to kill you, and you shot him—and saved his hat? *Señor*, that is strange."

"Well, now, hold on, deputy, you're getting out in front of your facts. He tried to kill me, that's the truth of it, but

Miss Garrison had no choice in the matter. She shot this man, 'Chuches,' you say his name is, in my defense. She did just what you'd done if'n you'd been there yourself. Let's be straight on that. As to the hat, well, of course, I saved it. And, his rifle, that damned shovel snugged on to his horse, and everything else that's crammed there in his saddle bags. I'm a US Marshal, so let's get inside. You need to take written statements from us. Then I got questions for you. We can start with the brand. Can you tell me straight out, is this *M/* the brand for the Mendoza string, the old man and his two boys, Ignacio and Onchero?"

"It is, Señor Angus. Come inside. I will give you paper and pencil, please."

We wrote out our statements. Mine was on one piece of paper, but Jill took up three pages. She dated and signed hers, along with her address in Chama. I just said my name and job. Mixed in with the young deputy's questions, Jill and I asked him some of our own. Turns out this little town is mostly Mexican, most of whom fear the Mendoza family. He and his boys carry swag in the little cantina, but the old man mostly stays out on his ranch, some twenty-five miles southwest, and on the other side of the Rio Grande. We took turns with him, Jill first.

"Did Mr. Chuches have a family, and if he did, do they live here in Espanola?" Jill asked.

The deputy, who had still not volunteered his name, said no, then changed his mind, and allowed as he did not know one way or the other because the man, Chuches, was not from here.

"I think he might be from over near Gallinas because the Baca Ranch over there has its brand on his saddle. The *caballo,* he's from the *M/*, but not so the saddle. Maybe he worked as a tracker for both ranches."

"How long has this Chuches feller worked for Mendoza Mendoza?"

"I don't know, Señor Marshal, maybe Jesús in the cantina could say. He's a cousin, I think."

"Chuches is a cousin?"

"No, Jesús, the bartender at El Bonito. He is cousin to one of the Mendozas. Chuches could be a cousin. Of that, I am not sure. The El Bonito, it is our only drinking establishment, *si hombre*? Maybe the Mendoza family owns it. No one in town seems to know who does."

"I'm familiar with the man; he sold me some mescal last time I was here. Reckon I'll have a talk with him after you're through with us."

"*Si,* you should. And, if you are looking for family for Chuches, maybe Hector Schwartz can say. He tends to all the people around here, before he makes their bodies look good in their coffins."

"Yeah, him, too. But, you can probably help me with one more thing. Where is the Mendoza spread?"

"*Si,* I went there once to serve a warrant for a *vaquero*. But, they would not let me in the gate. It's maybe twenty miles west of the Rio Grande, up against White Rock Canyon. I also went, two times, over there to Buckman, which is where you climb up the old Hay Road, up through Stonenail Canyon to the Pajarito Plateau. Do you know of the Cañon de Valles, señor?"

"Can't say as I've ridden it."

"It is the highest canyon anywhere around here, señor. You'd need a mountain horse to go all the way. I only went in to the bottom; my poor horse was not fit to make the climb up to the Valles Grande, and that was in the summer."

"So, exactly where's the *M/* ranch in all that?"

"I cannot say that in truth for you, since I am not sure. But, you know you are on Mendoza land if you can see the *Caja del Rio*. They own from there almost half-way to the Valles Caldera. They move sheep and some cows, too, in and out of there, depending on the grass on the plateau."

"*Caja del Rio? Caja* means box, don't it?"

"*Si*, Señor Marshal. The Rio Grande backs up into a box canyon somewhere up there. But, the drainage is from higher up, so it has its own name. Mendoza's family has lived there for a hundred years. That's what Jesús, the bartender, says. He knows about the land grant from España. There are some steep cones that stick up on top of burnt rocks."

"Rough country, would you call it that?"

"You need chaps and a horse that don't get too tired. When it rains or snows up there, the drainage goes down to the Rio Grande. All around you will see cliffs. So, his ranch is protected and his cattle stay. Some people say other men's cattle stay there, too. I don't say that myself, but that's what you hear."

"And, the other end of the ranch, the Valles Caldera, where's that?"

"Aiee, señor. It does not belong to Mendoza. It is grass-land surrounded by an ancient forest, Jesús says, where the volcanos blew up a long time ago. He called it the de Baca Land Grant. I don't know how big it is, but sometimes in the fall, we see the sheep they herd up there. Some are sold down here for the wool, señor."

"High snow country, you'd say?" I asked the deputy.

"It takes a horse and a man who don't feel the cold to go there in the winter. They say it was a volcano, but there is grass there in the summer for sheep and horses. Nobody lives up there in the winter. It is not easy, señor, to even go there."

The deputy read the statements that Jill and I wrote out and signed. He wrote things down himself on a little pad of paper on the desk. He put them all in an envelope and stuffed it in a drawer.

"Señor, and Miss Garrison. I will give these to Sheriff Romulo Martinez. He is the new sheriff of Santa Fe County, who has jurisdiction over Espanola. I don't know if he will want to talk to you or not, but can I ask you how long you will be in Espanola?"

I knew I was speaking for Jill on this, "Just long enough to talk to Hector Schwartz, and maybe a visit to Jesús, the bartender. Then, we'll be riding out, if you're satisfied this was a justified shooting."

"*Si*, I do. There is no one to say otherwise, *qué no?*"

Jill and I spent the night at the only boarding house in town. I slept in a sleeping room with one other man, and Jill got the front bedroom next to the owner, a recent widow who looked bewildered that we were even there. The next morning, I knocked on Hector Schwartz's door, and it opened before the sound of the knock hit my ears. He musta been standing inside watching us walk up the little boardwalk from the dirt street.

"Come in Señor Marshal, and Miss Garrison. So good to see you again, but it's too bad under these unfortunate circumstances, come in please," he said, stepping aside and waving his hand back into the little house.

He'd put a tea kettle on the wood stove in the kitchen, and it whistled as we sat on the upholstered sofa by the window facing the street. He asked if we wanted some, we said no, and he started apologizing, before I'd put a single question to him.

"I am very sorry I gave Mendoza Mendoza what he wanted, señor. He came here, in this room, the night you left, when I took your cast off. I should have been stronger about your private business. I'm very sorry about that."

"Slow down, Mr. Schwartz, I ain't sure I'm following this. Mendoza Mendoza asked what, exactly, about me?"

"He and Ignacio and Chuches; all of them were here. But, when Mendoza Mendoza is in the room, he does the talking. I was fearful for myself. Selfish, I know, but I'm not a man of the gun. I…"

"Just tell me plain. What did he say about me?"

"He wanted to know where you are—where did you go—all things like that. I said you and Miss Garrison were riding up the Rio Grande, and enjoying your time together, on the way to Chama. He asked if you were taking the stage road and I said no, you said you liked riding the bank of the river. Of course, I already knew that from when I fixed your arm and put that cast on. And, I told him that I took off your cast and that your arm was…"

"Is he tracking us? That's what I'm asking you."

"Yes, I think so. He didn't say that, but he is a man of blood. You humiliated his boys. Humiliated, that's a word he used—so he has to take Mendoza revenge. That's also what he said. That's why Chuches was with him. Chuches is a tracker, and a hunter of men and wild game. Everybody knows that."

"Does the deputy here know that?"

"Sure, everybody does. But, probably many are afraid to talk about Chuches or Mendoza Mendoza. You understand that, don't you, Marshal?"

"Well, I suppose. And, I ain't got no quarrel with you telling him what I told you. It wasn't a secret."

"Mr. Schwartz," Jill asked, "do you know it was me that shot the man you call Chuches? Can I ask you that?"

"Yes, the deputy told me that. By now, everyone here knows that. By tomorrow, Mendoza Mendoza will know it, too. Jesús will ride to tell *El Patron*. That's Espanola."

"Yes, but did he have a family? And, is he a killer, or just someone who does as he's told by Mr. Mendoza?"

"A killer? It is not for me to say those words about him. But, he is very beholden to Mendoza Mendoza. He would shoot me if *El Patron* told him to. He is not a Mendoza, but they treat him like he was one of the sons. And, they will see his death the same way. I have to get his body ready. I know when Mendoza hears, he will come here. Please, Marshal and Miss Garrison, go away from here. And, don't tell me, or anyone here where you're going. Just go, now, please."

"What will Mendoza do with the body? Bury him here in the cemetery I saw by that little church south of town?" Jill asked.

"No, Miss Garrison, he will take Chuches back to the ranch on the buckboard. He will bury him there, and the padre will follow on his burro. Then, after three days of mourning, he will come after you. Not with Chuches, but with many guns. Many. It will be *sangre de la Guerra*—war of blood."

I took Jill to the livery stable, then went to the general store and got supplies. On the way back, I tried the cantina.

Jesús was nowhere to be seen, and the front door of the El Bonito was bolted shut. When I got back to the livery, Jill was cleaning her rifle, and looking into the three boxes we'd packed on the mule. I hadn't seen the insides before. Turns out, they contained four carbines, three pistols, two spare gun barrels, bullet cylinders, and an assortment of springs, hinges, nuts, and tools. And three hundred rounds of assorted ammunition.

"I get why you buy guns, Jill, but why so much ammo?"

"Almost all of the ammo is for the general store in Chama. And, two of the carbines and one of the pistols, too. It's just a favor for them, the Wall brothers. One of them sells guns, the other sells ammo. They are strange, but somehow loveable. I keep the rest for use in repairing or trading guns myself."

She looked up at me and I could see another set to her jaw.

"Angus, I know you think I'm just a woman, and that you're intending on dealing with this yourself. But, I'm not just a woman, I'm your woman. I shot Chuches; it does not matter why. Schwartz said this would be a blood war. Well, here is what we need to fight one. And, we need more hands than just yours and mine. What's our plan?"

"Pack up. I'm going back to the deputy's office. I'll deliver those written statements myself. We ride south to Santa Fe."

"But, who will help us there?"

"Chuches fired on a federal officer, under the direction of Mendoza Mendoza. That's assault with intent to kill, and it's a federal crime. Marshal Knop will round up some men, deputize them, and we'll head off Mendoza Mendoza before he gets to hunting us."

"But, this is winter. I know you ride every day in the winter, but you said the *M/* ranch is west of here, up toward the Valles Caldera. It will be heavy snow up there."

"Reckon so. But, giving him time to plan and letting him pick the place where we square things ain't my way. And, I've spent more winters up that high than I have down here at six thousand feet."

"But, you cannot do this alone. Does the US Marshal in Santa Fe have enough men to form a posse?" she asked, as she repacked her boxes for the pack mule.

"We have today and tomorrow, while he buries Chuches. That gives Marshal Knop time to recruit some special deputies. Three days from now, come sunup, we're riding into the *Caja del Rio*. And, if need be, we'll chase him up into the Cañon de Valles, snow or not. I ain't one to wait till the fight comes to me. It's no place for a woman, but you ain't just a woman, are you?"

CHAPTER 33

Angus–Men Wearing Felt Hats and Badges

THE US MARSHAL'S OFFICE in Santa Fe was crowded with men in felt hats, wearing badges on their vests, and looking at me with questions written on their foreheads. Marshal Knop must have felt uncomfortable, too. "Now, look here, men, we are all officers of the law here, and I know this jurisdiction thing is mighty important, but we're getting off track here. The attack on a federal officer took place in Rio Arriba County. The intended victim was this man, a US Deputy Marshal from Colorado. But, like I said, he's been offered, and I believe intends on accepting, the position of undersheriff in that same county, and will be in charge of the office in Chama. Ain't that so, Angus?"

"Yes, sir, that is my intention, once this Mendoza Mendoza business is done."

Marshal Knop tried to continue, but Santa Fe County Sheriff Romulo Martinez interrupted, "Now, that's news to me. First off, what happened to my friend Joe Pete up in Chama? He's the undersheriff, ain't he?"

"Sheriff Martinez," I said to him, "this all happened just last week. I got a telegram from Joe Pete, telling me he was going to be appointed interim Rio Arriba Sheriff, until the next election. Don't know when that is. He asked, would I take on the job of Undersheriff in Chama, and report to him in Tierra Amarilla. I said I would."

"Well, that's good. He's a good man and you must be, too, or Knop here would not be vouching for you so strongly. But, you just called what we're about here as 'this Mendoza Mendoza business.' What exactly do you mean by that? I know his hired man fired on you, I read the report. I'll speak plain on this. Is this some kind of a vendetta with you?"

I was thinking on an answer, but Knop motioned me to be quiet. He laid it out.

"Their statements are here on the table. One by Angus, one by Jill Garrison, and one by the Espanola deputy. You all ought to read them. But, here's the nut of it. Marshal Angus came upon a criminal act in Bernalillo, and was drawed on by one of Mendoza Mendoza's boys. He returned fire and shot one son, name of Onchero Mendoza, and arrested the other, Ignacio Mendoza. Deputy Bo String, from Bernalillo was there, backing Angus's play. He saw it all, and his report is also there on the table for you all to read. Bo, you got anything to add to what I said?"

Bo turned to the group. "I might be the only one here that knows Angus in an official sort of way. He's a man to reckon with, and his word is reliable. I saw him face Mendoza's boys with a cast on his arm. So, I'm right happy to be backing his play again now."

That seemed to settle well with the men, so Marshal Knop continued his summary of the situation. "Now, we all have had some law enforcement matters with the Mendoza brand, the *M/*. Especially *El Patron* himself, Mendoza Mendoza. He tracked Marshal Angus from here up past the confluence of the Rio Chama and the Rio Grande. He had his fiancé, Jill Garrison, with him. Mendoza had his hired man, Chuches Martinez—who is no relation to Romulo, is he?"

Sheriff Martinez shook his head, and picked up the report from Marshal Bo String in Bernalillo. Knop continued.

"Chuches Martinez fired first, and Miss Jill Garrison, who is Angus's fiancé, returned fire, and struck Chuches with a mortal wound with a Henry repeating rifle. She is a well-known gunsmith in these parts. So, what we are dealing with here is the resolution of both federal and state crimes. What I propose is a joint posse, with men from Santa Fe County, my office, and maybe Bernalillo County, as well. We will need several well-armed men, because Mendoza Mendoza is a man known to resist any law that he don't control. And, he is on his own land. His spread is on both state land and private fee ground in two counties, and stretches up to, but does not include, the de Baca Ranch atop the Valles Grande. He will not likely come in peaceable."

"Yes, I know that country," Sheriff Martinez said. "It is canyon land called Caja del Rio, and feeds down into the Rio

Grande 'bout, I'd say, thirty miles from where we stand. But, I still ain't clear on our intentions here."

"Well, Sheriff Martinez," Marshal Knop said, "here's the intentions of the US Department of Justice. One of our officers is under mortal threat by Mendoza Mendoza, and we intend to arrest him, and bring charges against him before the federal magistrate here in Santa Fe, Judge Blakey, who as you know is also a state court magistrate of long-standing."

The Santa Fe Chief of Police, Frank Chavez, had not said a word, but he entered the fray, "Well, here's the thing, none of this involves my jurisdiction, the city of Santa Fe. What do you men expect of me?"

Marshal Knop answered, "Frank, we'd like you to give us one or two of your deputies for the posse. We'll be in Judge Blakey's office at one o'clock this afternoon, asking for an arrest warrant, based on the affidavits of Marshal Angus and Miss Garrison. Can we count on you, Frank?"

"You can. But, I have something that needs tending to, so just come on over to my office when you're ready and we'll discuss manpower."

When Chavez left, Knop asked whether anyone had further questions. Sheriff Martinez got up and paced around the room.

"It seems to me," he said, looking my way, "there's something that oughta be decided right now, before a posse is formed. That's whether Angus will be part of it. Marshal Knop, is that your intent?"

I got up and walked around to his side of the table, but Knop waved a hand at me, "Now, men, let's not move afield of the issue here. Romulo, I think you ask a fair question. I take it you ain't in favor of Angus being a posse member, for he's the victim. Am I figuring you right?"

"Well," Chavez said, "it's a question I'm raising, because this is an unusual situation we have here. If a civilian were the victim, of course, we would never let him be on the posse sent to arrest the wrongdoer. But frankly, I never heard of telling a lawman he could not arrest the man that attacked him. I see there's two sides to this. So, let's just hear from Angus himself. Son, can you take your personal views out of this, and treat this just like you would any other infraction of the law?"

I went back to my seat, sat, and tried to put a damper on myself.

"This all started when Mendoza's boys committed an assault on a woman in Bernalillo. They drew on me—well, it was actually a shotgun in Onchero's hand, but the intent was to kill me. I arrested the both of 'em, and turned 'em over to your deputy up there. Next, the old man and his boys, and his tracker, Chuches, followed me up the Rio Grande with the intent of avenging family pride. Chuches fired on me, and my fiancé shot him. But, for that, I would have arrested him right then and there or shot him myself, whichever he forced me to do. I guess I don't see the question about lawful authority. If I ain't got the authority under the law to arrest the man who hunted me and tried to kill me, who does?"

"You do, Marshal," Chavez said, "of course you got the authority. And, I ain't questioning your ability one bit. All I want to hear you say is this will be a lawful arrest. We ain't gonna hunt this man down and hear you say he ought to be strung up on the spot, are we? We're going to execute a lawful arrest warrant, and bring him back here for trial, right?"

"That's all I want—hell, if a jury sets him free because they don't believe my testimony, well, that's on them, not me."

Knop put a lid on it. "Mighty fine, men. Let's get the papers ready for the judge. If he signs the warrant, we can head out first light, day after tomorrow."

CHAPTER 34

Mendoza Mendoza–
M/ On a Pine Coffin

THE *M/* BURNT DEEP INTO Chuches's pine coffin was cold now, but the smell of it lingered in the back of the buckboard, as the twelve men walked alongside. Two old women and a small child followed us up to the small cemetery on top of the small hill behind the cook shack. I could see those five gravestones that were my family. And, also, the new hole for Chuches, my cousin.

I told Ignacio to fix the front seat so his brother could drive, and every man on the ranch to wipe the dust off their boots. When we got to the top, the men lifted the coffin down from the wagon and lowered it down into the grave. Then they stood, with bare heads, waiting for me to say the words.

"This man, Chuches, a loyal man to the *M/*, has been working this ranch, as his father did before him for I don't know how many years. A bastard with a badge spilled his blood. So, we're burying him. We will avenge him."

I waited for one of the men to speak, but they just kept looking at the box and the dirt.

"There's no padre here to give him blessings or comfort. Don't matter. He will see us, all of us, spill the blood of Angus. He shot Onchero, took Ignacio's gun from him, and killed this man. He's gonna die for all those things. *Que su alma descanse con Dios,* and may God help us kill the man named Angus."

As we walked back down to the house, Ignacio asked me, "Papa, do you want me to go to Espanola and see who knows where this Angus is?"

"You are still playing the fool, Ignacio. Don't you know where he is? What's the matter with you?"

We stopped at the bunk house, and the men were anxious to go inside, out of the cold.

"I don't know, PaPa, maybe he's in Chama by now. How can we kill him if we don't know where he is?"

"I will tell you where he is. He's riding from somewhere I don't know, but he's coming here! That's where he is! This man wears a badge, and he will come with lots of men with badges. Maybe from Santa Fe, maybe from somewhere else, I don't know. But, he knows one thing about me, Ignacio, my son. What is that one thing that this man knows about me?"

Ignacio stood without talking. No one else did, either. So I told them.

"He knows that if he does not come here in force, with many guns, I will hunt him down. Maybe in the summer. Maybe in a year. But, he knows I will kill him someday, if he don't kill me first. He has spilled Mendoza blood two times. We will spill his tomorrow, when he comes. I'm telling you, he'll come!"

"Maybe we should ride tonight and catch him with the other gringos, when they come to our gate," said Leopoldo, my foreman, the oldest man on the ranch, who had a big scar on his nose.

"No, Leopoldo, we will not charge them like soldiers. We will draw them to us, like our ancestors, the Yaquis. We will be out of here before dawn and leave an easy trail. All of you, listen to me now. He is coming here, but we won't be here so easy for him to find. We are going to set a trap for the gringo and whoever he brings with him."

"A trap, El Patron," Leopoldo said to me. "I'm not sure what you mean. Why don't we just meet them at the gate with all our guns. With you, Ignacio, Onchero, and Bonafacio, we have the number of twelve men with guns—seven vaqueros and me. You could jus' put us around the ranch like to watch for the gringo and whoever he has with him. Do you mean we are going to trap him here? "Leopoldo asked.

"No, I don't mean that. At dawn, all of us will ride out from the barns—twelve men together. Then, when we get a mile away, we will divide ourselves. I will take my sons, and Chuches's nephew, Bonafacio, with me. We will ride up the *Caja del Rio*, north and to the west. You will take all the vaqueros and ride the other way, southeast to the Rio Grande."

Ignacio spoke up. "But, PaPa, I don' know why we are going one way and the vaqueros the other?"

"Because, *mi hijo*, that's the trap. When the gringo gets here to the ranch, no one will be here. But, they will see all the tracks from twelve horses going away from the ranch for two miles. They will follow the tracks. But, then they will see that four of us went northeast up the *Caja del Rio,* and the rest went down the other way toward the Rio Grande. Do you know what they will think?"

"No, PaPa."

"They will think that I am running away from them, probably with my sons. They will think the vaqueros are going somewhere else, maybe to Espanola. But, they will follow us, not the vaqueros. I'm sure of that. Then the vaqueros will spin around and get behind the gringo and his men. So, we will lead the gringo to the trap, and the vaqueros will be behind the gringo so he don' get away from us up there."

"Watch you mean, up there?" Onchero asked.

"I mean up there where we will kill the gringo and his men. Now go inside. Clean your guns. Pick your best horses, ones with lots of hair.

"Tomorrow morning we ride. We ride to Valles Caldera! Vamanose!"

CHAPTER 35

Angus–The Posse Rides at Dawn

"JILL," I SAID, TRYING TO figure a way to tell her the Sheriff's decision, "the posse will be formed up at dawn. Sheriff Romulo Chavez will lead out, but I got to tell you something…"

"I already know," she said, waving off the reluctance on my face. "I'm to stay here. Of course, they won't let me go. A woman in a posse? The sky would fall down. Don't fret about it. I'll be here when you come back, with Mendoza Mendoza tied to his saddle, upright, or laid out across the horn. I'd prefer the latter."

We talked about it a good bit while she showed me the kit she'd laid out. She'd dug into my saddle bags and bed roll, and fished out double socks, long johns, my riveted Levi's (nearly new and store-bought), two shirts, my heavy vest, and a pair of gloves I'd never seen before. My sheepskin barn coat and oiled duster were hanging on the wall hook by the front door. My wool neck scarf was there, too.

"Those ain't my gloves."

"No, they were my father's. Pull 'em on, see if they fit."

The dark, blood-red gloves were of a kind I'd never seen before. The leather was stitched double, and the cuffs came up high over the wrists. Inside, there was a layer of what felt like silk lining, and the first finger was split, with the leather on the palm side of the glove tucked back inside. I pulled them on and realized I could free up my first finger with the gloves on.

"That's a trigger-finger glove. Been popular with deer hunters back in Missouri for years. I never saw a pair anywhere out here. I've been carrying them with me in the winter, ever since my father died. Take them, they will keep out ice and let you finger a trigger if it comes to that."

"I'll need them for sure. The ride from Fort Marcy to Mendoza's ranch is a good twenty-five miles, and it turns out there's a fairly good road from the fort up toward the *M/*. From there, the road narrows to a decent trail maneuvering up a steep canyon called *Cañon de Valles*. They say that's a passage up to the crest of the rim—the *Valles Caldera*. It ain't used much, and the last ten miles is purtin' near straight up, least that's what the sheriff said."

"Well, that's interesting," she said with a quizzical look on her face. "Why is there a road at all? There is no stage that direction, and except for sheep or cattle ranches, very few people live up there, right? And, I think someone once told me that no one lives on the Baca Ranch on top of the Valles Caldera."

"Well, there was a lot of talk about that in the sheriff's meeting. As I understand it, the caldera is a giant, open pasture created when the mountain top blew off in some other century. When it cooled down, the trees were gone, but the volcanic ash was perfect for growing tall grass. So, after the Civil War, when Fort Marcy was established, the Army used mule teams and soldiers to build a thirty-five-mile road for the teams to haul down fresh cut hay in the summer for horse feed. Turned out to be a good business for years. Anyways, the road is still used by the Mexican sheep ranchers that take their herds up to graze when the snow melts in spring. They called it the *Baca* Location. Guess location means a sheep ranch. Ain't no cows up there."

"But, it ain't spring yet," she said. "Is it passable now?"

"Don't matter. It's passable at least as far as the *M/*. We know that because the *vaqueros* ride back and forth from the ranch to Espanola, and to Santa Fe, too. Don't expect we'll have to chase them off their own ranch. Besides, we only want one man, *El Patron* Mendoza."

"Well, if what they say about him is true, you will have to fight his *vaqueros* to get him."

"Whatever it comes to, we'll be ready," I said.

An hour before dawn, I gathered up my kit, and snugged it all down inside my saddle bags and bed roll. Then I stuck the Winchester under my arm, holstered the Buntline Colt, and walked down to the livery. Two men were in the lobby and took up with me. Two more joined us across the plaza. By the time we reached the barn, there were five of us. Marshal Knop and Sheriff Chavez were already there, brushing their horses and tying down long guns in saddle scabbards, bed rolls, saddle bags, and extra tack. Nobody talked much. I got the feeling this was not the first posse for any of these men, but they fingered their badges like they were unfamiliar with the fit.

One man, a lanky bag of bones mounting a short-legged Morgan horse, plain out asked the sheriff, "Sheriff Chavez, do we have to wear these badges here in town, too?"

"Like I told you last night when everyone was deputized, this is not a pleasure trip. Wear the badge. We've got some unpleasant business to attend to."

Seven men in a posse riding north on the stage road just ain't all that quiet. We rode from the Plaza to Fort Marcy. Every man was riding a fit horse, and carried enough guns and ammo to get the job done. The cold mountain air made all the horses snort some. Saddle bags, rifle scabbards, water bags, and bedrolls tied down, and the loose shale under the horses hooves made a racket you could hear a hundred feet away.

Marshal Knop and I took the lead, riding side by side. The rest of the men spread out some, while Sheriff Chavez trailed, riding drag. We headed north by west, then turned off the stage road twenty minutes out of town. We headed up on the old fort road that sheepherders used fifty years ago. Sheriff Chavez rode up alongside Knop at a brisk trot on a long-legged sorrel with the big, white blaze on his head.

"Knop, you ever been up into the White Rock country?"

"Well, last summer we fished a stream up there. Hunted antelope two years ago. But, I've never had any business to attend to up there."

"How about you, Angus? I know your usual riding grounds are up north, Chama, Tierra Amarilla, and thereabouts. You seen the high ground up in the Jemez and the Valles Caldera?"

"No, sir, this'll be my first ride. Looks like a bit of a climb from here. What's the elevation top out at?"

"I'm told that Redondo Peak, that's the one on your left, is well over eleven thousand feet. Snowcapped until early summer every year. Where we just crossed the Rio Grande back about five miles, it's about five thousand feet. So, we got us a steady climb. Mendoza's home ranch is probably at sixty-five hundred, could be seven thousand. Can't say for sure. Only been by there once, on the trail of two men who'd robbed the stage down by Algodones, and lit out for the Jemez with a sack they thought was full of gold. Turns out it was a quarter-full. The rest was a supply of copper and nickel blanks headed for the mint up in Denver."

"How far you reckon before we come to the Mendoza ranch?" I asked from behind Chavez.

He slowed down the big sorrel's long trot just a tug. "Can't say for sure, we could be on the eastern edge of it in two hours. As I remember, there's a kind of territorial gate, with a branded cross beam maybe twelve, fifteen miles from the river. We'll be there midmorning. Then the ranch buildings are another hour from there. It'll be noon or later."

From listening to others in the posse, I learned we were headed to some high country that differed from anything else in the whole Territory of New Mexico. We'd cross a fifty-mile square area of ground they called Bandelier tuff, which was some kind of volcanic ash. And, there were well preserved cliff dwellings up there, too. Story was that ancestral Pueblo Indians lived there centuries before the Spanish came here about three hundred years ago.

The long, slow climb took all the sass out of the horses by midmorning. When we reached that gate, with no fence on either side, it looked like a monument. Adobe and stone work formed a foundation for two large logs propped upright by boulders, likely dug down into the earth. They were clean-scraped fir trees, cut more than fifty years ago. They'd spaced them twenty feet apart. Across the top was a crossbeam cut square with what looked to be a good-sized hand adze; the end cut marks were a good foot long. Two big, iron straps on each log had been placed to tie down the cross-beam. The straps were branded with the *M/*. A rusted, but still intact branding iron, hand-forged with the *M/* on the business end, was spiked onto the crossbeam with several bent-over, ten-penny nails.

The lanky cowboy, recently deputized, stared at it some and said, "Eye God, boys, I do believe we've come on land claimed by a proud man. He's giving us notice with this gate to nowhere that we're trespassing. I mean, this ain't just to welcome us, is it?"

Chavez had dismounted and cinched up his horse. Looking to the north and talking at us over his shoulder, he said, "Mendoza Mendoza is a man who recognizes the law in town, but believes he's the law on his own land. Perfecto Armijo-he's a cousin of Mendoza's, but of some distance—tole me once that the old bastard rarely comes to town, and prefers that the town never comes to him. We'd be told to git off his land, even if we weren't here with an arrest warrant. He don't take social calls; I expect him to be armed and ready. From here on up to his home ranch, keep a sharp eye. You might want to unsheathe your rifles."

It took most of two hours, but as we climbed up and over a rise, and around some rocky cliffs, we finally got our first look at the home ranch. Five, maybe six adobe buildings, a sizeable barn, half-a-dozen connected corrals and chutes, a smithy covering with a big anvil and stove, all just scattered around like they'd come together accidentally over the last fifty or a hundred years. A fresh water-well with a big, iron pulley and rope arrangement sat alongside what looked to be a cook house. Two or three privies stuck out in bushy areas. No smoke from the chimneys, except one, and no sign of men. There were burros, mules, and a half-dozen goats in the corral furthest away from the main house. There were maybe forty sheep penned, but everything looked quiet—an unnatural kind of quiet.

Sheriff Chavez held up his arm and circled his hand, motioning us to gather to him. We sat our horses, a quarter mile away, while he studied the ground and buildings. After a few minutes, he said, "Only smoke from one building, no visible horses or ranching activity, and a deserted sort of feel, that's my take on this. Either we're too late, or we're looking at an ambush. Knop, Angus, either of you got another idea?"

It didn't seem my place to talk, and no one else seemed of a mind, either.

Sheriff Chavez looked to a man two horses over from me.

"Odega, you probably got the most friendly look about you; why don't you ride half-way down the hill to that little stand of piñon and juniper over there? Then, stand your horse for a few minutes and holler something out. Make it Spanish and see if you get any attention. We'll cover you from here. The rest of you men, put some distance between you. And, don't draw any weapons unless something hostile happens to Odega."

Odega put his knees to the black stud, urging him downslope. He stepped out careful-like for about two hundred yards, leaving another two hundred between him and the buildings. From there he hollered, *"Buenos días! Yo estoy con Sheriff Chavez!"*

No response. Odega sat his horse like a stone on a boulder. Some time passed. Then, an old woman opened the door of the small building with a little smoke coming out of the chimney. She raised a hand to shade her eyes from the sun. He nudged his horse down to her. Dismounting and removing his hat, he looked to be talking to her. Couldn't make out the words from where I was, but whatever they were saying, it was taking some time. Odega walked back up the rise to his horse, fished something out of his saddle bag, and walked back to the old woman. He handed it to her, then snugged his hat down. Once there he jumped his stirrup, swung his leg over, and loped back up to where we waited.

"What'd you give her?" Chavez asked.

"Some chocolate. All old Mexican grandmothers love chocolate. She is the *abuela* to Ignacio and Onchero, and says she loves them. Don't think she approves of her own son. Even so, she's protecting all of them. I think she knew we were coming. The men rode out this morning, before she even stoked the cook fire. There's two other women, a baby, two kids barely walking, and a girl going on eleven. She told me all their names and ages."

"Well, nobody said Mendoza was a fool, he must've figured the law would be of a mind to look into the attack by Chuches," Knop said.

"Did she say how many men rode out?" I asked.

"I asked her that. She said her son, two grandsons, and two *vaqueros*."

"That'd be five of them, that's what you figure?"

"*Sí*, if she's telling the truth."

I turned to Sheriff Chavez and suggested we ride on down there and have a look-see in the barn and the bunkhouse. He pointed at two of his men.

"You boys go on down with Angus. One of you goes in the barn with him, the other stays mounted, gun cocked. Ready? We'll move down to good rifle range, but stay mounted from there."

I checked the barn first. Five indoor stalls, all with fresh horse droppings. The corral outside also showed fresh droppings and evidence of morning hay, mostly gone, but some still in the bins tacked to the barn wall. The *vaquero's* saddle rack inside was built to hold ten saddles, with blankets and hooks for bridles, ropes, breast collars, and such. All were empty, but there were four saddles hanging from hooks on the wall. Spider webs and winter dust on 'em. The bunk house was open, still warm from the embers under the grate, and eight of the ten bunks had blankets all a-strew.

We rode back up the rise, where I reported my thoughts.

"Sheriff, don't mean to call that old lady untruthful, but there's eight empty saddle racks in the barn, and that same number of freshly slept-in bunks, that had somebody in 'em last night. I'd guess Mendoza Mendoza and his boys slept in the main house. Could be we're lookin' at ten, maybe a dozen men that lit out of here a few hours ago."

He pondered less than a minute.

"Boys, let's do a big circle, starting here, completely around these buildings. Whether it's three, or ten, there will be fresh horse tracks made this morning. They will tell us direction and something about numbers. If it's a mob, it'll be easy to track."

Turned out there were two tracks leading out. Four horses, moving fast, based on the long stride between hoof plants. That group went northwest, up toward the Valles Caldera. A separate bunch, five, or maybe six others, walking their horses, looked to be headed mostly east, down toward the Rio Grande.

"Why'd they split up, Angus?" Marshal Knop asked me.

"Can't say with any particularity. Could be Mendoza Mendoza, his boys, and a top gun headed for the protection of the Valles Caldera, with the others headed to Espanola, up river. Seems awful strange."

Odega said, "Maybe, Sheriff, they want us to know they split up. Don't make no sense ."

"Or," I said, "could be that they are a ways off right now, waiting for us to do what they expect, based on seeing two tracks, half of us cinching up for the long pull up to higher ground, and the rest headed to town."

"Which is it?" Odega asked me.

"Mendoza Mendoza is shrewd, according to everything Perfecto Armijo told me. He might figure we'd know it was him headed up to Valles Caldera, and we'd set ourselves on his trail. Then, them other boys could circle back around in a big loop, cut our trail heading north, and ease in behind us. Sort of like a Chinese nut cracker, with Mendoza clamping down on both handles."

"Or," Sheriff Chavez said, "could be the *vaqueros* don't want to be involved with the old man's vendetta with Angus and drew their pay. Don't matter anyhow. We got a warrant to serve. I know one thing for damn sure. The old bastard ain't headed for town to make it easy on us. Tighten your cinches boys, and take a pull on your water bags, we got some hard ridin' to do."

As we spurred our horses from a steady walk into a fast trot, I couldn't help thinking 'bout how nice a ride this would be on my own, with only No Más to talk to.

CHAPTER 36

Mendoza Mendoza Rides to the Valles Caldera

"I AM RESPECTING YOU, IGNACIO, and you, too, Onchero, riding this fast with a gunshot leg."

The four of us, me in the lead, then Ignacio and Onchero, and last in line, Bonafacio, had just crested the southeast rim of Valles Caldera. I pulled back on my caballo, who was wheezing and starting to stumble the last hundred feet to the top. He needed to stop. Me, also. I told them to dismount, and explained this place to them.

"It is over ten thousand feet. Can you breathe good up here?" I asked my sons, not expecting an answer. Both looked pale. Ignacio was licking his lips and banging his gloved hands together. Bonafacio said nothing. Bonafacio never says nothing to me. Only Onchero spoke up.

"*Si*, PaPa," Onchero said, looking at me over the top of a bandana tied around the lower half of his face. "I know now why you never took us up here in winter before. I am very cold."

I ignored his complaints.

"So, Ignacio, can you tell me the name of those rocks there, where the snow has blown off during the night?"

"No, PaPa, but they look burnt."

"*Si*, they are burnt. You're looking at lava rock. All of this, from here down into the caldera, is a bowl left over when the volcano we are on blew up. Nothing survived that blow except burnt rocks. Later, the grass grew out of the rocks and the ashes. You remember, don't you, coming up here with our sheep. A few times. Only when the Baca family invites us to graze our sheep with theirs. You are looking right now at the highest mountain anywhere around here—it is called Redondo Peak. The Indians over there are the Jemez, and down below them are some other pueblo tribes. I don't know their names. But, they think this mountain is a church or something. Their gods are up here. That's what they think. The padre says God is in heaven. So, maybe this is their heaven."

"I hope their gods like ice and snow," Onchero said, shivering even under his heavy, sheepskin coat.

"And, steep canyons, too," said Ignacio.

"You boys are used to the cold and the canyons, but these ones up this high don't have too much air. It makes it colder. And, it's hard to breathe; that's what the padre says. Over there, toward our town of Espanola, is the *Pajarito* Plateau. It keeps the gringos away, I think. But, I'm proud you boys rode up here with me. We will do some revenge tomorrow on a gringo. He's after me, I can feel that even in the cold."

"*Si, gracias,* PaPa," Onchero said, "My leg is better now with the cast off and only these two wood splints left. I can ride with my right leg loose out of the offside *tapaderos.*"

"*Si,* but it will be harder for you going back. You must have your boot deep in the stirrup going down those goat trails we just came up."

Ignacio said he needed to get off for a minute. When he finished, he aimed his left boot into the *tapadero* and swung his right leg effortlessly over the saddle with both feet off the ground at the same time. All the *tapaderos* on our horses had little bits of spiny chaparral, cactus, manzanita, and cat claw from our ranch stuck into them. And, some of ice from the canyon we just climbed. It was a hard ride up.

"Don't forget to clean those spines off when we stop to camp tonight. It will be dark, but don't forget. Once it is dark and the smoke cannot be seen, there will be a fire, but only a small one. We will spread out on the rim before sunrise, and each man will have a clear shot at the gringo and his men as they try to come up that difficult part, right there at the top of the rim. They cannot come fast and will not know we are here. Once the bullets rain down on them, it is hard to even turn around on that skinny trail. You will lie down on the ground in the snow on top of those tarps each of you tied to his saddle. Every man must be listening with both ears open before the sun comes up."

"PaPa," Ignacio asked me, "how will we know that the gringo and his posse are coming? And, how will our *vaqueros* do what you said, 'close the gap' between us?"

"I will know."

In truth, right here, at the rim of the Valles Caldera, there is an echo coming from the trail we just took. If all is quiet, you can hear from maybe two miles away. I sensed they needed to hear me talk. These boys were young, and scared. I wanted to spike their courage, but only with words, not mescal. So, I spoke some serious words to them.

"Because, tonight, once we settle down and hobble the horses down there, maybe a hundred feet away, we can hear whoever is behind us. Even a lone horse can be heard from the top of the rim to maybe a mile down inside. It's nature, *mia hijos.*"

As I was talking to my two sons and Bonafacio, the sun was dropping behind the clouds in the west. The caldera had old snow and ice stuck to the rocks around the rim. But, down a mile to the bottom of the caldera, nothing could be seen but deep snow. The grass in the meadows was not visible. No streams or movement of any kind. I said to the men, "*Vaqueros*, we stop here. Unsaddle your horses, lead them down to those big rocks. Hobble them. Here is my plan. *Atención a mí!* When you get down off your horse, take those gunny sacks I made you bring. They are to tie over your horse tonight. It will get much colder before the sun comes up tomorrow. The men chasing us will track our horses up the trail. But, we will wipe the area clean with brush and some gunny sacks. When our tracks cannot be seen, here where we dismount, the gringo and his men will get off their horses to examine the ground carefully. Then, we shoot them. From four different places around here. We cannot be in a bunch because they might see us that way. And, also, if we are spread out in four differ-ent places, they won't see us. We can see them because they will all be in this little meadow. Shoot fast and don't stop till they are all dead."

The boys said nothing. Bonafacio, who was Chuches's nephew and just seventeen, was jus' looking scared, like he didn't want to be with us any longer. He looked at Onchero. Those two grew up together, swimming in the stock ponds in the summer, and always goofing around pulling pranks. Bonafacio could get away those things because Onchero could not be hit by the *vaqueros*. So, here tonight, he looked to Onchero for protection. From me and from what I was telling him to do: Kill all the gringos coming here tomorrow.

"Bonafacio, don't be scared. These are the men who killed Chuches. Are you ready to avenge your uncle? Or, are you going to piss your pants like a little boy? I put you with us, not the *vaqueros* following behind, for a reason. Do you know the reason?"

"No, *El Patron*."

"It is because I want you to see me shoot the *hijo de puta* that killed Chuches. That will be your signal. Then you, Ignacio, and Onchero will empty your guns into whoever is coming with him, the *hijo de puta*. You do not know him, only his name—the gringo. But, you can put some of your bullets into him after we kill them all. That is why you are here."

Ignacio slapped his hand down on his chaps, spooking his horse. The other horses just stood, hardly moving. He said, "*Si*, PaPa, now I see your plan. The *vaqueros* will be following behind the gringo. When we fire on the gringo, we might miss him, or some of the men with him. But, Leopoldo, and the vaqueros riding with him, which are now riding behind the gringo, will hear our bullets, and come to us on the run. The gringos will be caught in the middle, with all our guns shooting them. Aiee, we will kill them all!"

CHAPTER 37
Angus Sets a Signal Fire

I'LL SAY ONE THING FOR Sheriff Chavez, he knows how to pick a posse and climb a mountain. We'd been in the saddle purtin' near ten hours when Frank took his mare down from a trot to a walk. It'd turned cold, and we'd be out of light within the hour.

"Frank," Knop said, "you ain't getting tired are you? I don't know about the rest of these boys, but I think we oughta just push on till these ponies plain refuse to take another step."

We had nearly topped out on a ridge I'd later find out was just three or four miles from the rim of that old volcano, that's busted itself down into the Valles Caldera. I knew it would be awful peaceful at sunup, but even No Más was twitching and pawing the ground when we slowed down to a stop.

"All right, boys," Chavez said, "don't be listening to a federal law man. They all get funny when you take 'em up this

268

high. Air's too thin for federals. Dismount boys, and let's get a fire and coffee up."

Turns out, Sheriff Chavez decided on two fires. One right there where we stopped, and the other about a hundred yards up the switchback on a splayed, out piece of flat granite. The second one struck me as some crazy. It'd show our location for miles in every direction. *Hell fire, if we're being tracked by vaqueros who live up here, they'd have to be wearing blinders to miss smoke from a fire up here.* Marshal Knop rode up alongside me and presented his notion for the second fire.

"Well, I know it seems a poor idea at first, but look at his way. The sheriff's been worryin' and arguin' with himself all the way up here about the split of Mendoza Mendoza's men back down at the ranch. If you're right and they are now turned around and backtracking us, then we're at risk from up ahead and behind. But, what if you're only half-right?"

"Half-right?"

"Yes. Frank Chavez has been the law around here a long time. He's seen *vaqueros*, both Mexican and Anglo, come to town with a mind to raise hell. The boys riding *M/*-branded stock have always been ones to follow a hard line because that's the way old Mendoza Mendoza is."

"Yeah," I said, "Perfecto Armijo warned me about that. He said the man would rather die than be shamed about something."

"Well, that's likely the case here. That's the part I'll bet you're right about those boys backtracking us. But, Frank Chavez thinks that those boys might welcome the chance to take another fork in what could be a box canyon for them. Know what I mean?"

"No. Can't say that I do."

"Well, what if some of those boys are not fond of being part of what amounts to a family feud with the law? Frank figures that not all those boys ambushers. That second fire up there on the ledge is a sort of signal to them who might be thinking this way."

"Well, all right, then. I can see his motion. This little campfire down here will go out soon, and most of us will crawl into bedrolls. But, that other fire up there can be seen for miles down the mountain side. Someone will have to stay up a while and tend to it."

No sooner had we finished our talk then Sheriff Chavez walked around the coffee fire and made his way over.

"Angus, I have to say you are damn near tireless. I'm guessing you been ridin' these high ridges most of your life."

He had his coffee cupped in both hands, and looked up at the dark sky like it was a welcome sight for tired eyes. I got up, crooked my rifle in my left elbow, and swung my bedroll over the other shoulder.

"Sheriff, if you need someone to sit up awhile and tend to the other fire up there on the ridge, I'm your man."

Come first light, the sheriff and Marshal Knop roused the men. I added a few, green, wet sticks to the upper ridge fire. The white smoke drifted up the cliff, and then meandered slowly off to the north. Smelling coffee coming to a boil, I climbed down to the fir grove where the rest of the men were brushing the horses and sippin' on hot tins of coffee. Biscuits and cold cheese were breakfast.

"Men," Sheriff Chavez said, "it could be that we got riders behind us that aim to do us harm. Or, could be they're just doing the least they can to keep their jobs. So, I've decided to take a page out of that old bastard Mendoza Mendoza's book. We're gonna split this posse in two. I'm going to take Angus, Bo String, and two men on up into the caldera and smoke Mendoza Mendoza out. We figure there's four of 'em up ahead, probably dug in somewhere, rifles at the ready. Marshal Knop is going to form two pockets with three men. That'll work out to two men on either side of this trail, and one man working the head of the trail right about here. We got lots of horse droppings and other signs on the trail, so they will be coming along slow and easy through here. That little smoke fire that Angus tended all night long will have led them right to this spot. Questions?"

"Yeah," said Bo String, as he settled two saddle blankets snug up on his horse's withers," I ain't sure what you mean when you say we're gonna form two pockets here."

The sheriff liked to poke a little fun now and then. "A pocket is something you reach down into and find something you never expected to find. Maybe it's a turd or a lost bullet. I'm thinking those boys behind us will see the green logs smoking for the next couple of hours. So, if they are intent on backing up their boss, they might think… hell, I don't know what they might think. But, if we got two pockets of men on either side, and those boys ride through here, the men in this pocket can jump out and take them into custody. Or, if they are of a hostile mind, and one of 'em reaches for a gun, then you boys let loose on 'em. You will have your boots planted on the ground, looking around trees with rifles at the ready. Mendoza Mendoza's boys will be on horseback with their boots in stirrups. First shot and half those horses will bolt.

Take 'em or let 'em run back down the trail to Espanola. Just don't let 'em head up the trail to our backsides."

Marshal Knop spoke his mind, "Sheriff, you're the trail boss on this, and I'm putting my gun at your disposal. How about I put myself and the rest of the boys in the pocket right here? But, I ain't all that sure I understand how we'll know if they have hostile intentions."

Chavez nodded at Knop, and slowly scanned the face of the other men who'd be in the pocket with him. "A man with a holstered gun always has a choice. Draw or stand down. I believe in giving a man that choice. You holler loud as you can at the lead horse that he's under arrest, and he's not to proceed one more goddamn foot or you'll blow him out of the saddle! Or, such other words as you see fit. But, get your message across before you let any lead fly. The rest of the play is up to you."

Knop loosened the tie-down on his holster. "All right, then. That's it. Sheriff Chavez wants this fence gate tied down. Let's get to it."

"Well, Knop, thanks for the credit, but in truth I'm only doing what Mendoza Mendoza already did. Remember what Angus said? He called the play a Chinese nutcracker, with Mendoza Mendoza clamping down on both handles."

"Sure, but I guess I ain't never seen one of them nutcrackers. Mostly I just use my gun butt."

"Well, there you have it. We just don't know how much sand the men on our trail got in their grit. Some of 'em will be just boys, and one or two might be men with families. And, none of them will likely feel the blood rage that seems to be runnin' old Mendoza Mendoza to the caldera up ahead. Don't matter whether you boys are gun butts or fancy nutcrackers, it's gonna come out the same. If those trailin' us are prepared to let loose their bullets for the brand, then the pockets will hold cover with rifles cocked. If they stand down, then you men relieve them of their guns, hogtie 'em to a tree, and come at a fast trot up the trail behind us. I expect to come face to face with the old bastard when the sun's dead center in the sky. That's in five hours. Sound carries over big distances once you're in the caldera, so you'll hear the commotion."

"All right, makes sense." Knop said, sliding his Winchester out of the saddle scabbard.

No Más was stiff from the long pull yesterday, and from the cold, overnight stand tied to a tree. I rubbed him down with pine needles and a gunny sack, applied Jasper Horse Magic to his legs and hooves. Then I gave him a double sack of grain for breakfast. He took the saddle, headstall, and bit easy and snorted at every horse in the string. The sheriff mounted slow, but swung his leg over with authority. The rest of us followed single-file into place. I decided on the drag spot, thinking I'd best keep a look-see behind us. Besides, no one could see up-trail better than Frank Chavez.

One of the men asked a question, but Chavez hushed him, "Men, we don't need to give Mendoza Mendoza any advance warning we're coming. Up this high, sound carries a long way."

I noted the fact that every man had his rifle out of the scabbard, and had jacked a round into firing position before mounting. If Chavez was right that it'd take all morning to get to wherever Mendoza was holed up, there'd be several stiff elbows by the time anyone pushed rifle to shoulder.

We'd been in the saddle maybe two hours when I heard a tweet sound coming from behind us. It was not a bird. I'd been hearing them all morning, chirping, cawing, and whooshing by overhead. This was a man making a bird sound, poorly. I slid up alongside the deputy in front of me, and whispered that I was going to slip off here, but he was to keep going.

Five minutes passed before I heard the clink of horseshoe on rock, then more than one clink, and finally the telltale sound of saddle tack and horses snorting down-trail, likely not more than a hundred yards from me. I dismounted, left No Más with reins down on the ground, and found myself a little rock crevice where I could see a clear bend in the trail we'd left—forty feet of open view. Cocking the hammer back on the Winchester, I sighted in on what I guessed would be chest-high above the saddle horn of the first one to make the turn.

The breeze picked up some, and a critter crossed the path in front of me. I'd picked a low, dead branch on a big fir for a rifle stand. A gnat was picking at my ear when the big gray horse rounded the turn. Knop was a welcome sight. He kept his eyes peeled some, as anyone would expect of the lead in a posse.

Stepping out onto the trail with my rifle lowered and the cocked hammer let back down to safety, I gave him a wave.

"Angus, you were right," Knop said. "Five *vaqueros* walking their horses with reins held high just rode on into the pocket. I hollered at them to hold up, and they behaved handsomely. Hell of it is the oldest man in the bunch ain't but twenty. They look to be good cowboys, but they ain't gun hands. We collected two saddle bags full of pistols, and we stuck their rifles off up into a rock crevice a hundred yards from where we left 'em roped tight to winter aspen trees. It would embarrass them to hear me say it, but I think they are happy hogtied. Ain't that something?"

I remounted No Más and caught up to Chavez and the rest of the men. Now we were seven men strong again. Knop was sure that hogtieing Mendoza's *vaqueros* would be just fine with them for the rest of the day. Chavez took Knop's report in stride, then he kneed that dapple mare he favored. He began a slow lope up hill, trotting fast through the turns. Soon enough, we caught a glimpse of clear open sky up ahead. That signaled that we were getting close to the rim of the caldera.

CHAPTER 38

Mendoza Mendoza— Ambush in the Valles Caldera

"**P**ATRON," BONAFACIO ASKED me again, "how will we know when the posse is getting close?"

I had been thinking about that all night. So, I was glad Bonafacio was the one to ask. My sons had saddled their horses, and mine, and all of us were ready to ride. As I answered Bonafacio's question, I watched my sons, checking their guns and tightening their cinches.

"We will know, Bonafacio, because you will be the one giving us the signal. I am honoring you with the most important job. Are you ready to avenge your uncle Chuches?"

"*Si, Patron*, I am ready, what do you want me to do?"

"Onchero says you are the best turkey hunter on the ranch. Is he speaking the truth? Are you the most skilled with a shotgun?"

"*Si*, I guess so," he said, but he was not looking at me. He was seeking my son, Onchero, with his eyes opened very wide.

"Well, it is good you are so skilled. Come walk a little with me back on the trail we have left for the posse to follow. Bring your shotgun and your heavy coat. We will take your horse with us when we change our positions."

"But, Señor, I wish to go with you. I do not understand this."

"Just come along, goddamnit, you will see what honor I'm giving you."

My sons walked behind me. I walked with my hand on Bonafacio's elbow about fifty yards back down the little draw. We came to a point where two man-size rocks blocked the trail, which would force a man on a horse coming this way to pay attention, and take his horse off the trail to get around them. When we got there, I told him of his honor.

"Bonafacio, here is where you will lay down. Right there between those two big rocks. We will pull a dead log there so they can't see you. And, you will place your shotgun on top. It will give you a firm rest for both barrels. The honor of the first two shots will go to you. And, when we hear two big blasts from that sixteen gauge, we will know the posse is here."

He was young and wanted no one to see fear on his face. But, now, so quickly, all the color was gone, and he stood wobbling, like he was made of fresh-cut bacon, ready for the frying pan.

"We are going to attack the posse from up there, about fifty yards from here. Me, Ignacio, and Onchero will be covering the posse from both sides of the trail, but in the trees, where they cannot see us. Our horses will be tied way off the trail, down here behind you. We will attack them from the ground, like you. None of us will be mounted for this attack. Do you understand the plan now, Bonafacio? And, you boys also, Ignacio and Onchero. Do you see in your mind what we will do to the gringo?"

"Some of it, patron, but maybe not too clear," stammered Bonafacio.

Ignacio and Onchero were just standing there, letting Bonafacio for once be the one to face me. "Okay, listen to me again. I will be in front of you, back down that trail that the gringo will be riding. We will be maybe fifty or a hundred yards away from you. It will be a trap for the gringo. Can you see that?"

"*Si*, maybe," Bonafacio said to Onchero.

"Don't be looking at Onchero, goddamn you!" I said to Bonafacio. "Pay attention to my plan. Ignacio and Onchero will be up there almost with me, but off the trail, one on each side. All the horses except for mine will be behind you, far enough away so they won't whinny when the gringo and whoever is with him rides down the trail trying to find us. I will be further down the trail in front of you, but behind Onchero and Ignacio. I will be the first to see them walk their horses into our trap."

"So," Ignacio butted in, "you will be the one to shoot the gringo first, *si*, PaPa."

Sucking in a big breath to let them know my seriousness, I answered, "No! I will be behind the gringo, you, the men riding with him, and also Bonafacio. Don't you see this clear in your mind?"

No one said anything.

"You three boys will be like three points on the compass. One in front of the gringo—that is you, Bonafacio. Two others on the sides of the gringo as he rides into death—that is you, Ignacio, and you also, Onchero. I will be at the opposite end of the trap. Behind all of you, including the gringo. You boys with your rifles cocked will be waiting for Bonafacio to let loose both his barrels. Then the fight starts. Can you see how my plan works?" I said to them.

Ignacio, like always, was the one to speak first.

"Well, PaPa," he said, "it is good that we will shoot them when they are caught out in the open in this little plain right here. But, why are we not firing on them together? And, why is Bonafacio shooting them with a shotgun?"

Ignacio asked me the wrong question, because he did not see the plan.

"Who said Bonafacio was going to shoot the men with his shotgun? That's not why he is going to be here, lying low behind a log in the grass with a gun made for killing birds, not men."

I let my words out slowly, and waited to see if either of my sons would grasp the plan. They did not.

"Bonafacio, you will *not* shoot the man. You will shoot the *horse!*"

All of them opened their mouths at once, but no words came out. The air was cold and still. From somewhere, a tree limb cracked and the wind rustled an old acorn bush alongside the trail. Still, my sons and Chuches' nephew said nothing. Even with clear words from me, they did not see.

"Aiee, are you all *estúpido?* Here is what will happen. The posse has to come down single file through that little draw just down there. They will be coming slow, listening for sounds, afraid of an ambush. But, after you shoot both barrels, then they will hear the screaming of their horses, and the clanging of horseshoes on rock as they try to escape. Bonafacio, you must be patient and let the first horse get very close. Shoot at the first horse's legs. When that horse goes down, shoot the next one in line. The rest of the men will spin their horses and try to ride back down the trail, where we will be waiting."

Bonafacio, his voice like a girl's asked, "Are you sure, *Patron*? I dunno I can shoot a horse."

"Watch you mean, you can't shoot a horse? You are ready to shoot a man, the one who killed Chuches, but you can't shoot his horse? Goddamn you, Bonafacio, you are under my house and my command. Just do as I say, or I will shoot you myself, right now, before you bring any more shame to the memory of your uncle Chuches! I brought you here to do this thing, for him and for me. Are you refusing your *Patron*?"

Ignacio tried to speak for Bonafacio. "No, PaPa, I know Bonafacio and he is good, just unsure and maybe a little scared he will die, too, just like his uncle did. He will do as you say, but maybe you should let me do it. I can shoot a horse, and still shoot the man who falls off the horse. And, maybe…"

"Ignacio, *mia hijo,* you are a man, and maybe Bonafacio, he's still a boy. But, he can do this. I need you back down the trail, with your fast guns and your nerve like iron. You will be in charge of the middle with Onchero because those horses will spin and try to escape. That's all a horse can do when he's attacked. It don't matter whether it's a lion or a shotgun. The horse, he always runs away. To you. To Onchero. And, to me, blocking the escape. Don't you worry about Bonafacio. And, to you, Bonafacio, I ask again: Are you ready to defend your uncle's honor, and do this small thing for me—just to shoot a horse?"

"*Si, Patron.*"

"Bueno, *mia joven amigo,* you are young, but strong of heart. When you shoot the horse, immediately drop and grab this rifle. Here, I brought this extra one for you. It has six rounds in the chamber. I already jacked the first one in for you. Shoot at the men as they try to control their horses escaping the death trap. Don't worry, they won't be back. We will kill them all when they come to our guns, waiting for them. You will hear our guns. Just stay here in case one of them runs away from us back up to here. Shoot anyone who comes up, but do not shoot your cousins or me. *Que no?*

"The gringo posse will feel the rain of bullets from both ends of this trap. You can watch what I do with the gringo's head, with my machete! Then, we ride home, to the *M!.*"

CHAPTER 39
Angus—A One Horse Charge

I CAUGHT UP WITH SHERIFF CHAVEZ and the rest of the posse an hour later. They were just about up to the lip of the mountain. He'd told us while we were making that last long pull up the mountain that the Valles Caldera was visible from the top of the ridge. I'd ridden the tops of a thousand mountains, but the sheer power of this one took my breath away. No Más took the occasion to shake a little, and blow the ice off his chin chain. I gave him a comforting pat on the neck with my gloved hand. "No Más, we got us a new mountain to ride when this posse work is done."

The sky had opened up for us, with long plumes of gray clouds, streaked with a white so bright it hurt my eyes. Down the mountain side, it'd been clear that winter hadn't yet relinquished its hold on the landscape. But, up here, at winter's hem, a transformation was just peeking up through the snow. We were looking at the south side of the caldera, where the sun spent most of the day. The wind had blown all the snow off the tops of the trees, making a dozen shades of green sparkle in the morning sun. Rocks, blacker than the inside of a deep cave, took on the appearance of moving with the wind, which had picked up some.

The men had dismounted, giving their horses a blow, and everyone took a slug from leather or canvas water bags—one man had a tin canteen stamped "US Army." The two youngest posse men had been up here before, but this was the first peek for the rest of us. Chavez had hunted up here, and gave us a horseman's perspective.

"Once we top out, maybe two miles from here, you'll see a grassy meadow probably nine miles in diameter. They say the whole caldera, if you rode around it from rim to rim, would be about fifteen miles. The green atop the trees here, the little trees on the south side where we are, well, you won't see anything that shade of green anywhere else in the whole damn territory. On the far side, that's the warm side—the winter sun sits on all day. The mountain you see there is Redondo Peak. We won't get that far. Old Mendoza Mendoza knows the ground up here as well as anyone. It's not part of his holdings, but it's good hunting ground for everyone within forty miles."

Knop asked, "What caused the meadow to be that even, like a saucer? I heard a man say once that it looked like a star crashed down and dug a perfectly round hole."

"No," Chavez pointed out, "it was the mirror opposite. What you're going to see, when these horses get a few more minutes' rest, is a giant hole dug a half-mile deep into the crust of God's earth. Could have happened a thousand years ago;

I don't know. The preachers disagree, but the geologists say its millions of years. But, it was the biggest damn blow in the New Mexico territory, long before it even had a name. They call it the *El Cajete* eruption, and they named the crater after it."

"Questions, boys?" the sheriff asked. The youngest man, with peach fuzz on his upper lip, asked, "What happened to the top of the mountain when she blew?"

"Well, you'll recall us riding up through black volcanic rock and sizeable layers of pumice all over through the Jemez Mountains. There's your answer. It spewed all that down the slopes for fifty to a hundred miles or more. And, it created that huge rock formation over that way, too. It's called 'Battleship Rock.' I hope we don't have to battle Mendoza Mendoza, but if we do, well, we're in a place aptly named."

Once the horses were rested, we formed up again, and headed up the trail, following the sign made by Mendoza's men yesterday. There was some snow, but most of it had blowed off this rocky trail. There was a quiet to the trail I had not noticed earlier. The ground here was softer, not as rocky, with bits of grass trying to push through the frozen ground.

"Angus," Knop asked as he tugged on his reins and let me walk up beside him on a wider part of the trail, "what's your sense of this? I mean do you figure the man for facing us head-on in a running gun battle, or will we find him more or less dug in?"

No Más had his head up and his ears turned out. We'd been riding single file and a little spread out because of constant turns in the trail. What had been a mountain goat path was starting to take on an overgrown tangle that made me glad I was wearing chaps.

"Marshal, I can't say. Odds are against a running battle from horseback. The old bastard's reputation don't fit that. So, I'm guessing he'll be dug in, but on higher ground than this. The sheriff thinks we got less than a mile to go before we reach that *El Cajate* crater. I think I saw the actual rim once or twice up ahead through breaks in the tree line. It looked to me to have hard rock cover and a little pull up to the lip."

That's the last talking we did. He'd loped around the two men in front of me and moved up to the third slot in line. I was riding drag again, about fifty feet back.

Boom! Boom! The unmistakable thunder of a shotgun, and then the wail of rifle fire from up ahead. We were in tall trees here, with considerable underbrush. I could see maybe forty feet in front of me, but the riders further up must have seen more because one spurred his horse forward and the other spun his black mare back toward me, reaching for his rifle scabbard.

Crack! The sound of rifle fire from our right, up above me, but close. The shotgun went quiet, but the high ping and clink of rifle fire came from everywhere. I heard what I thought was a horse hitting hard earth. The shooters kept firing. I could hear horses crashing down, men cussing, and return fire flaring up. Sliding my left hand down the reins, I tightened up on No Más, and drew the Buntline.

Spurring him forward, we galloped through two turns in the trail, and came to an awful sight. One horse down, and three in full panic headed my way. Two men face down, just off the trail; neither one moving, but two others were still horseback, hanging on with bellies down over their saddle horns, heading downhill toward me. Both men were firing their rifles one-handed at trees and rocks on both sides of the narrow trail. I couldn't see what they were shooting at, but one had blood on his leg. So, I knew Mendoza's shooters were probably dismounted and firing from hidey holes. I turned No Más into the trees and spurred him from both sides crashing into the brush. I could still hear gunfire up and to my right. I emptied five .44-40 rounds in the general direction I was headed. I had not expected to hit anything, but as I let the last round go, I heard a man scream.

"I'm hit! Ignacio, I'm hit!"

Five seconds later, I jumped No Más over a fallen log and down into a little, frozen mud bog. There was Onchero, the shorter brother. His hat was gone, there was blood on his shoulder, and he'd lost his rifle down in the dirt. Blood was oozing from what looked to be a hole in his cheek. I was fifteen feet from him when he pulled his pistol and leveled it at me. But, before he could cock the hammer, No Más was on him. Full body-to-body crash. No Más won.

The man went down, and No Más jumped over him as I was yanking on the left rein to spin him back around. I had a hard pull getting him to settle, but I managed to jump off him as he slid to a stop ten feet on the other side of Onchero.

My rifle was still scabbarded, but I had the empty Colt in my right hand. Onchero was on the ground, but more or less sitting up as he strained to notch back on the hammer of his pistol with his left palm. I got to him in time, and crashed the Buntline's long barrel down on his head. As head blood spewed up at me, he bowled over like a pole-axed cow. His eyes were near closed, his nose had red blood squiggles, and his mouth twisted to one side.

"Where's Mendoza Mendoza?" I yelled at him. The last thing he did was point to the back trail, behind me. Then his head flopped back flat on a rock and he quit moving.

I reloaded the pistol with five new slugs from my vest, jumped on No Más, and gathered up his reins. The gunfire was fierce for another two, maybe three minutes, then a quiet came on, like a blanket thrown over a billowing fire. As I loped No Más back down the trail, I could see four posse men down. Dead or wounded, I could not tell which, yet. Frank Chavez was sitting up against a fir tree, bloody, but holding his grit, with wide-open eyes. Knop took one in the foot and another along his rib cage. Two other men were peppered with buck shot, and one broke his hand when it snagged under his saddle as his horse went town. Only one horse was badly hurt, but could be walked back down the mountain.

The shotgun boy behind the log was never gonna shoot another turkey. His body was riddled with entry and exit wounds. Ignacio, the other brother, was last seen afoot, headed north to the other side of the caldera.

I rode up to the sheriff, dismounted, and knelt beside him.

"What happened, Frank? I heard a shotgun, then rifle fire."

"Damned if I really know. That boy over there behind the log, he just jumped up thirty feet in front of me and fired his shotgun straight up in the air. Spooked every horse, including mine. Mine went down on his knees trying to get past the boy, but we opened up on him with rifle fire. And, one of the horses stomped him when he tried to jump over him and that damn log he was hiding behind. I don't know what he was doing. He could have killed both of us had he let go with the shotgun.

But he acted like he was trying to scare us, or maybe he was scared himself. Never know now."

"Did you see Mendoza Mendoza?"

"No, Angus. The shotgun scared the first horse in line, but that's all the little bastard got. I think Knop got hit from the other side, over there. They had rifle fire from up above the trail."

"Onchero was the one uphill. I silenced him."

From ten feet away, Knop said, "The one with the big beard, Ignacio, took off on horseback up the trail toward the caldera. Whoever can should take after him."

As we gathered up and took account, we had two men with bullet wounds and two with buckshot, which was painful, but not fatal. Two others took some bruises as their horses bucked when the kid fired straight up in the air. Then they went plumb crazy when the rifle fire came down as they were trying to back out of the ambush. But, they were unhurt.

"That leaves Mendoza Mendoza unaccounted for," Chavez said.

I had an answer for that.

"Onchero told me, just before he died, that his father was back behind us. Cagey old bastard. He might have figured that one or two of us might survive the ambush, and would likely head back down the same trail. He's back there, probably in a hidey hole."

"Well, wait up for me, and we'll go dig him out."

"No, he ain't your problem now, Sheriff. He's mine."

Sheriff Chavez gave me a nod with the front of his hat. Knop holstered his pistol, and went about digging into his saddle bag for something. They said nothing to me as I tightened up No Más's cinch, added a sixth .44-40 to the Colt's chamber, and jacked a fresh round into the Winchester. I untied my bedroll and both saddle bags, then dumped my kit on the side of the trail.

"He'll be waiting for you, Angus. He's shown some talent for ambushing. Don't go at him head on."

"Good advice, Sheriff Chavez, but my aim is to rattle him. If I can get him to rush things, he might make a mistake. In any case, I intend to put him down, or gather him up, which-ever way he wants it."

With that, I remounted, tied a square knot in No Más's reins, and laid it on his neck about a foot below the back of his head. Then, with my left hand, I cocked the Buntline Colt, full back, and took the Winchester in my right, cocked. I kneed No Más around back up the trail without reining him, gave him a sharp jab with both spurs, and in a few seconds he had jumped forward to a steady lope. Laying my gut down low over the saddle, I talked to my horse, "Git, son. Git!"

He could feel me down over his neck, guiding him with my knees, and getting into the rhythm of his long stride. We covered a quarter mile as loud as we could, me hollering *HeeHaw* and No Más's big, iron hooves pounding the trail. Maybe, I thought, Mendoza Mendoza might mistake my one-horse charge for a run at him by the whole posse. That's apparently what he thought, because as we rounded a tight turn in the trail, I saw him astride that big dapple stallion, spinning him around to the south, and spewing loose rocks back at me. I knew I could not hit him with both of us moving fast downhill, but I fired a shot at the back of him, anyhow. It missed, but the sound must have been enough, because I could just see him sticking his rifle back into its saddle scabbard. He spurred down the trail like a man gone crazy.

The distance between us widened some because he was on softer ground, facing a wider trail with no short curves in sight. The sound of that big horse of his pounding the ground grew faint. I pulled No Más up, and let him blow. As we sat gathering ourselves, I lost the sound of a running horse. Then, the quiet of the Valles Caldera returned. As I topped a little rise, I saw something I'd missed on the ride up here. There was a small creek, frozen over with ice now, but angling off on the north side of this mountain goat trail and running parallel to it. It was craggy and thick with overgrown brush on the sides, but the ice channel down the middle was wide enough for a horse and downslope on an easy angle. It looked to be a shorter ride down to a flat place maybe a half-mile down from me. Seemed worth the chance; it would get me off the trail facing a back shooter in front of me.

No Mas's ability to break trail came to life as he navigated us down the little ice channel. The ice broke free, the rocks gave way, and he never missed a step. Fifteen minutes later, we came on a flat place where the downslope view was clear. I could see the original trail about a hundred yards away, snaking back down to the canyon country below us. And, there the old bastard was. He'd tied his horse to a broken branch on a tall ponderosa pine, and laid his fat body down on a ledge looking back up the trail. He had a long-barreled rifle out in front of him, and was eyeballing the ground in front of him like an elk hunter who'd just spied a bull headed his direction. He was looking for me, assuming I'd still be on his back trail, instead of forty yards behind him.

I tied up No Más. Deciding not to take the Winchester, I drew the long-barreled .44-40 Colt and hunkered over, stepping slow and quiet, rock to rock, down the hill behind him. I got about a hundred feet away from him when I remembered Jill's shooting lesson. I dropped flat to the ground, planted both elbows in the dirt, and wrapped my left hand on top of my right on the gun butt. I fingered the trigger through Jill's dad's shooting glove and settled in. So had he. Only difference was I knew where he was; he'd not yet spotted me. I give him time to make a move. He was patient; I'll say that for him. He stayed still a good five minutes. Then, letting the rifle stock settle into the rocks, he got up, first onto his hands and knees. He was showing his age and bulk because he could not jump up with the rifle at the ready. He got up into a crouch from the bent-over position, still focused on what he could see up the trail in front of him. He reached for a water jug beside him. As he pulled the cork and began a pull, I yelled at him.

"Get up, Mendoza, you're under arrest!"

Sound is clear up this high, but direction is always hard to place. And, he was in a crouch. He dropped the water bag, cupped his left hand to an ear, and leaned forward. I made no sound, but he must have sensed I was to his left. I wasn't. Focusing that direction, he picked up the long rifle again, listening hard, trying to get a front-sight fix on me. Then, not seeing anything, he began a slow swing back to the right. In my direction.

I fired. My first shot missed, clanging off a rock two feet beside him. I thumbed the hammer back, feeling the cylinder turn and lock into position. Then, adjusting the rear sight an eye-wink to my left, I squeezed off another .44-40 slug his way. As the muzzle blast screamed back at my face, the slug tore straight through the left side of his pelvis. 'Course I didn't know that at the time because I was more or less on automatic, pulling the hammer back, breathing out slowly through my lips, cocking the third round, not breathing out, and squeezing easy down on the trigger. The third round blew open the right side of his chest, a few inches below his clavicle. He looked surprised, shuddered some, and died before I made the hundred-foot climb down to him.

CHAPTER 40

Angus–Holding on Tight and Leaning Back

JILL AND I MARRIED in the spring, and I became Chama's new undersheriff. The marriage took, but the job didn't. That was okay with Jill. She knew before I did. A full-time town job would have stifled near everything important to me. But, our marriage holds on tight to both of us. Looking after a whole town is a different ride, best done by a man who likes living in town.

The town council found another man more suited to a full-time badge, and one who didn't mind sitting behind an oak desk. Turns out Bo String was tired of cowboying, and fond of keeping the peace in small towns. Chama took advantage. They gave up having an undersheriff beholden to another man down in Tierra Amarilla. Bo String got the full title—Town Marshal, Chama, New Mexico.

The Mendoza clan turned out to be better than most thought they would. Ignacio spent a year in jail before the judge felt sorry for him—said he had not killed anyone—and let him out. He took over the Mendoza Hacienda, buried his father's machismo in the grave with him, and—so they say—has become a solid citizen. They dug two more holes in that little cemetery; one for El Patron and one for Onchero. Don't know what they did with Bonafacio's body; someone said it wasn't up there in that little cemetery. The *M/* brand is still in use, but Frank Chavez suggested they ought not to brand everything in sight with it anymore. The *vaqueros* that we hogtied to a tree just shy of the Valles Caldera rim went back to cowboying. One of 'em, the youngest at sixteen, became New Mexico's first rodeo star. They say he hangs onto a bucking horse like his britches was glued down right out of the chute.

Milton J. Yarberry gets more attention now than he did when he was alive. Back-east newspapers picked up the tale about burying him in a pine box with the hanging rope still noosed up over his Adam's apple. They say it was a lesson to law breakers all over the territory. Others still say he must have shot those fellows in self-defense, and that he was a lawman deep down inside.

There remains considerable skepticism about New Mexico's chances of becoming a state anytime soon. It's anchored to Arizona, and some say it has not yet gotten over its lawless ways. The Santa Fe Ring might still be holding sway, but there's other men whose importance is up the upswing. Some are named Chavez and some named Simms. So, statehood is possible, I guess.

No Más takes my advice, or not, as long as he gets a nose bag of grain a day. He seems to have accepted what I told him about the meaning of life. He thinks riding on a narrow mountain ridge, or alongside a mountain river is how everyone ought to live. Getting a good rub down with a gunny sack, and not having the mules in the back corral braying at him is good enough.

Jill more or less insists that I saddle up every other month, and find a new river bottom to scout or an old mountain ridge to ride. Those are the times that the truth comes to us—No Más and me—life just ain't all that meaningful on its own. We just ride for the sake of riding. I explain things to No Más that he's never thought of before. It's a great comfort to both of us.

The End